TALON

This book is a work of fiction. The characters, incidents, and dialogue are drawn from the author's imagination and are not to be construed as real. Any resemblance to actual events or persons, living or dead, is entirely coincidental.

Copyright © 2023 by Jayden Jelso

All rights reserved.

No part of this book may be used or reproduced in any manner whatsoever without permission except in the case of brief quotations embodied in critical articles and reviews.

"During times of universal deceit, telling the truth becomes a revolutionary act."

~ George Orwell

CHAPTER ONE

MAY 1ST, 2492

The morning sun beat down on the cragged streets of Borough IV, and the sounds of a hovercar's whirring engine filled Talon's ears as he crouched behind the wall of the tavern. He blinked the stinging dust out of his eyes, sighed, and shoved a hand through his hair, the heat of the day making sweat appear on the back of his neck. He peeked around the corner, gazing at the drunken man standing at the tavern's entrance.

Len couldn't see him, and Talon wanted to keep it that way. He couldn't afford being extorted today. Not unless he wanted breakfast. Boredom flooded the fifteen-year-old's mind as he leaned his back against the wall, straightening the collar of his black overcoat.

Alger stood close by on his four furry legs, his soft muzzle buried in an overgrown weed sprouting from a crevice in the dirty sidewalk. Talon's dog trotted up to him, a scrap of greasy paper resting in his mouth.

"Where'd you get that?" Talon asked, wrenching the paper from Alger's jaws and tossing it aside. "That's gross… don't eat things like that."

Alger whined.

"*Shh*," Talon whispered. "Len's over there. I don't want him to see me."

His dog ceased the noise immediately. Even Alger knew how annoying Len was. Talon peered around the wall once more, painfully bumping his reddish nose on the rough corner. Len cast his extinguished cigarette onto the street before clumsily stumbling off in the other direction.

"Okay, buddy," Talon beckoned, "let's go."

He stood, brushing dust off his black pants, and Alger followed him into the tavern. The wood planks creaked underneath Talon's boots and the large, cobweb covered windows let morning sunlight pour in. A few old tables stood here and there, accompanied by metal stools.

Josef, the bartender, stood behind the stomach-high counter, cleaning a misshapen glass with a towel. Despite having an unwarranted dislike of him, Talon thought he was rather welcoming, a rare quality in people these days.

"Hey, Talon," he greeted with a smile when he saw the boy. "What can I get you?"

Talon shrugged, avoiding eye contact. "Anything new?"

"Not much… for you at least," Josef replied. "Same old, same old. Coffee, water."

"I'll take the coffee," Talon chose. Josef nodded, retrieving a white mug from the rack above the counter.

Talon sat on one of the metal stools at the bar and rested his elbows on the wood, rubbing the last of the morning weariness from his ocean blue eyes and swiping a bit of lingering dust from his thick, red-brown hair. Alger lay beneath him, his pink tongue hanging from his mouth.

"How have you been, Talon?" Josef said as he filled the mug with the dark, steaming liquid from a silver tap. "I haven't seen you in a few days."

Finally, Talon looked at him. His gray hair hung in tangles, leading into a clipped beard. He wore the same white shirt, the same brown apron, and the same ripped pants he always did.

"Fine," he responded simply, but didn't ask the question back. Josef handed him the mug. Talon sipped the warm coffee. To most people, it wasn't much of a breakfast, but it was all he could afford.

Alger whined, and Talon noticed him licking at an ugly image tattooed in his furry side.

"Is that still bothering you?" he asked him, before remembering dogs didn't talk.

"You need a rag?" Josef said.

"Yeah."

The bartender crouched behind the counter and reappeared with a wet towel. He lathered it with a soap that smelled strongly of seaweed.

Talon took the rag and knelt beside Alger, dabbing at the simple blue square tattooed in the dog's flank. He hated the symbol. Hated it every time he saw it. And he was sure every *other* citizen hated it, too.

After a few moments, the swelling around the image went down, and Talon returned to his coffee.

"I've never asked," Josef said, "where did you find that dog? I don't see too many German shepherds anymore… and there's no dog pound anywhere nearby."

"I found him in an alley a few years ago," Talon explained, still not focusing on the bartender. "He was hurt… I think he was abused."

Josef shrugged. "Well, that would explain the scars."

Alger *did* have scars, and they had been fresh lacerations when Talon found him, a few years after… no, he wouldn't think of that.

A sudden wave of horrible memory plagued Talon's mind, and

he rubbed his forehead with his hand.

A flash of light… a scream… thick smoke.

He dreamed about it every night, the terrible thought… the terrible *memory* infesting his nightmares like a plague.

"You okay?" Josef asked.

"I'm fine," Talon said, harsher than he'd intended. He withdrew a bronze token from his overcoat pocket and placed it on the counter.

Josef shook his head kindly. "It's on the house."

"No," Talon protested. "I can pay."

"Please, I insist."

"I'm not leaving here with the token… take it."

Josef shrugged before accepting the coin and shoving it in his apron pocket.

"Well," he said, "thank you, Talon."

I'm not doing it for you… I just don't need you to pamper me, Talon thought, but he kept his mouth shut.

"I've gotta get to work," he claimed.

"If Futz gives you any trouble," Josef said, "be sure to let—"

Talon interjected, "I'll be fine."

He slid off the stool and, without thanking the bartender, made his way toward the door. However, before he could open it, he stopped, then rolled his eyes with a lengthy groan.

Len stumbled drunkenly into the tavern, sporting a ripped scarlet long-sleeve half covered by dark brown overalls, his stained white beard hanging past his bulbous stomach.

"You," he said with a hiccup, stabbing a finger at Talon. "Gimme a token… I need my whiskey."

Josef straightened. "Didn't I tell you to get out?"

"When?" Len asked gruffly.

"Ten minutes ago."

"That was *today*?"

Josef rolled his eyes. "Yes… Do you want me to draw you a map to the door, or will I have to call the Bluecoats?"

Len let out a particularly large belch, and Alger growled.

"Fine… I'll leave."

He turned and bumped into the doorframe before finding the handle and disappearing onto the street. Talon beckoned Alger out the door, ignoring Josef's friendly goodbyes as they began their journey down the road.

Josef. The man who constantly tried to help him. Talon didn't *need* his help… he didn't need *anyone*… he didn't *want* anyone.

His shoulders slumped as he pulled on his thick hood, almost as if to try and shield himself from the repulsive surroundings. He could smell the thin cloud of dust hanging in the air and, at one point, felt sparkling glass shards crunch underneath his feet. He felt dreary being out here, and he assumed the distant rain clouds forming in the sky was the cause.

Abandoned ammunition shops dotted the area—they weren't used for anything except, perhaps, temporary shelter. Guns were a rarity now, and most citizens resorted to blades or other handheld weapons for self-defense. Talon wondered why the government hadn't taken the guns when they had taken so many other things. Then he realized they didn't *need* to; their power stretched to the point that citizens with guns would barely scratch them.

Broken streetlamps, and numerous food stands lined the road. Shady looking people, both men and women, stood on one of the corners, directly beneath a tall sign that read *No Loitering*.

"Beat it, kid!" one of them shouted, even though Talon walked over five yards away. Alger barked, but Talon stroked his head.

"It's okay, buddy."

Through the gaps between buildings, Talon could barely make out the hazy skyline of Borough I, or—as a lot of people still called it—Manhattan.

The roof of the Empire State Building shimmered in the sunlight. He remembered reading, before the government had taken the books, that the building once bore a tall metal spire, helping establish it as a symbol of wealth… a symbol of *strength*. Despite its visible scars, Manhattan was left off in a much better physical condition than other cities after the Great Quake. His gaze drifted toward the Chrysler Building but didn't stay there long because of a massive white tower casting its own arrogant shadow upon it.

Prime Tower. The newest building in the city, constructed within the last twelve years. Its angular design and sparkling windows would catch anyone's eye, being much more appealing than any of the older buildings. Talon tore his eyes away from the skyline and focused on where they were supposed to be headed.

He and Alger passed junkyards, the decrepit bakery, and the ruins of aged buildings until they came to a large wooden sign standing on the left side of the road. The sign Talon loathed with all his heart, yet the one he had to see every day.

DRUDGEN
SECTOR 83

Drudgen… such a stupid name, Talon thought. Whomever had named this sector must've had a sad life… he could relate to that. It began to sprinkle.

Two burly men, dressed in navy blue uniforms, stood next to the sign. They bore white badges on their breast pockets and donned black helmets veiled by transparent face shields.

Each gripped a truncheon.

In Talon's eyes, they seemed ready to attack *anyone* who questioned them.

As he and Alger made their way toward the entrance of the sector, the Bluecoats stepped forward.

"You know the drill," said the shorter of the two in a gruff voice.

A cold fury swept over Talon as he reached inside his own pocket and withdrew New York's *new* symbol of strength... its *new* symbol of wealth.

Its symbol of control.

He gripped the little book tightly, staring at its dark blue cover, its silver designs, and its ribbon bookmark. Imprinted on the front in gold lettering was the Greek word $\mu\pi\lambda\epsilon\beta\iota\beta\lambda\iota o$. Bluebook.

Talon raised the book, and the Bluecoat aimed his scanner at the cover.

Beep.

"You may proceed, but do *not* let that dog out of your sight," the Bluecoat dictated.

Alger growled.

Without a word, Talon beckoned his dog to follow, and the two of them entered Drudgen. A city of tents met their eyes as soon as they turned the corner, some of them pressing against the short, stubby buildings.

Over two-hundred citizens, most of them rail-thin, stumbled

over one another, cradled small children, and shouted obscenities. Talon kept his head down as numerous people followed him with their eyes, as if looking for a good chance to pick his pockets.

Posters plastered in the windows of buildings flashed a variety of phrases, laws, and mandates.

EVERY CITIZEN IS REQUIRED BY LAW TO CARRY A BLUEBOOK.
CITIZENS WILL BE INCARCERATED IF FOUND WITHOUT A BLUEBOOK.
LOST YOUR BLUEBOOK? BUY ANOTHER HERE!

He and Alger ambled past sleeping people passed out on the sidewalk and purposely avoided the streets they knew not to go anywhere near.

Sudden shouts rang in their ears as they rounded a corner, and an uplifting sight swarmed before them. A crowd of people lined the road, gripping banners protesting against the Bluebook… the oppression… *everything*. Talon silently cheered them on, but he had seen enough peaceful protests in Drudgen and it wasn't anything he wanted to be near.

Sure enough, five truncheon wielding Bluecoats bolted around the corner and plunged into the crowd. The protestors scattered and screamed. Talon and Alger raced away before it could get any uglier and continued on their way through the sector.

A few minutes later, Talon groaned; they had reached their destination. His workplace… the meat market.

It was much more a stand than a market, but Talon's boss never let anyone call it anything else. A bald, brute of a man wearing a stained white apron crouched behind one of the wooden counters. Talon sauntered up as the man hacked into a massive lump of meat with a messy cleaver. His porky face filled with boiling blood when he laid eyes on him.

"Late again, boy!" he roared.

He always says that.

"Sorry…" Talon replied without an ounce of apology in his voice.

Enock Futz had only hired Talon as his assistant because he'd claimed a desperation for an assistant. Talon only *accepted* because he needed a living. Sometimes he wondered what had happened to Futz's last assistant before deciding he probably didn't *want* to know. Futz never called Talon by name… just *boy*.

"Start on the beef over there," Futz ordered thickly.

"That's pork."

"*Whatever!*"

Talon made his way over to the fully intact pig carcass lying on its side on the counter. He stripped off his overcoat, hung it on the rack next to him, and retrieved one of the many blunt knives.

As he began slicing, his eyes drifted to the blue square tattooed on the pig's side. Identical to Alger's. Not surprising, since Talon knew every animal was imprinted with a Bluebook image at birth.

He continued cutting the meat and pulling the larger strips off the bones before Alger whined and gazed up at him hopefully.

"Oh, I'm sorry, buddy," he apologized, grabbing a few slices of meat. "Here you go."

Alger happily gulped down the pork. Futz rounded on Talon.

"No feeding the mutt until your work is done!"

Talon breathed. "Then can I work quietly, please?"

"Excuse me?" Futz roared. "*I* am your boss, and *I* tell you how I want things done! It's all written, right here!"

Futz plunged a hand into his dirty breast pocket and withdrew his copy of the Bluebook.

"I know," Talon said. "I've read it. Everyone has."

"Then you'll do best to follow the laws written inside it!" Futz continued to shout as he turned back to his current meat chunk. "Don't forget! *I* hired you! *I* gave you this job! Without *my* generosity, you'd be on the streets! You'd be penniless! You'd be starving!"

Talon mouthed these phrases and counted them on his fingers as Futz yelled. It was officially the millionth time he'd heard them.

"You'd be *nothing*!"

I already am nothing, Talon thought.

"And," Futz ranted, "I'm paying you! Without me, you wouldn't have anything!"

Talon ignored Futz and his incessant rambles and continued slicing the meat. His life wasn't like this when he was younger... Why did it have to be now? Why couldn't his life go back to the way it was when—

Another flash of memory struck his brain like a lightning bolt.

Flames, ash, desolation...

He clenched his eyes shut and attempted to force it all out of his mind. He didn't need the memories... he didn't *want* the memories.

"*Ah!*" he gasped. Sharp pain slithered up his finger as blood seeped from the fresh cut he'd unintentionally given himself. He grabbed a towel from the counter and balled it around his wounded finger.

"Don't ruin that towel!" Futz seethed.

Talon threw the stained rag aside, bandaged the bleeding cut with a spare bit of greasy cloth, and continued working.

The hours ticked by, and the rain with it, until the golden sun began to hide behind the horizon rimmed with breaking clouds.

A woman spoke over the loudspeaker, filling the streets with a voluminous echo.

"Thirty minutes to curfew. Please finish up any activities now. Anyone found to be outside of their homes after seven o'clock will be arrested."

Her voice was like poisoned sugar, sweet but deadly.

Talon pulled on his overcoat before ambling over to Futz, who busied himself wiping down the dirty counter with an even dirtier cloth.

"Can I go?" he asked.

Futz grunted and dropped a single oily token into Talon's open palm.

"That's *it*?" Talon exclaimed.

"Unless you'd rather me pay you nothing… and you'd better not be late tomorrow, or you'll see just how little I'm willing to pay!" his boss threatened. Talon sneered, shoved the coin in his pocket, and beckoned Alger to follow.

The two of them traveled past the sea of tents, past the posters enforcing the Bluebook mandate, past the bars and ammunition shops, and past the truncheon wielding Bluecoats standing at the entrance to Drudgen.

They finally arrived at a three-story building with a flat stone roof, a tiny ground floor, and grungy walls. A shelter designated for underpaid citizens, laid out in an old, abandoned apartment complex. Talon knew he should be thankful; there was rarely another place with free housing, and he wouldn't be able to afford a *real* apartment otherwise. At least he had his own room, where Alger lived with him.

The duo ascended the rusty fire escape, right past the window that led into their room, before emerging onto the roof. Talon breathed deeply, gazing at the skyline, and sat down on the edge of the building. Shimmering light rays peeked through the gaps between the skyscrapers and reflected off the windows, making them twinkle like orange stars.

So many emotions… so many *feelings* crawled through his mind as the sun continued to descend. Sadness, anger, fear… all of them spun so fast through his brain, making him unsure of which he truly felt.

Alger whined and rested his furry head in his young owner's lap. Talon stroked his dog's soft ear and finally let his mind settle on the one question he asked himself every night.

Will anything ever change?

CHAPTER TWO

MAY 5TH, 2492

Officer Zedah Kahzak brushed a strand of black hair from her green eyes, gazing out the shimmering window, ninety stories up in Borough I's tallest building.

Prime Tower: the tallest and most luxurious building in New York City.

Though standing in the governor's massive office, Zedah *felt* the building's elaborate and imaginative design.

Constructed of white stone, the angular walls and expansive windows stretched toward the clouds as if the tower itself thought it could touch them. She had a birds-eye view of the circular courtyard below, vibrant hedges lacing themselves along the cobbled bricks, and sparkling fountains dotted strategically throughout.

Zedah fidgeted with her gray, knee-length cloak and pursed her red lips. She blinked, then laughed at herself.

I must be nervous, she thought. Zedah brushed the feeling away and allowed her mind to grapple with more important matters.

Why had the governor summoned her here? She hoped it was to discuss the growing unrest in the city — a much larger issue than it had been just months before.

The citizens rebelled like never before. Riots, protests and sabotages infested the city like ants.

What would happen if everything went to hell? If the city fell from its glory? If the extremists turned into an army? An army large enough to overthrow the government?

What would happen then? She knew she wouldn't be able to bear it if anything happened. If her life went back to the way it used to be…

"*No,*" she said to herself.

Zedah surprised herself when she spoke out loud, but the shock didn't last long. She turned her attention back to the city and stared through the morning fog casting a thin drizzle across the skyline.

A loud click startled her, and the automatic doors behind her whirred open.

Fear pierced her heart like a shard of poisoned ice. Her legs felt weak, and her breathing pace quickened. Nerves made Zedah's entire body shake as she turned and subconsciously let a spurt of breath escape through her mouth.

Governor Irnal Kresh strode into the office.

He wore a dark gray suit, matching the color of his long, tall shadow. A blue tie hung from his neck, its tip disappearing into his tailored coat, and his hands calmly rested behind his back.

Zedah stood as frozen as a statue, and Kresh gazed at her through eyes so dark they were almost black. His salt and pepper hair fashionably streaked over the top of his head. He would've been handsome, were it not for his pleasant features being overshadowed by his permanent sneer.

"Officer," he acknowledged in a deep voice.

"Governor," Zedah said weakly.

Only now, with herself and Kresh occupying it, did Zedah appreciate the impressiveness of the massive office. Dual wooden staircases, each placed on a separate side of the room, wrapped themselves around the governor's oak-wood desk that stood in the middle of the floor. They led up to two separate landings, the left dotted with bookshelves and the right with cushioned chairs and a round white table. Both walls, left and right, were constructed entirely of glass, letting in as much natural light as possible and offering a panoramic view of the vast city.

Kresh seated himself in the tall leather chair behind his desk.

"Please, sit," he stated, gesturing to one of the two seats placed across from him. Less of a request, more of a command. Zedah obeyed, her boot heels clicking on the white tile floor as she made her way toward the smaller chair.

For a short while, silence hung about the office as Kresh's shiny pen scratched away on one of his sheets of paper. Zedah soon grew restless, bouncing her knee and tapping her fingers on her leg.

Finally, Kresh set the pen aside and laced his fingers together. He gazed at her shrewdly.

"Coffee?" he offered, grasping the handle of the metal pot sitting next to him on the desk. Zedah nodded.

He poured her a cup, then one for himself. His brow was so furrowed that Zedah couldn't help but wonder if something was troubling him. Kresh turned back to her.

"It's been a while, Zedah. I trust you are holding up well?" he inquired. The question caught her off guard, being the last thing she expected.

Was she in trouble?

"Oh… yes, sir," she answered. The look Kresh bore on his face terrified her, and Zedah had to remind herself the expression wasn't angry or frustrated. It was deep and hungry, and she knew he was searching. Kresh could see through a person's soul as though it were made of glass.

"I see," the governor responded. He stood and stalked to the window, surveying his massive domain like a lion. Zedah couldn't imagine anyone else standing in his place. How could they? No one could ever be as good of a governor… as good of a *ruler* as he was. And yet, she *did* wonder why he had sat down if he was only going to get up again.

"I'm sure you're wondering why I summoned you here," Kresh stated.

A short pause.

"Yes, sir," Zedah answered.

"Well…"

Another pause, one that worried Zedah. Kresh had never been at a loss for words before. Not in *her* presence.

"Is—is everything okay, sir?" Zedah asked cautiously.

Kresh turned from the window and stared her directly in the eye.

"Walk with me," he said softly.

Zedah's surprise must've shown because Kresh came close to a smile. He led her to the doors, and she obeyed his gesture of *ladies first* as they swung open automatically.

Silence passed between them once again as they strolled down the elegant glass hallway before stopping to stand and stare at the harbor of the Hudson River, gleaming ninety stories below. Zedah fixed her eyes on the same thing she always did whenever she looked at the harbor.

The build site.

Colossal cage-like structures surrounded the half-built cargo ships resting in the shimmering water. Giant cranes lifted heaping amounts of metal and glass and other materials Zedah didn't recognize.

Even from inside Prime Tower, way up on the ninetieth floor, she could hear the faint bangs, booms, and rumbles that could have told her, even without the visuals, of the laborious construction.

Governor Kresh initiated the build over a year ago and, according to him, it progressed slowly but smoothly. It would be completed in less than a month.

He'd said they could increase New York's income if they achieved a greater ability to trade with other countries. To do that, they needed ships.

Kresh had dubbed it, without the Bluehouse Prime's approval, the Third Borough Project, which confused Zedah since its development commenced in Borough I's Harbor.

"I called you to my office today," Kresh began, and Zedah turned toward him, "because I desire to speak with you about something very serious."

Zedah furrowed her brow. "Yes, sir?"

There's definitely something wrong, she thought.

Kresh fixed his eyes on hers and said, "The Falcon's Nest is not dead, Zedah."

Zedah couldn't have been more shocked if he had hit her. Her mind spiraled, her hands shaking uncontrollably.

"*What?*" she responded in a near whisper.

Kresh pursed his lips.

"You remember Elijah and Hazel Chambers," he said. Not a question—a statement. Zedah would *always* remember them, and not in a good way. She'd once thrown all her attention... all her thoughts toward them, and she was still haunted by what she did to them.

"Yes, sir," she affirmed after she'd gathered herself.

"They had a *son*," Kresh explained.

Another wave of nauseating adrenaline rushed through her like a tidal wave. She was stunned to the fullest extent of the word.

"A *son*?" she repeated.

"Yes," Kresh said, turning back to the window, "and he is a teenager now... a Fourth-Class citizen, practically living on the streets."

A long moment of a festering silence followed, finally broken by Zedah.

"Sir, what *exactly* are you saying?"

"I am saying, Zedah, he could be a problem... and a large one at that."

She did a double take before responding.

"If he's just a *boy*, then—"

"I am also saying," Kresh interjected, "if he learns of his importance, his actions could spell the end of the Bluehoue Prime as we know it."

Zedah's mind started to connect the pieces of information. "So... he doesn't know what his parents were involved in?"

"No, he doesn't," Kresh said simply and straightened his tie. "If he did, he would have acted out already."

Zedah didn't know if she believed that. Kresh wasn't the kind of man who brushed aside an issue. Not unless he was stressed. Then again, she remembered his attitude toward the growing unrest in the city.

But she knew she had to trust him.

"I wanted to get your opinion on the matter, Zedah," Kresh said, his dark eyes meeting her green ones.

Startling. Again. He'd *never* asked her opinion before. She didn't know what to say—perhaps that he might have overlooked something, and this boy wasn't the child of Elijah and Hazel Chambers. Or the boy could have known the truth of his parents' activities and chosen to ignore it.

"I think," she began after a moment, "that we should leave the matter alone."

She prepared for Kresh to explode with anger, to shout she didn't trust him, and he regretted asking her in the first place. Then she remembered Kresh never had reason to be angry with her before and wouldn't raise his voice to *anyone*.

He stared at her blankly. To her, it was almost worse than an angry monologue.

"Why?" he asked simply.

Zedah pondered for a moment.

"Well, if he doesn't understand his importance, then we should keep it that way and focus on more important matters."

"Such as?"

Again, she thought about her answer.

"Such as gaining the respect of the people."

Kresh stroked his chin and turned back to the window for what Zedah felt like was the fiftieth time.

"I don't care if the people respect me so long as they *fear* me," Kresh declared.

Zedah stood silent and rolled his statement over in her mind. She'd never thought of it that way. The creed of a *true* leader.

"I understand your concerns, Zedah, but we cannot leave this matter alone. The boy must go… permanently. And you are going to carry this out."

A third wave of adrenaline curdled Zedah's blood, this one the worst of all.

"But, *sir*," she stuttered. "You mean—?"

"Yes, officer," Kresh declared.

She nearly started shaking again. "But... the boy's just a—he's just a *boy*!"

Kresh glared at her so fiercely that goosebumps of intimidation appeared all along Zedah's neck.

"You're right. He is. But if you truly care about this city... this *state*... I suggest you adopt a more agreeable attitude."

They stared at each other for what felt like hours to Zedah. She wanted to protest. She wanted to say *no*. But she knew openly defying him would mean imprisonment, possibly for life. His mind was made up.

Zedah inhaled deeply and nodded her head ever so slightly. Kresh relaxed.

"You may go," he granted.

She turned and departed from his presence, traveling down the hallway. She turned a corner and exhaled, leaning her back against the marble wall. She gritted her teeth, scrambling to overcome the internal war raging inside her.

Painful questions raced through Zedah's mind, too many to count.

Was this *good*? She supposed it was good for Kresh and the Prime.

Would she regret it? *No*, she wouldn't—she *couldn't*. She'd fought for Kresh before, commanding his units. This felt completely different.

Stop it! her mind shouted at her.

She couldn't take her thoughts off it. She knew why Kresh was making *her* do this. He was testing her loyalty… testing *her*.

Zedah closed her sea-green eyes and twirled a finger through her black hair. She pursed her red lips and prepared herself to do the deed.

She spoke into her com-link, lifting her wrist toward her mouth.

"Get my ship ready," Zedah ordered.

She unclipped a metal handle, wrapped in serrated rubber, from her belt. Zedah clicked the minute button implanted in its side and the blade unfolded.

Separate sections of sharp, gleaming metal pieced themselves together like a puzzle until she held a curved sword that reflected light from the many windows.

No going back. Zedah gripped the razor-sharp weapon and began her journey down the maze of elegant hallways that would lead her to the hangar bay.

CHAPTER THREE

MAY 5TH, 2492

Talon shot awake with a broken yell and nearly toppled out of bed. Hot sweat drenched his body, and it took him a moment to realize his hands were white from gripping the sheet so hard.

He sucked in large amounts of breath, sat up on the uncomfortable cot, and swung his legs over the edge before burying his face in his wet palms.

Breathe... breathe, he told himself repeatedly.

The dream... *again*... as always. His sleeveless shirt stuck to him like a soaked magnet, and he hugged himself tightly, embracing his shivering torso. No matter how hard he tried he couldn't get the images out of his head.

The explosion... the searing heat... the ash... the smoke...

And the screams... *their* screams...

He pulled his face from his hands and turned his attention to his surroundings. His tiny apartment.

Rays of morning sunlight streaked through a large window. In the right corner stood a sink with a dirty basin, and a small wooden cupboard—where Talon stored the little food he could afford—sat next to it. Its contents consisted mostly of hardtack and dried fruit.

Talon rested his elbows on his knees and shut his eyes. He slumped over, unable to tear his mind off the horrific nightmare.

A timid whimper sounded from his right and he turned his attention toward the decrepit white door. Alger stood staring at it, as though it were some suspicious thing no one in their right mind would dare cross. His muscles tensed. He panted heavily and, for a moment, Talon worried his dog might have been hyperventilating.

"Um… are you okay, buddy?" he asked.

Alger didn't look at him. Instead, he pricked up his pointy ears, listening hard.

Talon furrowed his sweaty brow, threw off the sheet, and gathered a bundle of clothes. Alger was stuck like a nail and stiff as a board for the next few moments. As Talon prepared to leave the apartment, he allowed the cot to draw his gaze. He almost stepped toward it… almost reached underneath.

No… stop.

He shook off the temptation. It would only cause pain. Only cause the memories to resurface.

Talon retrieved the Bluebook and reached for the doorknob.

His dog turned and yapped at him.

"Alger, what's up?" Talon asked incredulously, but Alger just stared at him. He reached for the door again and Alger's fur stood on end.

"I've gotta go get a shower… look at me," he told him, gesturing to his soaked body.

Alger didn't budge, his barks echoing through the room.

"Stop it! *Quiet!*" Talon shushed.

"Hey! Keep that dog quiet!" yelled the gruff voice of his neighbor whom he'd never met, muffled by the walls. Talon knelt, attempting to stroke Alger's head, but the dog wouldn't permit him. He just continued to bark. Talon didn't have time for this… not *now*. He shoved both hands through his wet hair and massaged his temples.

"I'll be late for work, Alger!" Talon exclaimed. More shouts from the neighbor echoed through the walls. He tried to sidestep him, but Alger continued to bar the way.

"I can't bring you today, buddy!" He forced his way past Alger and out the door. As Talon made his way down the hall, he heard Alger's claws scratching at the wall, pleading his master to come back. He tried not to feel guilty, but there was no stopping the sorrow he felt. He would make it up to Alger later.

He made it to the locker room and attempted to wash away his disturbance under the cold shower. After shutting off the water, drying, and pulling on his clothes, he descended the stairs to the ground floor before finally pushing his way out the grimy glass doors.

"Where's the dog?" Josef asked kindly when Talon arrived at the tavern.

"Back home," he responded almost robotically, avoiding eye contact. He drank his coffee in silence, placed a token on the counter, and without saying *goodbye*, departed from the bar.

The Bluecoats scanned his copy of the little book, and he made his way through Drudgen, attempting to ignore the hideous tents, and the posters restricting citizens of all freedoms.

"Glad to see you forgot the mutt today!" Futz shouted when he saw him approaching. Talon didn't reply and began to work, ignoring the soreness in his hand that surfaced after repeatedly slicing large chunks of beef.

Neither the sound of Futz exchanging tokens with a customer nor the distant rumble of a massive and mysterious construction project could take Talon's mind off the strangeness of Alger's behavior. He hadn't even thought of his nightmare since he woke up.

Talon knew Alger would calm down in time. He might've just been going through a phase. Everyone went through phases, right?

But what if something was *wrong*, and Alger's behavior was a warning? Dogs had a sixth sense. They could sense danger. That was common knowledge.

Questions he knew might never be answered continued to jab at his thoughts like a relentless woodpecker until an idea suddenly sparked.

Carrots!

Alger loved carrots. Talon resolved to pick some up at the market on his way home. He nearly smiled at the thought, knowing Alger would be back to normal in no time.

A brown haze blanketed the surroundings for the rest of the day, and the air smelled strongly of dirt. Futz ordered Talon to hang the tarp so that the loose dust didn't ruin the meat. After thirty minutes of tirelessly clipping the rubbery black cloth to the roof of the stand, he was sure the aches would never leave his arms. However, the shade from the boiling sun was a plus.

The following hours showed a hard laboriousness. By the end of the day, Talon's hand was so sore from slicing meat that he couldn't make a fist, barely able to hold onto the two tokens Futz dispensed thirty minutes before curfew.

The descending sun cast a golden light on the grungy buildings as Talon searched for the market on his way home. He had to take a detour down a few unfamiliar streets, reminding himself to keep his guard up.

Finally, he found it… the puny market.

The few baskets holding dried fruit had barely any contents, and the vegetables they had didn't exactly look appealing.

He told the hostile, frizzy-haired cashier he wanted some carrots. She only grunted, searching through one of the buckets below the wooden counter. Finally, she reappeared with a bag containing three and a half of the large roots.

"Who eats carrots?" she mumbled to herself.

"They're for my dog," Talon blurted before he could stop himself.

She glared. "Well, roots are about the only food that grows well these days."

"Um—" Talon stuttered.

"I don't have time to answer all your questions!" The cashier exclaimed.

"But… I didn't ask a ques—"

"*Whatever!*"

Talon immediately dropped one of his tokens onto the counter and left the market, making his way back onto the familiar streets. On the bright side, he'd gotten the carrots and knew he would see Alger back to his usual self in no time. He turned a corner and nearly tripped over a woman cradling a small baby. She scowled at him.

"What do you want?" she asked harshly. She might as well have said: *if you want money, I don't have any*.

Talon glanced down at the bag full of carrots. He extracted one and held it out to the woman, whose eyes widened ever so slightly. Slowly, she took the carrot and nodded with a small but gratified smile. Talon didn't know what inclined him to do it. It was almost an impulse.

He continued past.

I hate broken glass, he thought as he stepped over a pile of the gleaming shards.

"*Ten minutes to curfew,*" rang the sweet, evil voice over the loudspeaker.

He froze. *Ten minutes?! I can't have taken that long!*

The sky gradually darkened as Talon raced through the streets, the bag of carrots swinging at his side. The Bluecoats scanned the book, and he sped around the last few turns before the apartment complex came into view.

He pulled the heavy door open and leaped inside, sweat dripping from his face. Talon smiled and took a deep breath, wiping his mouth on the back of his sleeve.

That was close.

Relieved, he focused on the surroundings, his smile melting off his face. Something felt strange. Something felt *off*. Something filled the building that unsettled him, tugging painfully at his stomach.

Silence.

Pure, raw, eerie silence seemed to slither its way through the ground floor of the complex, laughing, jeering, tickling Talon's ears and mind. There was no one there, no noise emanating from *anywhere*. Everything stood eerily still and unnaturally quiet.

Talon crept through the lobby, past the dusty seating area and toward the carpeted staircase.

"Hello?" he whispered.

He emerged onto his floor, immediately knowing something was horribly wrong. The neighbor's drunken shouts always echoed through the walls when he came home.

And where were Alger's barks? Had he calmed down? Was he back to normal? Would he find him resting in front of the door, anxiously awaiting his owner's return?

Talon's heart pounded against his chest as he attempted to convince himself nothing was amiss, everything was okay, all was normal.

He arrived at his door, and his stomach turned when he laid eyes on it.

It stood slightly ajar.

Talon laced his aching fingers around the cold handle and gently creaked it further open. Night had set in, moonlight streaking through the large window. Everything was exactly the way he'd left it. His cot was still there. So was the tall cupboard, and the sink.

But something caught his eye… something on the floor, right at his feet.

Talon bent down, his head spinning, and touched it.

Warm, wet…red.

His pounding heart stopped.

Blood.

A broken, mournful whimper sounded from the other end of the room, and Talon snapped his head upward, a thousand terrible revelations violently reeling through his mind.

Alger lay beneath the window, a trail of dark blood winding across the floor and up to a wound in his stomach, like a river leading to its gaping mouth.

No!

Talon tried to yell, but no sound came out. He stumbled across the room, over to his dying friend. Alger still moved, but barely. His terrified eyes peered right into Talon's. He choked out a timid howl as Talon shook his head, rejecting the fact that *another* loved one was to be taken from him…

No! Please! Not again! Please!

His pleas did nothing. He felt his precious friend's head go limp as he scooped him up, holding him tightly.

"Alger?" Talon whispered. But Alger didn't move. His beautiful eyes were a million miles away.

Talon hugged Alger's head close to his chest and stroked his soft ear, not wanting to admit it… not wanting to let in the pain. He continued to clutch onto him, the tears beginning to break through, knowing it would be the last time he'd ever hold him close.

But he was suddenly aware of something else… another presence. Something… no… some*one* was in the room watching him, stalking him.

He lay Alger's lifeless body gently on the wooden floor and stood up slowly, his heart beating faster and faster.

Talon let his eyes settle on the corner of the room, right next to the door. Through the moonlight, he could barely make out a sinister figure standing in wait, shrouded in the shadow cast by the open door.

"Who's there?" Talon demanded fiercely.

The figure moved…

Talon stepped back as it revealed itself.

It was a woman, and Talon instantly hated everything about her. He hated her shoulder-length hair, black as midnight. He hated her red lips, hated her green eyes, hated her knee-length cloak.

Rage boiled inside him, waiting to explode. He wanted to attack, ignoring the fact she stood taller than him… ignoring the fact a long, thin sword rested in her hand, rimmed with Alger's blood.

For a moment, the woman didn't speak. She only stood there contemplating him, staring him up and down.

"Who are you? What do you want from me?" Talon yelled, loathing in his voice.

"I don't want anything from you," she answered simply. Her

voice was deep and dark and… conflicted. Talon didn't care.

"What did you do?" he shouted.

She didn't answer him, but still spoke. "I am Officer Zedah Kahzak, and I am here on behalf of Governor Irnal Kresh."

All the hate… all the rage Talon felt increased, now fueled by utter shock. The governor? No, she had to be lying. But why would she lie? Why would he be of interest to the governor?

"He gave me a mission, one we both regret."

Talon's heart raced even faster. A mission? It couldn't have been to kill Alger. Why would they need to kill Alger?

Yet, one word from the endless supply of horrible thoughts jammed in his mind: *kill*. The sword in Zedah's hand began to look much more intimidating. His mind whirled even faster, clouding his thoughts—Alger was dead, the pain digging deeper into his heart.

Zedah straightened, her body rigid as a wooden plank. The officer clenched her fingers around her sword's serrated handle. Fear replaced Talon's anger, his chest spasming as though some horrific creature was trying to burst from it. Panic welled up inside him. Painful tears filled his eyes.

What did I do? What did I do wrong?

His mind screamed these words over and over until…

"Please," Zedah whispered. "This will be so much easier on both of us if you don't try to run."

She raised her sword…

The razor-sharp blade came swinging toward him, slicing through the air, headed for his neck. In a split moment, Talon hurled himself out of the way as he felt the blade graze the hairs on the back of his neck. She swung again and Talon dodged, tripping over Alger's body and landing right next to his cot.

Now was the time… the *only* time.

His fingers spidered under the bed, closing around something hard and round. Talon pulled at the object and—from beneath the cot—drew out a battered, dusty sword.

He hadn't looked at it in years. He'd never *wanted* to… he didn't want to *remember*. Zedah stood frozen on the spot, her eyes widening as they fixed themselves on the sword.

"That—that sword," she stuttered.

Talon's breathing leveled as he gripped his weapon.

Zedah snapped out of her trance and struck again. The edge of her blade connected with the edge of Talon's as he brought it to bear. A deafening ring echoed through the room and the impact sent a violent shockwave of adrenaline through Talon's arm.

Again and again, she struck, swung, sliced, and stabbed, but Talon continued to deflect with barely the grace of a child just learning to walk. The edge of her blade slid right across his bicep and stinging pain exploded up and into his shoulder. He held his other hand over the wound, blood seeping through his fingers, trying not to yell from the pain.

Zedah raised her sword, preparing to deliver the fatal blow…

Just before the blade would have slid through his heart, Talon dodged, rolled, and leaped out the door. He heard her pursuing him as he bolted through the hallway, tears still stinging his eyes.

So many thoughts… so many *emotions* swam through him.

What had he done wrong? What had he done to warrant this?

Zedah's fingers closed around the back of his collar, and she pulled him down. He fell to the ground, hot blood trickling down his arm.

Talon gripped his sword and deflected her next blow. He rolled to the right, lunged, and threw himself against her. Zedah grunted as he pushed her off balance and sprinted down the hall.

Using the termite-eaten rail, Talon pulled himself up the spiral staircase before bursting out another door and onto the stone roof. He sprinted to the edge, but there was nowhere to go. A fifty-foot drop led to the street below, where barely anyone stirred.

A loud bang split the air as the door behind him burst open. He whirled around. Zedah stood there, her face stoic, her sword ready.

"Please!" Talon yelled. "Please… what do you want?"

Zedah seemed not to hear.

She pressed a button on her wristband.

The screaming sounds of an engine assailed Talon's ears as he turned back toward the street. A slim, black aircraft rose from below… and it was *hideous*.

Long dark wings protruded from its sides and its viewing port stared at him menacingly. Three giant engines sprouted from the rear, spitting out shafts of red flame. Four rotating guns turned to face him, and Talon could see right through their metallic barrels.

Through the viewing port, he could see the pilot. A gray flight outfit hung about his shoulders, and he wore a chilling mask with a cylindrical breathing apparatus. The aircraft revved, and Zedah distanced herself as the guns began to spin.

This was it… Talon froze in terror.

He closed his eyes and prepared for the cold embrace of death.

A deafening *BANG*….

Blistering heat….

But death didn't come… *nothing* came.

Zedah yelled in horror and Talon dared to open his eyes.

His mouth fell open when he beheld the sight before him. Her aircraft spun uncontrollably, and he could see the pilot struggling to regain command over the ship.

A cloud of fire erupted inside the aircraft, engulfing the pilot and shattering the viewing port. Black smoke obscured the sun as the vessel continued to explode, sending ear-splitting bangs through the air.

A silver aircraft emerged through the swirling smoke, casting a long shadow across the building. Zedah's hideous ship crashed to the ground below and vomited up a curling ball of fire.

The strange new aircraft had an oval-like shape and bore three massive thrusters at its stern, shooting out columns of blue flame. Two large wings jutted out from each side, then curved toward the bow in the shape of crescents. The rectangular viewing port shimmered in the front, positioned in the exact middle.

The ship rotated to its port side as short spurts of steam erupted from all sides of the vessel, its gray boarding ramp lowering with a buzzing whir. A girl appeared on the ramp, clutching one of the spokes holding it in place, her long blonde hair whipping around in the wind like a curtain of gold.

"Come on!" she called, extending her hand. Her voice was like music. After a long moment, Talon recovered his sanity and turned back toward Zedah, who rushed toward him, sword in hand.

What else could he do?

What other option was there?

Before Talon knew it, his feet were moving as fast as they could. All he could hear was the beating of his own heart as he reached the edge of the building… and *leaped*.

He felt the tip of Zedah's sword graze his leg as the girl caught his hand and pulled. The impact against the ramp knocked his breath away.

"I've got him!" the girl shouted to the pilot.

The wound in Talon's arm seared with pain as she pulled him up and into the ship, leaving Zedah stranded on the top of the apartment complex, standing over the remains of her burning aircraft. The ship lurched, and Zedah disappeared as the complex grew smaller and smaller.

The girl steered Talon through the ship and sat him down on a ripped leather seat before either of them could catch their breath.

"You're bleeding," she stated. "Castor, get a bandage!"

"On it," a boy's voice called from the front of the ship.

The girl turned back to him. "Are you okay?"

He didn't know. So many emotions surged through his body. Confusion, fear, sadness, exhaustion. But he nodded.

"Yes," he managed to say.

The girl looked around his age, maybe a little younger, and the first thing Talon noticed was how pretty she was. Her startling green eyes sparkled in the pale blue light that filled the ship. She wore fingerless gloves and a fringed cloak around her shoulders, hiding the fact that she had a thin dagger strapped to her waist.

She had the means to kill him on the spot, but that wasn't what was at the forefront of his mind. A slight pause hung over them as he noticed her studying him, and he studied her.

Talon heard a small ding come from a door to his right. He assumed it led to the cockpit. A teenage boy stepped through the door, swiping the unkempt black hair out of his gray eyes.

He was tall and handsome, his hands scabbed and smudged with grease. He wore a dark red, leather flight jacket and black cargo pants, frayed in some areas. He had a somewhat mischievous glint in his eye, only making him even more suspicious.

Who were these people? Why had they rescued him? How did they know he was in trouble?

"Well, *that* gave us a bit of a scare. You alright?" the boy asked him.

Talon merely nodded, avoiding eye contact with either of them.

"Who are you?" he inquired suspiciously.

"I'm Amber," the girl introduced.

The boy opened his mouth to speak, but Amber cut him off.

"And this is Castor, but don't encourage him."

"Hey!" Castor snapped.

Amber took the bandage and tried to wrap it around Talon's injury, but he pushed her away, still avoiding either of their gazes.

"I can do it," he claimed quietly and began tending to the wound himself. Once he'd finished bandaging the bleeding laceration, he lifted his eyes and focused on them.

An awkward silence filled the aircraft.

"What do you want from me?" Talon asked.

Amber blinked. "Nothing."

"We just wanted to help," Castor explained.

"Why?" Talon asked.

Another pause, this one much longer.

Instead of answering Talon's question, Amber inquired, "What's your name?"

His mind reeled with uncertainty. Should he tell them or not? They'd given him no reason to trust them. Besides, perhaps, saving his life. But they hadn't even answered his question.

"Talon," he revealed, against his will.

"It's nice to meet you, Talon," Amber responded kindly.

He couldn't say the same… not *yet*… probably not *ever*.

"*Why* did you save me?" he repeated with more force. Amber and Castor glanced at each other.

"Uh…" Castor stuttered, almost as if he were trying to find the right way to say it, "We… um… heard you were being attacked… and—"

"You were spying, weren't you?" Talon snapped. How many people had to be spying on him at once? The government first… now *these* people?

Amber shot a look at Castor that obviously said *shut up*.

"It doesn't matter right now," she said. "We're just happy you're safe."

Talon's eyes stung, courtesy of the anger welling up inside him. What did she *mean* it didn't matter? Of *course* it mattered! How could he trust them if he didn't know?

After a moment's silence, Amber gave him a soft smile and stood from her seat.

"Well," she said, "maybe we should give you some time."

She tapped Castor on the arm and practically dragged him into the cockpit. Talon glanced around, taking in the surroundings for the first time.

The ship didn't look as welcome as it had when it first emerged from the smoke. Stuff was strewn about randomly, like a teenager's bedroom in which cleaning had been neglected. Then he remembered the ship was occupied by two teenagers.

There were buttons here and there and the walls were constructed of various kinds of scrap metal. In the back were two hammocks, one hanging above the other, and a small workbench littered with tools and complex tech. Viewing ports dotted the walls, and the dirt and grime acted as an orange filter for incoming moonlight.

The raised boarding ramp stood to his left, and a yellow lever used to operate it protruded from the wall. On the right stood another door, leading to a small bathroom complete with a shower, toilet, and sink.

A ladder made of hollow metal bars led upward to a separate, unrecognizable room casting a column of white light into the belly of the ship.

Talon realized he gripped something in his hand, something smooth. He forced himself to look at it. The sword still sat between his palm and fingers. Once he had his eyes on it, he couldn't take them away, not even by force.

Smooth leather wrapped around the handle, fringed at the sides. There was no guard, but a strand of thin cloth laced itself around the upper rim of the handle, covering the seam that connected it with the blade. The scratched finish on the blade itself shimmered in the pale light.

It was the very sword he'd avoided for so long, and now he'd been forced to use it. He still remembered the expression on his father's face when he'd first gifted it to him, over six years ago. The very day of the tragedy... of the horrible accident...

No.

He forced it out of his mind. Talon didn't *want* to remember. He wanted to *forget*, never to feel the pain again.

After studying the sword, another terrible truth stabbed him in the heart.

Alger was dead.

His loyal, lovable dog was gone and there would be no bringing him back. If *only* he'd taken Alger to work. If *only* he hadn't left him in the apartment. If *only* he had paid more attention to the dog's warnings. *Both* he and Alger could've survived.

It's all my fault…

Why had he chosen to rescue him that day he found him in the alleyway? Why did he take him in?

If he had listened to his better judgment back then, he would have been spared this torment. Now, there was no stopping the raging fire of grief accumulating every second, that seemed to coalesce within his heart… consuming him… *suffocating* him.

He'd made a mistake in rescuing Alger, and he swore not to let anything of the sort happen again. He clenched his eyes shut and suppressed the whirlwind in his head, tightening his grip on his mind like he tightened the bandage around his arm.

CHAPTER FOUR

MAY 6TH, 2492

The sounds of swirling water rushed through Talon's ears as he broke through the surface of the lake, treading with his arms and legs. He laughed as his father swam over and lifted him onto his shoulders.

He could see his mother, sitting on the bank, her feet barely touching the little waves.

"Mom! Are you gonna get in?" he called to her.

She laughed, a warm smile spreading across her face. "It's a little cold for me."

Talon leaped off his dad's shoulders and splashed back into the water, swimming over to the sand and sprinting toward his mother, her bright orange hair gleaming in the sunlight. She retrieved a towel for him, and he wrapped it around his bare shoulders before sitting down next to her. She reached down and swiped some of Talon's soaking hair out of his eyes as he leaned against her.

"What's wrong, Talon?" she asked after seeing the look of longing on his face. He answered almost immediately.

"I just wish I was taller... then I could touch the bottom of the lake like dad does."

His mother laughed again, the sweet sound rolling off her tongue. "You will be. Very soon. Sooner than I'm ready for."

She didn't say anything else. He knew she was probably right, but *soon* felt like a long way away. He couldn't wait to be grown up.

Just then, his father climbed out of the water.

"You ready?"

Talon nodded.

His mother said, "We'll need to hurry. Patrol might come by soon and we don't want to be caught."

Talon looked back at her, and she smiled once more with a rebellious glint in her eye. *That's* where he got his rebellious side. His mother.

He fixed his eyes on her hair. Brighter than his, but still somewhat the same color. The sun shined bright against it; it was almost like fire.

Wait… it *was* fire. Suddenly, the brightness was too much. It burned his eyes, and a terrible ring resounded through Talon's head, shadows rushing by in a blur. Waves of blistering heat seared his body, and a blinding glow danced within his vision. Muffled crashes and dull bangs swam through his ears, an agonizing shout striking his attention like a bullet.

He came to, vaguely aware he sat on the ruined ground of a burning building.

Through the tears in his eyes, he scanned the surroundings.

He couldn't see them. Where were they?

He called out to them… no reply. His own voice sounded cracked and hoarse, distant and broken.

The ground caved in. He screamed as he fell to the lower floor. Something struck him on the head, and everything went dark and silent.

Talon gasped and shot into a sitting position, his chest rising and falling as cold breaths poured from his open mouth.

He mentally put the pieces together, glancing around, his vision still coming into focus.

The dream, Talon realized.

He'd fallen asleep in the leather seat Amber placed him in the night before. Flickering daylight streamed through the viewing ports as the aircraft sped through the air; he didn't know where they were, or where they were going.

Talon rubbed his face before the memories of the previous day flooded his brain. A sick, nauseating feeling twisted in his stomach when he realized yesterday's terrifying events hadn't been a dream.

He'd half hoped he'd wake up in his cot at the apartment, Alger lying across the room from him. Talon swallowed back his anger… swallowed back his pain.

Why did Alger have to be taken from him, too? Why couldn't things be the way they were when he was younger. when *they* were alive?

Castor ambled out of the cockpit, breaking Talon out of his thoughts, his disheveled dark hair matching his black long sleeve.

"Morning," he yawned, scratching at his shoulder.

Talon only gave a slight nod.

"I hung another hammock last night, but we didn't want to wake you."

Talon nearly cringed when he realized he'd fallen asleep in the middle of the ship, but quickly brushed off the embarrassment.

"Thanks," he mumbled.

Castor smiled. "Hungry?"

Talon shrugged.

Castor turned to a metal cupboard and flipped open the creaky doors. He extracted an apple and tossed it to Talon.

An apple? A real apple? He hadn't had an apple in years. The Drudgen market didn't even carry apples.

Again, he nodded his thanks and bit into it. Juicy, sweet, and—though Talon would never outwardly admit it—*delicious*. Castor fished out one for himself and sat across from Talon.

"That's an interesting sword," Castor gestured after he had finished. Talon nodded.

"It's not mine," he responded quietly, breaking the uncomfortable silence.

"You stole it?" Castor guessed with a mischievous grin.

"No," Talon explained. He was tempted to say *I don't deserve it*.

A loud bang erupted from underneath the floor, causing both Talon and Castor to jump in surprise. Amber's muffled yells echoed through the ship. A metal trapdoor, implanted in the floor to Talon's left, swung open and she pulled herself up and out. Talon noticed the thick layer of dark liquid covering her face, which she wiped at with a greasy rag.

"Castor, I thought you fixed the propellant tank!" she exclaimed. Castor looked guilty.

"Oops," he muttered.

"I just finished cleaning the engine, and now it's all dirty again!"

"Why don't you fix the tank, then?"

Amber scowled. "You know I don't know how. Technology is *not* my forte."

"The propellent tank isn't really technol—"

"Can you just take care of it please?"

Castor rolled his eyes. "Fine, I'll clean and fix the tank myself."

"*Thank* you," Amber threw back with mock politeness.

"But," Castor reasoned, "just remember that this is still *my* ship. I'm in charge."

Talon could tell it wasn't the first time he'd said that. Castor disappeared into the engine room below, and Amber breathed, taking his vacated seat, but Talon thought he saw charmed amusement flash across her face.

She laughed softly. "Sorry about that…"

Talon shrugged again.

"Typical day here on *The Independence*," Amber explained, before noticing Talon's look of confusion. "That's what Castor's father named the ship."

"This was his father's ship?" Talon asked before he could stop himself.

Amber nodded, then hastily changed the subject, "I guess I shouldn't complain. I mean, Castor helps me all the time… a lot more than I deserve."

Her voice trailed off, almost as if she were speaking more to herself than to him. She fidgeted with her long golden hair.

Talon realized she'd put another question into his mind: did they have parents? She and Castor weren't siblings, he could tell that much. They looked *nothing* alike. And yet, they were still only his age. How long had they been on their own?

"Well," Amber said, "make yourself at home, feel free to roam around."

What did she mean at *home*? Surely, he wouldn't be staying here. Amber shuffled toward the trapdoor, calling out Castor's name, and she too disappeared below.

Talon blocked all other questions from his mind and stood from the seat, stretching his tight legs. He left the sword resting against the wall and turned toward the cockpit.

When he entered, he immediately noticed multiple shelves lining the narrow walls, bearing curious items like a glass cube and a flip-out knife.

Two worn swivel-chairs sat in front of the console, which was layered with multicolored buttons, knobs, and levers. The steering mechanism—a metal wheel with a rubber grip—protruded from the console, tilted slightly to one side.

To Talon, the viewing port overshadowed everything else in impressiveness. A tall, wide window that slanted outward, letting pale morning sunlight streak through and illuminate the front of *The Independence*.

His heart sank when he focused on the view through the window. They were Upstate, and Talon immediately decided he never wanted to come here again.

Green grass was nowhere in sight. All he could see was gray.

Gray dust, gray dirt, gray *everything*.

The pine trees had been snapped like twigs, their crooked branches bare. A hideous river of mud wound its way through the dead trees. Just looking at it was nauseating.

Turning away, he exited the cockpit, making his way to the back of the ship.

The hammocks were simple pieces of substantial, magenta-colored cloth, hanging in front of three immense fuel tanks situated horizontally against the wall.

Three large touchscreens were perched on the workbench, blinking lights rimming their frames. Multiple oddly shaped tools were littered across the bench, providing a more chaotic space to work. Castor didn't strike Talon as the tidiest person.

Beneath him lay the metal trapdoor with a turn-wheel, leading to the engine room below.

Talon glanced inside the bathroom before sitting back down on the leather seat, leaning his head back and momentarily closing his eyes.

He suddenly became aware of something sitting in his pocket… a small item. Talon reached inside, his face falling before even seeing the object, knowing the feel of it all too well.

The Bluebook. The beautiful little item sat comfortably in his hand, its gold lettering reflecting the light, its silver designs snaking across the cover, its ribbon bookmark protruding from the bottom of the spine.

A surge of anger swept over him as he stared at the book's little cover and flipped the pages, every law Governor Kresh had ever written invading his eyes.

"A Bluebook?" came Castor's voice. He pulled himself out of the engine room, clutching a dirty cloth. Talon glanced at him before shoving the book back into his pocket.

He nodded. "I only have it because I live in New York…"

Castor smiled slyly. "Well, you won't need it here. We can burn it for you, if you want."

Intriguing….

Talon shook his head, and Castor shrugged before wandering into the cockpit. Amber climbed out after Castor and, without looking at Talon, also hurried her way into the cockpit.

Castor's muffled voice snagged at Talon's ears. Should he listen to this? It could be private. Yet something drew him nearer, and he listened through the wall.

"We need to tell him," he heard Castor say.

Amber responded with a concerned voice. "But what if he tries to run off?"

"Amber, where's he gonna go? It's not like he can hike thirty miles back to the city on his own, especially through Upstate. And, even if he tried, the Prime would catch up to him, like, *immediately*."

Silence. Talon sat rigid.

"Fine," Amber said, "I'll tell him about his parents. And the governor. Put the ship down."

"Why?"

"Just do it."

Talon froze… his parents? What did they know about his parents? *How* did they know about his parents?

The Independence slowed and lurched before descending, roughly setting itself on the dusty ground.

Amber exited the cockpit and shuffled her feet when she laid eyes on Talon. He tried to seem like he hadn't heard anything, but it was difficult.

"Come with me," she beckoned softly, before turning and pulling the lever to lower the boarding ramp. Talon stood from the chair and hesitantly followed her down the ramp, into the morning light.

The ship rested in the middle of an expansive clearing. Talon could taste the dust in the air and feel the soft soil beneath his feet.

A few trees stood about forty yards away, twisted at strange angles, their branches hanging by just a few black twigs. The river of mud wound its way across the ground, making a sickening noise as the muck shifted. Harsh rays of sunlight peeked through the clouds, tinged with brown.

Way in the distance, Talon could make out the faint skyline of New York City. He'd seen the skyline from Drudgen, the buildings towering over the Hudson River, but he'd never seen it from this far away. It gave him an exhilarating feeling to be away from the horrible city and among the silence of Upstate, even if it wasn't exactly beautiful.

Talon stood next to Amber, who seemed lost in thought as she stared at the vast city in the distance. She bowed her head and took a sharp intake of breath.

"Talon," she said, and he flinched when she said his name. No one had addressed him by name in years. Except Josef, but he didn't count. "I know this is confusing for you, so I wanted to talk to you."

He stared without saying a word.

"I want to talk to you about… about why that woman tried to kill you."

Talon bit his lip. "Who was she?"

Amber's green eyes pierced his blue ones.

"Officer Zedah Kahzak," she explained. "The New York records say she was imprisoned in the Danyorian concentration camps when she was just a child. Governor Kresh took her in when he destroyed the camps, and she became his officer later."

She said all of this very fast, and they stood there for a moment's silence. Castor appeared in the doorway of *The Independence*.

Talon said, "How do you know all this?"

Amber smiled. "Well, Castor is very adept at… um… *hacking*, I guess you could say."

"I got inside the system. We overheard the governor talking to Zedah." Castor added.

Talon tilted his head expectantly.

"They were planning on killing someone," Amber continued. "Killing someone because of their lineage. So… we tracked Zedah's ship and… that's when we saw you on the roof."

Confusion still permeated Talon's mind. "Why would you do that? Why hack into their system?"

"We're like everyone else," Castor stated. "We *hate* the Bluehouse Prime."

"But," Talon continued, wishing to clarify, "why *you*? Why are you two doing this?"

There was a long beat of silence before Amber changed the subject.

"Our parents are dead, too, Talon."

He snapped his head toward her so fast he popped his neck. His heart raced. Sweat broke out on his forehead. A terrible knot formed in his stomach.

"My… I never said… how do you…?" he stumbled.

"I can see it in your eyes," she explained softly. "I can just tell, and even if I couldn't, the pieces wouldn't be hard to put together."

Talon turned away and fixed his gaze on the muddy river, a hurricane of emotions assaulting his mind, attacking his heart. He'd sworn to himself he would forget. He'd sworn he wouldn't remember. He'd sworn he wouldn't let himself feel the pain.

Talon clenched his teeth together, trying to hide the emotion written on his face, trying to form a wall between himself and the grief. He'd been pulled back into the past, pulled back into the nightmare that plagued him every night, pulled back into the horror of that winter day.

"What does the governor want with me?" he declared fiercely, after grasping a firm grip on the present.

"That's just it," Castor replied. "We don't know."

"Based on what Castor and I heard," Amber stated, "we believe your parents may have been part of something. Something bigger than themselves. Something that possibly could have overthrown the Prime. The only problem is we don't know what it was or where it went."

Talon listened intently.

"You knew your parents better than anyone. We thought you may have known what it could be."

His heart sank deep into the pit of his stomach.

He said, "I'm sorry, I don't."

Amber's posture sank a little, too, but she continued speaking.

"Then we could really use your help in discovering *what* they were a part of. And what they were trying to stop."

Hope laced her voice, and Talon considered this. He assumed a normal person would feel excited at this chance of adventure. He'd always wanted things to change. But not like this.

This was *terrible*.

He wanted to be back home with Alger, wanted his life to go back to the way it was, but Talon knew he couldn't have that… he could *never* have that.

But if he discovered the answers to the questions about his parents, something inside of him might be fulfilled… he just didn't know what. So many questions flickered through his mind.

Would happiness finally be achieved when he discovered what his parents could've been fighting for? Would he feel accomplished? Would it satisfy him?

Then the flip side. What if Amber and Castor were lying? What if he couldn't trust them? Not that he could trust anyone. Not *anymore*.

What if they turned out to be frauds, or spies, or something even worse?

Battles raged inside him, each side trying to convince him of which road to take. What to do and what *not* to do.

Almost subconsciously, Talon slipped his hand inside his pocket and withdrew the Bluebook, vaguely noticing Amber's green eyes go wide.

He stared at the cover that seemed to be laughing at him, jeering at the fact he had to follow all the rules inside. All the torturous laws.

In one fluid motion Talon swung his arm behind his head, flung it back outward and released the wicked book from his grip.

It tumbled through the air like a feather in the wind before splashing into the muddy river, where it sank beneath the thick, wet soil.

Castor whistled. "Cool."

"I take that as a *yes*?" Amber confirmed, a slight smile crossing her lips.

Talon continued to stare at the river, avoiding eye contact with either of them.

Quietly, he affirmed, "Yes."

Amber gave a soft smile, reached up, and placed a hand on his shoulder. Talon flinched, and he knew she noticed because she pulled her hand away soon after.

Her touch was warm and… *comforting*.

Talon hated the feeling.

Compassion? He didn't need compassion.

"Well," Castor stated, "If we're all in on this… we may wanna get started. Unless you wanna wait for The Children of Ledger…"

Amber rolled her eyes as Castor disappeared into *The Indepen-*

dence.

"Um… Children of Ledger?" Talon mumbled.

"They're only legends," Amber mused. "*Fake* legends."

She entered the ship, leaving Talon outside. He wondered how many *fake legends* they were going to have to face before this was all over.

CHAPTER FIVE

MAY 6TH, 2492

Pale sunlight drizzled through the towering windows as Governor Kresh stalked through the long hallways in Prime Tower, escorted by two soldiers dressed in gray. The marble floors and walls reflected the sun's illuminations, casting a crystalline glow onto the surroundings.

Kresh walked with dignity, determination, and a good sense of powerful arrogance. As they passed through another glass hall, he inclined his head toward the shimmering Hudson down below.

If only they knew. If only anyone knew what was *truly* being built. If only they knew *why*. Kresh smiled internally, a wide grin spreading across his black heart.

He and the soldiers rounded a corner, coming to a large corridor, at the end of which stood two oak doors. Kresh's never-ending feeling of pride increased every time he saw the image implanted just above the doors: a small blue square.

The Bluebook wasn't just the Prime's symbol; it was *his* symbol. A symbol of everything he had built. Everything he had accomplished. Everything he *needed*.

Control. A symbol of control, and he reveled in the wondrous idea of totalitarian authority. Soon, absolute control would be accomplished. Soon, no one would defy him. He only needed more time.

The mechanical doors swung open, and Kresh entered the room. He gazed around the massive chamber, as he did every time he entered.

The smell of polished wood and soft carpet immediately met his nose. Velvet curtains hung from the white ceiling, partially obscuring the wood-paneled walls which reflected light from the massive crystal chandelier. Decorative marble columns lined the room, surrounding a broad rectangular table. Kresh had a perfect view of the Empire State Building through the wide window that stretched from the floor to the ceiling, rimmed with more heavy curtains.

Four faces turned to look at him, their owners seated at the table, and a rush of contempt swelled within the governor.

"Members of Prime," Kresh acknowledged.

"Governor Kresh," Mayor Xian said coolly, squinting his almond-shaped eyes. Kresh took his seat at the head of the table, sitting up straight, his hands on his lap. The soldiers took their places on either side of him.

He glared at the four men who sat staring at him expectantly. Every time he saw the members of the Bluehouse Prime, Kresh could not stop the unquenchable surge of hatred from boiling inside him. Consuming his every emotion. He gazed at them with his dark eyes before standing and placing both hands on the table in an authoritative manner.

"The operation is proceeding smoothly," he stated.

"And yet," declared Davith Coronil, the assistant city manager, "you're no further along than you were a week ago."

Kresh's anger rose but he maintained his composure. "I only need more *time*, gentlemen, and the ships will be finished."

"We don't *have* time, governor," Xian said. "We need to increase New York's trade, or bankruptcy will become inevitable."

Kresh's internal grin manifested itself again. If *only* they knew.

They will soon enough, he surmised, *and they'll be sorry when they do.*

"Mayor Xian, please," Kresh breathed. "My workers are doing the best they can. These things take time."

The city manager, Raul Barrios, stood and glared at Kresh through piercing gray eyes.

"You *dare* to tell us how things take time? We have put up with *you* for many years as you bide *your* time."

Kresh experienced a second surge of hatred. He hated them all but, if there was one he hated more than any of the others, it was Barrios. He was loud, he was rebellious, and he was the most unfiltered of all the Prime. He had no problem with questioning Kresh's tactics.

The city attorney, Tykeim Mills, also stood and motioned for both Kresh and Barrios to sit.

"Let us discuss this rationally, gentlemen."

The governor and the manager sat, neither of their gazes drifting from the other.

"The citizens are out of control," Mills said. "They are breaking laws at an extensive rate. If we continue to do nothing, the crime rate will increase and so will the protests."

"They will be dealt with soon." Kresh explained.

"You say that as if you have a plan," Barrios spat.

Kresh squinted. "Perhaps I do."

Dead silence. The governor glared at the council, his pride swelling at the fact he knew something they didn't.

If only...

Barrios said, "*We* are the Bluehouse Prime. You run your plans by *us* first."

"This is not a democracy. That chaos was abolished long ago. I ask you, gentlemen, what kind of man would I be if I did not keep my own secrets," Kresh inquired.

A longer beat of silence. Neither Barrios nor any of the others had a response to this. Kresh stared out the wide window, directly at the Empire State Building.

That is exactly what New York was. An empire state.

Or at least it would be, when Kresh's plan was finished. He would finally accomplish his ultimate goal. His ultimate *belief*.

It had failed the first time, and he'd paid for it dearly. He would do everything in his power to make sure it didn't happen again. He used to care about others, but he had discovered care was overrated. His ambition to do the right thing had cost him everything. Now, he knew only one ambition was worth his while: *control*.

"The cargo fleet will be completed by the end of the month," Kresh stated with finality.

"The end of the month?" Xian snapped.

Kresh nodded. "It has proven more difficult than I first believed it would."

"Don't forget, Kresh," Barrios said, "that it was *us* who helped raise you to this position. We helped you achieve this. I would expect you would be a little more grateful."

Kresh inhaled. "I am, truly."

It felt good to lie.

The oak doors swung open, and a third soldier entered the room, moving toward Kresh.

"Officer Kahzak has requested to see you, governor," the soldier announced. "She says it's important."

Kresh nodded, then turned back to the council. "I am afraid I must cut this meeting short. The Seventh Annual Bluebook Day is nearly upon us, gentlemen. Perhaps we should focus on preparations."

They stood simultaneously, acknowledged each other, and departed from the room. As Kresh and his guards made their way through the halls, a wicked joy ignited inside him.

The boy must be dead.

No more risk. The possibility of failure? Gone.

He entered his office and dismissed the guards. Zedah stood with her back toward him, peering at the vastness of Borough I.

"Zedah," Kresh said. "I trust it is more good news."

She hung her head before turning to him and, from the expression on her face, Kresh instantly knew something was wrong.

"Sir, I…" Zedah stuttered.

"Well?" Kresh huffed dangerously. He noticed her eye twitch.

"The—the boy escaped."

Rage shot through Kresh's veins, and he nearly lashed out. Composing himself, he stalked toward his desk and took a seat in the cushioned chair.

"Tell me," he ordered with false interest.

Zedah relaxed, but Kresh knew if she understood his true feelings, she would have died of fright.

"He was rescued."

Rescued.

The word pierced his mind. Who would've rescued the boy? How would they have found out?

Zedah continued, "I only saw one of them, a girl. She looked young."

So, Zedah had gotten outsmarted by a couple of kids. So unlike her.

"They destroyed my ship. I had to call an escort."

Kresh almost laughed, but the serious matter still tugged at his emotions. Anger swarmed through him. Zedah had *failed* him. He had given her *one* job, and she couldn't carry it through. He had put so much faith in her throughout the years, and now she stood here, a failure in his eyes… all because she couldn't kill an underage boy.

"Are you tracking them?" Kresh asked, avoiding her gaze.

Zedah straightened. "Yes, sir."

"Good. You must find them. I expect you will not fail me again."

Zedah retracted and—though she may not have noticed—let a spurt of nervous breath escape from her mouth.

"Sir, is—is death *really* the solution?" she stuttered. Pulsating anger consumed Kresh's emotion. She was questioning him again.

He stood and walked to a section of the giant window. "Death is the best solution to all problems. If there is no man, there is no problem."

She didn't respond. Kresh marveled at his prized ability to silence people with words.

After a moment, Zedah spoke softly. "Sir… I want to apologize for doubting you earlier today. I didn't think the boy could've been whom you thought… but I now know you were right about him."

Kresh squinted. "And why is that?"

"Well," she answered, "the boy had his father's sword. I recognized it."

A wave of dread washed over Kresh as her words hit him like

separate punches. Then, one thing replaced it.

Fear.

"I see," Kresh said, trying with all his might not to let his voice crack. "I'm glad you see your error and I hope you will not allow him to gain the upper hand."

She nodded vigorously. "No, sir. Never."

"I will send help with you this time, Zedah," he decided.

"Help, sir?"

"Yes, it is time we use our most vital resources."

Zedah paused, then nodded.

"The Entity Project?" she asked. Kresh tapped the touchscreen sitting on his desk. It beeped quietly.

"They await you."

The governor dismissed her, and she departed from the room. He sat at his desk and rested his elbows on the polished wood, gazing out the massive window, hoping—*pleading* the boy would die before he learned of the sword's importance.

CHAPTER SIX

MAY 13TH, 2492

A week passed by, and they were no closer to answers. No closer to *anything*. At times, Talon saw Amber messing with a couple of the touchscreens on the workbench, her fingers flying over them as quick as lightning.

Nevertheless, he noticed a heavy blanket of boredom set in.

Every day repeated itself. They woke up, flew to different areas so as not to be so easily found, and went to sleep. Soon, Talon realized his days in Drudgen hadn't been much different. Castor and Amber lived by this routine and didn't seem fazed by it.

Moreover, Talon didn't have a change of clothes; they had all been left behind at his apartment. Castor offered to loan him some. At first, he refused, but when he realized his clothes were beginning to smell despite frequently showering, he finally accepted.

Talon used the hammock most nights, but often found himself unable to sleep. He always ended up sitting awake in the cockpit, where Castor and Amber found him each morning.

He noticed they seemed to have an interest in him, but he also realized they appeared a little uncertain as to how he might respond.

In truth, he felt the same about them.

It was a strange feeling, having two other real people around. People he couldn't get away from. Back in Drudgen, only two people clung to him, two he truthfully couldn't escape: Futz and Len. But he'd hated them, and they had hated him, so their presence didn't bother Talon.

This was different.

Castor and Amber certainly didn't hate him. They seemed to enjoy the extra company, even if he barely spoke a word. Talon couldn't relate to that.

He didn't dislike them, but he didn't like them either. Their kindness felt abnormal. He hadn't experienced *kindness* in years. Not since his parents...

No.

He wouldn't allow his mind to go there. He'd already had the painful reminder, the reminder of that horrible day. Not that he wasn't reminded every night, in the nightmare that deprived him of sleep.

But the truth was that Castor and Amber were just two other people to him, two strangers who were just... *there*.

He didn't trust them, which he assumed to be the source of his interest in them. How could he trust someone he didn't know? And, even if he did know more about them, would he be able to trust them?

Early, on the morning of Talon's seventh day aboard *The Independence*, Amber shook him awake and he nearly tumbled out of his hammock in shock. She'd shaken him right out of his nightmare, cold sweat covering his neck and chest.

"Sorry!" she gasped. "I didn't mean to scare you."

"S'fine," he mumbled, wiping his forehead with his sleeve.

Amber half smiled before forcefully punching Castor's hammock.

"Hey!" he said when his eyes snapped open. "Okay, I'm a-wake!"

"Good," Amber remarked. "Because I found something."

Talon inclined his head toward her.

"Have you been messing with my computer again?" Castor scowled when he noticed the touchscreen was on, sliding out of his hammock.

"Well, I figured if you *still* don't want me touching the turret, I might as well mess with your touchscreens, which are *still* running slow." Amber said simply, sitting down at the workbench.

Castor countered, "You know why you can't touch the turret."

"I'd be fine, I wouldn't break anything!" Amber replied.

"Hey, don't play dumb… it's dangerous, that's why. Not because you would break something. Plus, we've never had to use it, and I don't want to waste ammunition."

Amber rolled her eyes. "We used it when we rescued Talon."

Talon started when his name was brought into their argument. He could tell they'd had this conversation many times before.

"Correction," Castor said, "*I* used it."

Amber waved him off. "Whatever."

She focused on the screen, clicking through a digital network of what looked like names. The screen suddenly froze, and Amber tapped at it.

"Castor, you really need to fix your computer."

"It's as good as it's gonna get."

Talon heard Amber mutter something that sounded suspiciously like *uggh, technology*. He grabbed his overcoat and let it hang loosely over his shoulders.

"You gonna tell us what's going on?" Castor asked with a yawn.

"In a minute."

"Look, it's still dark outside, Amber. If you're gonna wake us up this early to argue about a turret and a stupid computer, there better be a valid reason. Why are *you* up so early, anyway?"

Amber flinched. "You know I don't sleep well."

Talon saw Castor's face fall before he mumbled, "Sorry…"

Silence hung about the ship for a short moment in which Talon's mind reeled with questions. Why didn't Amber sleep well? Did she have dreams too? He refocused when she began to speak.

"I found something that might be able to help us."

"What is it?" Castor inquired.

"A person… look."

She rotated the screen and Talon saw something resembling an informational profile. A profile for a person.

"Orson Rye," Amber stated. "I found this in the New York archives. Apparently, they have every past and current citizen on record."

"How did you even get in there?" Castor exclaimed. "I thought I was the hacker!"

"You were, and still are. When you broke into Prime Tower's security system you opened a lot of other routes… too many to count."

She swiped the screen, now displaying a giant digital web Talon understood to be the government's supposedly secure information.

Castor shrugged. "Well, I guess that's a good thing."

"It is. We have access to everything, and it'll make things so much easier. But this is the *wanted* database, which has information on all the people who've committed crimes against the government."

Amber swiped back to the profile.

The name *Orson Rye* projected from the screen, but there was no image to prove his existence. Talon noticed the two other information slots just before Amber began reading them aloud.

"Offense: A known conspirator and member of The Falcon's Nest. Status: Unknown, last seen alive in Blackridge."

There was a short pause.

Castor scratched the back of his neck. "And *why* is this important?"

Amber took a deep breath and stopped for a moment. She turned toward Talon, staring at him in contemplation. His stomach turned uncomfortably, feeling her gaze piercing his. What was the matter?

"Because of this," she faltered. Amber swiped to the right, revealing another profile, and Talon's mouth fell open in stunned shock. Two faces stared back at him as a hard knot formed in his chest. All the memories returned, all the horrible thoughts, emotions, and feelings.

His father… his mother… their faces gazed at him through the screen, staring with stoic expressions. He knew, without asking, how Amber had discovered them as his parents. He had his mother's hair color, and her blue eyes, and his father's handsome features.

Tears stung his eyes, but he couldn't… *wouldn't* let them fall. He wouldn't show his true feelings, he wouldn't exhibit his emotions.

Talon couldn't bear to look at them anymore. He stared at the ground, focusing his gaze away from both Castor and Amber.

"Elijah and Hazel Chambers. Offense: Known conspirators and members of The Falcon's Nest. Status…"

Amber didn't finish. Her face told Talon she'd noticed his pain, but he already knew what it said.

He could feel both sets of eyes on him.

Another short pause. Amber spoke in an almost pleading voice. "I'm sorry, Talon. I didn't mean to…"

"It's fine," he interrupted. It wasn't fine, but he couldn't say that… he *wouldn't* say that.

From his peripherals, Talon could tell she studied him with more than just sympathy. Almost… *empathy*. As if she could truly relate to his pain. How could she? He knew both she and Castor had lost their parents, but their pain wasn't as bad as his… was it?

But something else hung in her eyes. She stared at him, but he could tell she wasn't thinking about him. Her mind was somewhere else… somewhere *dark*. Talon could see it in her eyes.

"So," Castor said, "what's The Falcon's Nest."

Amber shook her head. "I'm not sure, but it sounds like some sort of organization. It must've been an issue for the Prime, or they wouldn't have it listed as an offense."

Was that what his parents were? An offense? Felons? Talon didn't want to believe it, but the truth sat right before him. The truth he never knew. The truth his parents kept from him all along. He couldn't blame them. He'd been so young, so naïve. How could he expect them to tell him the truth? The truth that they weren't just ordinary people. The truth there was something more to them.

But there was a part of him that was upset… almost angry. Angry that he didn't truly know his parents. Angry that his life had been a lie up until they died. But had it been? Had they really loved him as their own, or were they too preoccupied for it to be real?

No, he knew that was a lie. His parents had loved him. They'd *always* loved him. He'd never doubted that, and he never would.

Amber continued. "Blackridge is a sector in Cantatonia, and from what I've heard it's completely lawless. There's absolutely no government. And the citizens aren't exactly the *greatest* people," Amber groused.

Castor muttered, "Great."

Another long silence followed, in which all three of them sat still, deep in thought. Talon knew it was worth checking out. His parents and this Orson person had been labeled as part of the same organization. If he was still alive, maybe Orson could help them. Maybe he could give them insight. Maybe he'd actually known…

No. He wouldn't have. He *couldn't* have.

That thought was horrible.

Someone who had truthfully known them?

What even was The Falcon's Nest? What did they do?

"Look," Castor doubted, "I know that we're trying to find answers and stuff, but don't you think this is a little early?"

Talon and Amber remained silent, waiting for him to finish.

"I mean," he continued, "we don't even know who this Orson person is. How do we know he'll help us?"

"We don't…"

This time, it was Talon that had spoken, and he immediately wished he hadn't. He stared at the ground as they continued to contemplate him.

"You're right," Amber stated. "We don't. But we have to try. If we don't, we may never know anything."

Talon remained silent.

Castor shrugged, then nodded. "I'll get the ship ready. I think we have enough fuel."

He made his way through the belly of the aircraft and disappeared into the cockpit. Amber stared after him until he was out of sight, then turned her attention to Talon.

"You okay?" she asked quietly. He moved his head forward, barely nodding. She continued, "I know this must be hard for you…"

What did she know about it? Her parents *were* dead, but her pain could be nothing compared to his. How could she understand? How could *either* of them understand?

"But I want you to know we're on your side. You can trust us…"

"I didn't say I don't trust you," Talon declared bluntly.

"But you don't, do you?" Amber queried with a small frown.

Silence. He still didn't look at her.

"I would be skeptical, too. You don't know us, we don't know you, but that doesn't mean we can't work together."

He almost believed her… he *did* believe her. But he wouldn't let himself start to *care* for them.

The thought of care made him want to vomit.

There was danger in care… danger in developing a bond. He couldn't bear it if he had to feel that pain again. First with his parents, then with Alger. Talon wouldn't let it happen again. Not if he could help it. And he *could* help it.

"I…" he began in a near whisper, "I just don't think it's a good idea for you—either of you—to be around me."

He barely glanced at her when he said these words, catching a glimpse of her puzzled face.

"Why?" she questioned.

"I… I'm not gonna be here forever," Talon explained. He thought he saw her shake her head.

"Where else is there to go?"

Talon noticed she said these words with something more than just interest. Almost pain.

"I don't know," he stuttered, almost desperately, "but I'll... I'll figure it out."

"On your own?"

Yet another moment's silence. He nodded ever so slightly, and Amber seemed grieved. She seemed to think he was making a mistake, seemed to think he was wrong.

But Talon knew he wasn't wrong, *she* was. She didn't understand. He met her sparkling eyes, which stared back at him with sympathy. The thought of sympathy made his head ache. He hated sympathy. Didn't they understand he didn't *need* their sympathy?

"Talon, if this is going to work, then we need to be around you. You want this, too, don't you?"

"I do," he related. "It's just..."

He faltered.

"Just what?" Amber inquired.

He couldn't tell her. He would *never* tell her. He wouldn't let her know that he was afraid...

Talon breathed. "Nothing."

She continued to watch him through her pretty green eyes, and Talon stared right back. It wrenched his gut to focus on her this long, but he maintained his gaze for what felt like hours.

"I should probably go help Castor," she reckoned. She broke eye contact and stood, following Castor into the cockpit. Talon heard them exchange conversation, and though he couldn't make out their words, he assumed they were speaking about him.

The computer screen still shined bright, displaying the image of Orson Rye's profile. Talon made sure Castor and Amber were still in the cockpit before standing from the hammock and slowly stepping toward the workbench.

He reached his finger out, prepared to touch the screen.

His eyes stung. The temptation to swipe back to their profile was painful. Agonizing. The temptation to lay his eyes on them once again.

In the blink of an eye, Talon placed his hand on the frame and forced it, screen down, onto the workbench. He stepped backward, sat on the hammock, his eyes burning as he tore his gaze from the back of the screen.

CHAPTER SEVEN

MAY 13TH, 2492

The Independence's engines revved to life as Castor's hands flew over the controls, prepping the ship for takeoff. The ship rocked and swayed, and Talon felt it leave the ground, rocketing into the sky.

After pulling on his boots, he made his way to the heart of the ship and took a seat on the tattered leather chair. Castor poked his head out of the cockpit, his eyes seeking Talon.

"You coming?" he asked. Joining them in the cockpit intrigued him for a fraction of a second, then turned his stomach. It almost sickened him, the thought of the company, and he made up his mind almost immediately.

He gently shook his head, and Castor shrugged before disappearing again. Talon heard him ask Amber for the coordinates, which she began to relate after bringing it up on yet another touchscreen. It was strange for him to hear and not see them, but he knew it was for the better.

He turned and gazed out of a small circular viewing port spattered with grime. The skeletons of the trees below whipped past in a blur as the aircraft sped over the plateau of filth.

Miles in the distance, the outline of the Laughing Highlands, a mountain range with gray peaks, glistened in the sunlight. Talon remembered reading about the mountains years ago, and that the Highlands wove a long line through the top of the country, cutting through multiple states, empires, and cities, all the way to the shoreline of Danyor on the west coast. He recalled they held the record for the largest and longest mountain range to form as a result of The Great Quake, the disastrous event that forever changed the geography of the earth.

Despite the fact no one in his life ever talked much of the Laughing Highlands, Talon found it very interesting to look at. He'd rarely been outside of New York City, and it was strange seeing something new, strange having an entirely different view of the world. Some place other than Drudgen, even if it was still the same state.

He heard Castor tell Amber the ship was clocking at around two-hundred miles an hour, setting their journey at a little over three hours.

After close to thirty minutes, Talon noticed the scenery begin to change. The landscape became greener, though not by much. An adrenaline rush coursed through his blood when he realized they were out of New York.

He'd left the state... left the one place he'd never *ever* left. Though the landscape was still less than beautiful, the shocking revelation passed over him that he'd crossed the border. Now that this moment had come, he didn't know what to feel. Scared? Interested? Glad?

Another half hour passed by, but Talon couldn't stop staring out the window. Expansive hills, dressed in yellow grass, rolled by like a sea of pale gold. Occasionally, he saw thatched roofs and dirt roads, belonging to a village or small settlement. Talon tried to imagine what it was like living in solitude, reminding him he could relate to the villagers. Though he lived in the city, he *still* led a life of aloneness.

Wasn't that exactly what he wanted? To live alone, to not have to deal with anyone, to not have to risk the pain?

Yes, he decided adamantly.

And yet, something still nagged at his mind, tugged on his heart. If being alone was what he wanted, why was it such torture? He thought he'd achieved true happiness by his self-inflicted solitude, but now he wasn't so sure. If being alone didn't bring true happiness then what did?

Stop, he told himself. *Happiness can't be anything else for you.*

Talon said these words over and over in his head, ingraining them in there, hammering them into his mind. Soon, the rolling hills transformed into miles of expansive nothing.

Dirt. Everywhere he looked.

Not a single mountain, tree, or settlement stood within sight. All Talon could see for miles was a massive blanket of brown. He had a distant memory of reading, in an old geography book, about this place. What was it called? The Ochre Prairie? It lay in the Empire of Xanitough, as it had been renamed. He remembered it used to be called Ohio. Over eighty miles of yellowish dirt stretched as far as the eye could see.

I wish I had a book right now.

Talon knew that couldn't happen, at least not in New York. The Prime had taken the books over seven years ago, and Drudgen rumors told him they had burned them. He hadn't read a book since he was very young.

After almost ninety minutes the landscape began to change again, and in the most stunning manner. Enormous rock spires, the height of skyscrapers, sprouted from the ground like blades of grass in a world of giants. Some of them stood crooked, some shorter than others, some missing their sharp tips. Castor weaved *The Indepen-*

dence around the monolithic stalagmites which were sandwiched between two massive cliffs.

The Durinian Canyon, Talon realized.

It was one of the most famous and unusual places to be formed as a result of the Quake. All the memories of everything he'd learned at a young age flooded back to him. All the geography books he read, the ones he'd keep going back to as a small child. He nearly smiled at the thought.

Talon turned his head from the viewing port and subconsciously reached for his sword. He found himself staring at it again, as he always did whenever he laid eyes on it. He ran his fingers along its leather wrapped handle, and the blade shimmered in the light.

A sudden powerful *BANG* shocked Talon out of his thoughts, and he heard Castor curse before handing the controls to Amber. He rushed out of the cockpit and to the back of the ship, where he threw open the metal trapdoor and disappeared inside it. Another, even louder *BANG*.

Castor yelled, "Amber, could I get a little help?"

"I'm flying the ship." she called from the cockpit.

"Just put it on autopilot."

"I don't know how. Piloting is *your* thing."

"You just press the green button."

"There are a million green buttons!"

Talon heard Castor groan, and he felt stupid just sitting there. Slowly, he stood and made his way toward the trapdoor, where he bent down on his knees and peered through the opening. He saw Castor pressing on a metal pipe, attempting to force it into place. Oil dripped from a serrated tube.

"It's the connection rod," Castor stated when he saw Talon, relief in his tone. "Could you hand me a wrench?"

Talon nodded, keeping his eyes down.

He craned his neck and found the silver tool sitting on the workbench amidst the other scattered items. Castor took it and began to crank it back into place, oil dripping onto his hands.

He wiped his forehead when he finished. "That could've been bad… if the rod had broken, it wouldn't have been able to transmit the force between the piston and the crankshaft, so—"

He stopped himself.

As Talon moved to stand, he felt his foot collide with something. He turned just in time to see a tall object fall from behind Castor's hammock, and a loud metallic ring resounded through the belly of the ship. He froze, realizing he'd just knocked something over.

Castor's eyes widened.

A long, silver spear lay on the ground below the hammock, shimmering in the pale light. He hadn't noticed it before… had it been hidden?

"Oh… that's nothing," Castor stated even though Talon hadn't asked. He pulled it from the ground and pressed a small button on the felt-wrapped handle. The glistening weapon folded into a small cylinder, its metal head disappearing into the handle.

Talon stared, and Castor gave him a side-eyed glance.

"Just a gift from my dad," he said quietly as he placed the folded spear back behind his hammock. A pit formed in Talon's stomach, leaving as quickly as it had appeared. He nodded without saying a word, but inside, his mind yelled at him.

Castor had been left a possession by his father, too, but it wasn't as if… it couldn't be like Talon could *relate* to him.

He wouldn't allow his mind to go there.

Castor shoved a hand through his thick black hair, half-smiled, and disappeared back into the cockpit, leaving Talon standing alone, deep in thought.

Spears weren't common weapons. Not anymore. They were reserved for the highest ranked members of the military in some states. Had Castor's father been a general? A commander?

Talon sat back down, remaining in his seat until Amber poked her head out of the cockpit.

"We're here," she said softly to Talon. She wore a sadness on her face that Talon only understood when he got up and gazed out of the cockpit viewing port.

Cantatonia was like no place he'd ever imagined, and not in a good way. A dull, heavy mist covered the city, filtering the sun and casting a drearily sinister light on the buildings.

Talon noticed the city seemed to have been constructed with a very organized design. Smaller buildings stood on the outskirts, taller buildings in the exact middle. Ten cylindrical buildings formed a circle around a massive, black skyscraper that looked to be twisted on its axis like a strip of curly ribbon.

The tall structures in the center were strong and sturdy, but the small residences on the outskirts looked like they'd been built by a child who'd obtained a few slabs of rotting wood, some rusty nails, and a hammer. Even from twenty thousand feet in the air, Talon could tell how much of a terrible place this was.

He remembered that, when the Quake came centuries before, a young Cantatonia had been leveled by the disaster, then rebuilt by all different groups of people. It was complicated, but what his old books had told him was that absolutely no one got along. The result was... *this*. A dark, sinister city anyone in their right mind would stay away from.

The Laughing Highlands towered in the distance, about thirty miles from the edge of the city, their peaks vanishing in the low clouds. As they descended toward the city, the sinister details became even more apparent, and they cruised above the buildings for almost five minutes before Castor spoke.

"Where's Blackridge?"

Amber glanced at her touchscreen. "It's a few miles northeast, close to the outskirts."

The ship veered to the right as Castor turned them northeast, the inertia making Talon queasy. Soon, he saw a modest section of the city with aged stone buildings, cobbled streets, and metal spires that could only be for radar.

"There's a landing dock over there," Amber stated, pointing to her right. *The Independence* descended toward the docking port, touching down with a loud mechanical thud.

Castor stood and, with the click of a few buttons, the ship's engines went quiet. The three of them stood in a small circle, though they were silent for a few moments.

"Okay," Amber started. "We don't know what these people are like, and I don't think we want to find out."

They gathered their things, Talon pulling on his overcoat and retrieving his sword before turning and seeing Castor slip something into his pocket, leaving nothing behind but a curious gleam of silver. Amber fingered the handle of her dagger before securing her cloak around her neck.

Castor pulled the lever. The boarding ramp lowered with a resounding creak and the first thing Talon noticed was how incredibly loud Blackridge was.

As they descended the ramp, the awful sounds of rageful shouts, shattering glass, and rumbling machinery invaded his ears. A security guard in a red uniform stalked up to them and held out his palm before they even had a chance to survey the environment.

"Payment?" he huffed.

"What?" Castor asked.

"You have to pay to land here," the man exhaled, growing irritated. Castor cocked his head.

"We… um… have to *pay*?"

The guard nodded once, grunting angrily, and Castor and Amber frantically felt around in their pockets.

Talon remembered something with a start; he still had half of his last earnings from Futz in his overcoat pocket. It had been in there for a week, and he hadn't even given it a thought. Without hesitation, he withdrew his final bronze coin and placed it in the guard's meaty hand.

"Is that enough?" he asked quietly.

The man nodded and stood aside to let them pass, and there was a brief wave of confusion that jammed in Talon's brain. He nearly reached in his other pocket for the Bluebook, half expecting the man to withdraw a scanner.

He stopped when he remembered he'd destroyed his Bluebook, and he wasn't in New York. The feeling was exhilarating, and a fleeting rush of mischievous joy ran through him. He felt like a young child committing a sneaky act of rebellion.

"Thanks for that," Castor said. Talon shrugged.

Two shaggy black dogs bolted past them, reminding him painfully of Alger, before disappearing down the cobbled street. Both men and women lay unconscious on the walkway, empty liquor bottles resting in their firm grip. Citizens shouted at each other, brawling and scuffling everywhere they turned. Talon noticed the citizens of Blackridge wore a brutish and unpredictable expression, as though contemplating if they were worth murdering. They donned many different types of clothing; rags, sleeveless-shirts, and some of the women wore dresses that looked several hundred years out of fashion.

The sun dipped behind the Highlands, casting the orange light of golden hour on Blackridge, but Talon saw the physical environment didn't help the mood. The buildings were hewn out of blocks of limestone, with door and window openings carved crudely into them. Citizens appeared in second story windows, wringing out dirty towels or emptying disgusting chamber pot contents onto the street below. The smell was abominable.

"How are we going to find him in this place?" Castor asked with a sigh. "We don't even know what this Orson person looks like. There was no picture on the profile."

"I guess we should ask around," Amber suggested.

Castor gulped. "Oh, sure... just ask one of *these* people, as if they won't even kill us for bothering them."

Amber rolled her eyes.

Talon noticed a mousy haired mechanic working on one of the spires with a rusty tool set. As Castor and Amber bickered, he slowly approached him.

"Excuse me?" he asked quietly.

"Eh?" the mechanic replied gruffly. Talon took this as an invitation.

"We're looking for someone named Orson Rye. Do you know

him?"

The mechanic paused, studying Talon before finally shaking his head.

"Never 'eard of 'im. Look, this isn't the southside, but if yeh're smart, yeh'll still keep yer mouth shut 'round 'ere, kid."

Talon sighed and shrugged before making his way back toward Castor and Amber, who were only now finishing their bickering session. He suspected they hadn't even noticed him leave.

Before he could speak however, Talon saw, with a surge of unsettlement, a tall, hooded figure standing twenty yards away at the entrance of one of the buildings. The doorway framed his mysterious shape as he stood perfectly still, facing their direction. Though the depth of his hood shrouded his face in shadow, Talon could see his short, scraggly white beard and weathered hands.

What startled him most about the figure… what unsettled him terribly… was that he stared directly at them, stiff and frozen. Talon averted his eyes and motioned for Castor and Amber to follow.

"What is it?" Amber whispered when they were a few steps away.

Talon shrugged. "Probably nothing…"

He glanced over his shoulder.

It's definitely something.

The figure followed them, his face still hidden beneath his thick hood, his cloak billowing menacingly in the wind.

Castor and Amber glanced around and finally laid eyes on the man. It took them a moment, but Talon realized they eventually understood his worry. They turned down alleyways, hurried up streets, and twisted around confusing roundabouts.

Soon the figure disappeared, and Talon finally relaxed.

"Who was that?" Castor asked, concern etched in his voice. Talon shrugged, but his mind whirled. There was something about that man's presence that ignited some sort of familiarity.

No, that couldn't be. Where on earth would he have encountered a man who lived in Cantatonia?

Amber was first to recover her wits. "I guess we should start."

"Start what?" Castor asked.

"Asking around."

"Didn't I already say that was a bad idea?"

But Castor didn't complain any more.

They split up, making sure to remain in each other's line of sight.

For hours they asked around, and nearly everyone told them to get lost (one man tried to club Castor on the head with a large rum bottle). A few people seemed like they may have wanted to help, but when they learned there was nothing in it for them, they lost interest.

As the time passed, so did Talon's energy. He wore himself out continuously asking for directions, help, anything. But he hadn't forgotten about the startle they'd had earlier. He turned to speak to one more person, thoughts of the hooded figure still plaguing his mind.

The sun had hidden behind the Highlands, darkness covering the sky. Amber glanced at her holo-band and told them it was half past eight.

In the distance, Talon could see the lights of the city, and came to the realization that Cantatonia looked much more appealing at night. Multicolored lights dotted the buildings in perfectly symmetrical patterns. Turquoise, red, green, and purple illuminated the exteriors of the skyscrapers, as though made of long sticks of light

Blackridge shined bright as well, though not as elaborately. Blue lights shone from behind signs, streetlamps, and windows, casting a pale color on the surroundings. There was no curfew here; Talon hadn't been outside while it was truly dark in over a year, and the chilling air made his skin crawl.

Amber sighed. "Maybe we should go back to the ship and continue tomorrow."

"Yeah," Castor yawned. "I'm tired."

Talon wasn't. He was wide awake, but he knew he couldn't continue on his own. They wouldn't let him.

But Amber suddenly screamed, staring at something right behind Talon. Before he could even look, he felt a man's cold hand clamp itself over his mouth. The shock nearly made him pass out, and his adrenaline spiked painfully.

He tried to move but couldn't; whomever had grabbed him had gotten him into an unbreakable hold. Castor yelled and leaped toward the attacker but fell back as the man thrust his foot out, kicking him to the ground. Talon's breathing quickened as he realized it was the hooded figure from before. He struggled even harder at the realization.

But the man didn't do anything. He didn't attack, didn't try to do anything to him. He just held him there, waiting for him to stop struggling before leaning forward and whispering into Talon's ear.

"Follow me," he said. His voice was deep and hollow, as though it had seen better days. The man released him, letting him scramble away as Castor lifted himself to his feet. After staring at them for one more moment, the man turned and strode toward a rugged building.

The structure had a large neon sign placed above the door.

Kupo's Inn

Loud music emanated from the place, muffled by the limestone walls and cracked windows.

The figure's shadow was rimmed by flashing lights coming from the interior of the building, and Talon could just make out a head nod before he turned and disappeared inside.

Talon started to follow, but Amber grabbed his arm.

"What are you doing?" she asked exasperatedly.

Castor nodded. "Are you crazy?! He just attacked you! We don't even know who he is!"

"He didn't attack me… he just wanted us to follow." He immediately knew these words wouldn't go over well.

"What are you talking about?" Castor exclaimed. "You're going to *follow* this guy?"

"He could know Orson," Talon explained. There was a beat of silence, broken only by a dog's bark in the distance.

Amber cut in. "It's dangerous."

"I'm not saying it isn't," Talon explained. "But we could give it a try. That's what you said right? That we have to try?"

He wasn't sure why, but something inside him drew him toward the man. That same familiarity he'd felt hours before.

Amber fixed her eyes on the building before releasing his arm. The three of them stared each other down for another moment before Talon saw Amber inhale deeply.

"Okay, but I'm going in prepared," she hesitated, fingering the handle of her dagger. Talon let his hand fall to the hilt of his sword.

This was insane. This was a bad idea. He knew that without a doubt. But at least it was a *chance*. Talon stepped toward the entrance, the flashing lights blurring his vision, before the three of them walked inside.

CHAPTER EIGHT

MAY 13TH, 2492

The first thing Talon noticed about *Kupo's Inn* was how incredibly crowded it was. Hordes of people clambered around, leaving them no place to move. They squeezed their way through walls of drunken men and women, and the smell of drugs permeated the air.

Shouts echoed from every corner of the room as blaring music made the floors and walls shake. A diversity of drinks splashed and splattered everywhere as people cackled maniacally, shouting obscenities at each other. White lights flashed, making Talon's head spin and causing him to squint.

Castor instinctively stepped in front of Amber.

"You stay between us," he said. She half shoved him.

"You always do that, stop trying to protect me from everything."

Castor seemed offended, speaking over the noise. "I let you do your thing all the time! I rarely try to protect you!"

Amber coughed something that sounded suspiciously like *turret*. Castor didn't seem to hear, staring darkly at a couple of drunken lunatics throwing violent punches at each other.

An old wooden staircase stood at the back of the bar, leading up to a separate landing where the cloaked man stood, surveying the chaos below.

The three of them pressed their way through until they made it to the base of the stairs. Talon kept his eyes glued to the man, watching for any sudden moves, anything that could tell them he had a sinister motive.

They climbed the last step, where he peered at them, standing a few paces away. The music and shouts still echoed everywhere, but Talon hardly noticed.

The figure turned and stalked swiftly down the hallway. They followed him along dimly lit corridors as the loudness of the lower floor slowly began to muffle behind the grungy walls.

Talon was reminded of his apartment complex in Drudgen, though they didn't have a bar on the ground floor.

"Come," said the man. He turned and unlocked a wooden door with a rusty key, beckoning them to enter.

Talon hesitated. What if this was a trap? What if they couldn't trust this man?

He followed him anyway, thinking himself stupid, Castor and Amber at his heels.

Clutter filled the room. A small cot rested in the far-right corner, hidden behind stacked boxes and used paper, as if sleep wasn't important. A small wooden table with two antique chairs stood in the middle of the room, and a food cupboard shrouded half of the window with its bulk. Another door led out to a small wooden balcony overlooking the street below and offering a panoramic view of the skyline.

Silence hovered about the room as the man shuffled to the back, opening drawers and placing the contents of his pockets inside them.

Talon nearly pulled the door shut, then thought the better of it. He didn't know if they would need to make a quick getaway.

"Who are you?" he managed to ask, trying to sound fierce. It didn't come out the way he'd hoped.

The figure turned and stared at them for a long moment. Finally, he lowered his hood. His eyes were dark brown, a kind of sadness to them, rimmed with small wrinkles. His nose was thick and lumpy; evidently, he'd broken it at one point in his life. His short hair was white, matching his beard, and the faded creases in his cheeks told Talon he used to smile a lot.

He opened his mouth to speak, and what he said stunned Talon to the core.

"Hello, Talon."

Dead silence.

Talon caught his breath, a burning sensation erupting inside his stomach. This man knew his name… he knew *him*.

"H—how do you know me," Talon stuttered in disbelief. "Do you know… Orson?"

The man waited a moment before responding, staring directly at Talon, dark emotion written on his face.

"I *am* Orson."

Talon's mouth fell open, and he heard Amber gasp. This was the man they were looking for? He'd imagined someone strong… almost *mighty*. Now, all he saw was an aging man, whose expression told him he'd seen too many sorrowful days.

Orson stepped toward them slowly, and Talon could feel Castor and Amber stiffen.

"How…?" Talon stuttered.

"How did I recognize you?" Orson finished. "Because of your parents… you look so much like them."

Parents.

The word stuck in Talon's mind, as though a bullet had crashed through his skull. No words would form. He could only stare back at the man who was gazing at him with sadness and remorse. He could only stare at him in bewilderment.

"How… how do you…?"

Another pause, and Orson smiled at him before saying softly, "Your parents were my closest friends, and I theirs."

A spike of adrenaline rolled through Talon like a tidal wave of shock. He couldn't think, he couldn't *feel*. He didn't know what was happening. It was as though he was tumbling through a black void of darkness.

"I haven't seen you since you were a baby," Orson explained, taking a deep breath.

Now he knew why Orson seemed familiar. He *had* seen him. As a baby.

Talon tried to seem stoic, he tried not to *feel*. It was no use. The wave of memory was there before he could stop it… and it was horrible. It took all his might to shut it out again. To shut out the vast hole of grief, sucking in all goodness he'd ever felt, sucking in *everything*.

"I'm sorry, I only have the two chairs," Orson apologized.

He scrambled to find seating arrangements for two more people. Eventually, he pulled a wooden box and a decrepit stool from the back of the room, arranging them next to the other two chairs.

"Please," he beckoned. "Sit."

He took his seat at the table, and so did Castor and Amber, both of whom seemed shocked and perplexed. Talon was the last to sit, but he immediately wanted to stand up again. He wanted to shout, stunned and almost terrified at the fact he had now met someone else who had known his parents.

"Who might you two be?" Orson asked, directing the question toward Castor and Amber. They each glanced at the other before speaking.

"I'm Amber."

"Castor."

Orson nodded and repeated, "Amber and Castor."

His eyes found the wooden table. He looked to be in deep contemplation. After a long moment he turned his attention back to Talon, his eyes glazed.

"I'm so sorry," he said.

Talon didn't have to ask what he was talking about. He knew he was talking about his parents… about how they were *gone*… how they were *never* coming back.

"I… I don't…" Talon stumbled. His mind wouldn't let him form a sentence. All four of them sat in eerie silence, staring at each other, hearing nothing but the sounds of the music below. A long moment passed before any of them spoke.

"All this time, I never knew you were still alive," Orson said. "I thought you were dead."

"I don't understand," Talon finally declared. "How do you know me?"

Orson stared at him with more than compassion: *care*. "You wouldn't remember me… you were just a newborn… but what's to remember?"

His gaze fell back to the table.

"I was the first besides your parents to see you."

Nothing could have prepared Talon for this moment. His whole life had turned upside down.

"How did you know them?" he asked breathlessly.

"We worked together," Orson replied, his face somber and flushed with memory.

What were the chances Orson would've recognized him purely by his looks? What were the chances they would've found him in this way?

"Sir?" Amber questioned, and Orson directed his attention to her. "We—we're looking for answers."

Orson nodded delicately, and Amber seemed to take this as an invitation.

"Something happened… and, well, I should let Talon explain."

Talon stared at the table.

"If he wants to," Amber added hastily.

This moment was everything. This was his chance to know… his chance to understand. Now that he was here, Talon wasn't sure he *wanted* to know. What would it bring him? Content or anguish? Joy or sadness?

"I'm sorry," Amber apologized in a sorrowful tone. "I didn't mean to—"

"No," Talon interjected. "It's fine. I need to know."

A relieved yet joyous expression passed over Amber's face as Talon lifted his eyes and stared directly at Orson.

"A… there was a woman…"

Orson turned his head, ever so slightly, wearing an expression that made Talon assume he knew more than they did.

"She was… she was sent to kill me."

"Who sent her? Who was she?" Orson asked immediately, the words coming out swiftly and darkly.

Talon breathed. "Governor Kresh sent her. Her name was Zedah Kahzak."

Their names tasted sour on his tongue. Orson stood from his chair and walked, as if in a trance, to the window, where he stared out at the vast city in the distance.

"What is it, sir?" Amber inquired.

Orson lifted his head. "I know her all too well. I know *both* of them all too well."

Talon's mouth parted. "You... you do?"

"Yes," Orson said, turning back toward them.

"How?"

"They were our most powerful adversaries. Kresh was the whole reason we were fighting," Orson explained, his words twisting their understanding.

"Adversaries in what?" Castor asked.

"In the war... our *secret* war."

Orson seemed to be lost in thought, turning over memory after memory in his mind. His face was gaunt and disturbed, like a child's after a nightmare.

Amber's eyes widened, and Talon knew she'd had a revelation. "Sir, does... does this have anything to do with The Falcon's Nest?"

Orson turned to her, a smile barely crossing his lips.

"It has *everything* to do with The Falcon's Nest. How did you discover it?"

"Well, Castor broke through the Prime's security system, and we found... well, we found you in the *wanted* section. It talked about something called The Falcon's Nest."

A beat of silence followed.

"It takes a lot of talent to do that. Well done," Orson said. A gratified smile fluttered across Castor's face.

Talon mumbled, "What *is* The Falcon's Nest?"

Orson took his seat across from them and laced his fingers together before meeting his eyes. His voice was strained as he forced the words out.

"It was an organization dedicated to overthrowing Kresh and the Prime."

Talon's head began to spin again. If his parents were part of The Falcon's Nest, as their profile had claimed, were they dedicated to ending the Bluehouse Prime? But *how*? How could that be? How could *they* be secret soldiers fighting against Kresh?

"Your parents, Elijah and Hazel, were the leaders," Orson explained, and the loudest silence Talon had ever experienced swam through the room. He nearly fainted from the shock. His vision blurred, his head ached, and his stomach cramped painfully. His parents… the leaders of a rebellious organization? He didn't want to believe it.

"They founded it soon after you were born, Talon," Orson said, "and they named it after you."

Talon's body stiffened and his eyes stung, rimming with tears. He swallowed, but it only made the pain worse.

"What happened to it?" Castor asked eagerly. Orson's expression darkened, and he rested a hand over his mouth in deep contemplation.

"We lost."

There was a horrible silence. It was as if the air had turned to ice, and a cold sliver of it had slipped down Talon's back. Orson stood once again and turned his back on them.

"How?" Amber pleaded shakily. Orson's expression told all three of them he hadn't spoken of it in years and hadn't been planning to.

"Governor Kresh. He and Zedah focused all forces against us… and wiped us out," he explained before glancing back at Talon. "A select few of us escaped, myself and your parents included, but I don't know how many more."

Amber said, "But, *why*? Why did they focus everything at The Falcon's Nest?"

Orson neither looked at her nor spoke. Talon, Castor and Amber had their eyes fixed on him, waiting with bated breath.

"The Nest wanted to make right what the governor had made wrong, and when they learned what he was—*is* going to do… they couldn't stay silent."

"Sir," Amber said, "what is he going to do?"

Orson stroked his temples as though he were in some sort of trance.

"They… they wanted to make it right…"

His voice faltered, and Talon understood he was speaking more to himself than to them. It was almost as if Orson hadn't had a happy thought in years. The past haunted him… disturbed him… and, even now, it shook him.

Castor said, "You keep saying *they*… as if you weren't a part of it."

"I didn't deserve to be." Orson lifted a finger and stroked his lumpy nose. "I wasn't as committed to the cause as the rest of the Nest, and I made… *mistakes*. Your father had to teach me a lesson."

He looked at Talon and a meager smile came to his face.

"We had a disagreement… a heated one… and he broke my nose."

Orson laughed quietly. A mixture of surprise and shock swam through Talon's blood, and he nearly smiled, but stifled the urge violently.

"I won't say I didn't deserve it," Orson continued. "He and I had been standing on thin ice for a while, and I was the foolish one. I suppose he lost control… something very rare in him."

Talon bit down hard, trying to barricade his mind against the influx of emotion.

"Sir," Amber said, "you said the governor is going to do something. What is he going to do?"

Another cold bout of silence as Orson drew in a hoarse breath, and by the tone in his voice, Talon understood this story would change everything he thought he knew.

"Have any of you heard of The Third Borough Project?" he asked.

This caught Talon off guard, not because he hadn't heard of it, but because he *had*. It was a project the governor had initiated over a year before, to build a fleet of cargo ships that could help increase New York's trade and income. He had seen banners advertising it in Drudgen. If it was only a trade project, what could be so terrible about it?

"It…" he stumbled, "it's a trade project, right? A fleet of cargo ships?"

Orson shook his head immediately. "No, it is not. The trade project is a lie. A trick meant to mislead everybody. I doubt even Zedah nor the council understand what Kresh is really building. Only he and his army of workers know what is truly going on."

"What *is* going on?" Amber said in one breath, a pleading eagerness in her eyes.

"The governor is building a fleet of armored and weaponized battleships," Orson explained, his body going rigid.

After a short while, Talon asked, "Why would he need them?"

"For one reason," Orson murmured, his eyes shining with despair. "He is going to destroy a fifth of New York... the entire third borough."

Chills ran up Talon's spine, and a wave of pure horror swirled through his veins, curdling his blood. He could feel the room grow even colder, and the others sat as still as statues, their faces as white as snow.

"Wh—what?" Amber stuttered, her voice nothing more than a choking whisper. Orson nodded once.

"But," Castor said, "all those people... why would he... how could he...?"

"There is much unrest in New York, and there has been for years," Orson continued. "He wants to put an end to that. He wants to scare the people... scare them into submission. By showing them the kind of power he has and what he is willing to do with it, Kresh believes they will all submit to his rule. That is why it is called The Third Borough Project."

Silence filled the room and remained for a long, long time. They sat for minutes, so stunned that, when Amber broke the quiet, Talon was truly startled.

"Sir," she asked, "is there any way to stop him?"

Orson blinked and shook his head ever so slightly. "No."

Talon's last thread of hope snapped under the weight of that word. *No*. The word had never hit him as hard as it did now.

Orson finished, "Not anymore."

Amber leaned forward. "You mean... there *was*?"

"Yes, there was. The Nest developed a way to stop the governor by using one of his own inventions against him."

"What was it?" Castor coaxed.

"The Key," Orson declared simply. Castor squinted.

"The… what?"

Orson turned to him. "The governor's battleships are loaded with shells that are powerful enough to—if fired in tandem—destroy the entire borough. The shells are on automatic timers that will begin their countdown when fired, meaning they will detonate whenever ordered. Kresh invented a device called the Key… an emergency override drive, only to be used if all other operations fail. It will detonate the shells wherever they are, even if they are still in the ships. The Nest discovered it years ago, and we orchestrated a raid."

He turned to Talon again and finished, "Your father managed to steal it."

"Where is it?"

"Hidden. It was too dangerous to keep at our headquarters in case Kresh discovered us… and he *did*. So, your father hid it, but only he knew where. I don't believe he even told your mother its location, in case something slipped."

Talon tried to keep the tidal wave of memory at bay, but the struggle was so much that he began to shake.

Castor's eyes went wide, and he seemed to be putting the pieces together. "So, you're saying that if we have the Key, and if we use it while the shells are still inside the ships…"

"Then the fleet will be destroyed," Orson concluded. "But there is no way to stop him anymore."

"Why?" Amber asked with a hint of dread.

"No one from the Nest is left."

Talon said, "You are."

Silence. Orson bowed his head, then stood from his chair and made his way to the back of the room, where they heard him rummaging through different boxes and drawers. He returned carrying a modest holo-device: a half-sphere encased in a solid and reflective cylinder, three separate connection ports dotted symmetrically around its smooth surface. Orson blew on it, thick dust curling into the air.

"Your mother gave this to me the last time I saw her. She told me that your father invented it in case everything went south."

Talon stood and peered at the little device, knowing that his mother had touched it once before. The thought of it made his stomach cramp even more.

"This is a holo-map that will lead you to the three different pieces of the map to the Key."

"How does it work?" Castor inquired.

"Somewhat like a puzzle. Once you find one of the pieces, you plug it into this device, and the location of the next will appear. When you've obtained them all, it will give you the location of the Key itself. But there is a passcode; a four-digit number. Even I don't know what it is, so I can't break into the device. Only your parents knew what it was."

Talon stared at the device for a long while before turning his attention back to Orson.

"Where have you been all this time? Why haven't you tried to find the Key yourself?"

Orson stared, sorrow in his face. "It's hopeless, Talon. There's no assurance where the Key truly is, and someone may have already discovered it. I am an old man, not an army. There is no way that Kresh can be stopped."

A sharp surge of anger rocketed through Talon's blood. "So, you're just going to sit here and let Kresh destroy Borough III?"

A shadow passed over Orson's face, and Castor and Amber watched anxiously.

"I don't want this, Talon, but I can't stop him… no one can."

Talon twisted up his face, a stronger wave of frustration coursing through him. "You're a coward. You were right when you said you didn't deserve to be part of the Nest. My parents would've never backed dow—"

His thoughts jammed. He'd let the memory of his parents escape off his lips. Orson smiled at him, but his somber expression returned soon after.

"You're right, Talon, they wouldn't have backed down. Your parents were so dedicated to the safety of others they were willing to put *themselves* at risk to stop the governor's tyranny."

Talon pressed his lips together, his mind fighting a war littered with sorrow. Castor and Amber stared at him with something more than just sympathy… *empathy*. He didn't need it… he didn't want it. They could relate to him, relate to the sorrow. Somehow, that made the pain even worse.

"But they loved you even more, Talon. They would've given up everything if it meant one more day with you," Orson said.

Talon's thoughts were anguish. Before anyone could say anything else, he whirled around and made his way onto the balcony, the chilling wind rustling his hair.

The multicolored lights of Cantatonia's skyline shined brightly as he rested his hands on the wooden railing. All the memories… all the pain… all the sadness… it collected inside of him, forming a dark cloud of grief.

A tear rolled down his face as he clapped a hand over his mouth, trying to quench the whirlwind that was his mind. He hunched over as another tear dripped onto the wooden balcony. He wanted it to stop, to *end*, to never return. None of his willpower could overcome it, nothing could stop it. He was hyperventilating. His hands shivered with cold. His own mind was against him.

"Talon?" came a soft, kind voice. Talon gasped and instinctively turned. Amber stood behind him, shutting the door as she gazed at him with glassy eyes.

He spun back around, trying to hide the tears, drying his wet face on his overcoat sleeve. Talon avoided looking at her, but he could feel her warmth as she moved to stand next to him. He felt her rest her soft hand on his, and he tensed, but Amber didn't let go.

"I know how you feel... so does Castor," she stated.

"How?" Talon said, before he could stop himself, his tone coming out sharper than he'd intended. He knew they had lost their parents, and that she was probably right, but he didn't care. He still couldn't get over his *own* sorrow.

"We've been without a family for a long time," she explained. "The closest thing we have to a family is each other. It took me a while to realize that."

Talon waited. Amber fidgeted with her hair. It was beautiful in the moonlight, her golden locks flowing in the wind. He could see something in her eyes. Something almost content... settled. She looked peaceful.

He wished he could be like her. Wished he could feel the same settlement she did. But there was something else behind her eyes as well. A hauntedness, a guilt, as if there was something she wasn't telling him.

"Your pain, Talon… I've felt it before. I *still* feel it," she claimed.

"You don't know my pain. You don't know what I've been through," he challenged. Amber breathed before glancing upward and meeting his eyes. After a long moment, she turned and stared at the skyline.

"My father was…" she began. Her voice dropped off. Her eyes were intently fixed on something in the distance. Talon squinted, momentarily forgetting about his own pain when he saw the expression on her face.

"What is it?" he asked quickly. She didn't answer, her gaze pointed toward the skyscrapers. Talon turned his eyes back to the city, trying to locate what she was so focused on. He saw it almost immediately.

The dim outline of an aircraft, rimmed with red light, was heading directly toward them. Talon's heart dropped into the pit of his stomach.

Zedah.

No, he told himself, *it might not be. It could just be a patrol ship.*

It was a new ship anyway, since Castor and Amber had destroyed the other. It looked completely different, so could that mean that it *wasn't* her? He knew his hopes were unwarranted. Only Prime aircraft had that kind of design. He'd seen them speeding through the sky every day while living in Drudgen.

"Oh no," Amber whispered. They caught each other's eye and rushed back inside, where Orson and Castor sat at the table, evidently in conversation.

Castor's face fell when he saw their faces. "What?"

"We have to go… *now*," Amber declared.

"Why?"

"It's Zedah," Talon explained.

Orson stood slowly, his face ridden with seriousness.

"Are you sure?" he asked.

"Yes, she's—"

A flash of light, a deafening bang, and the air exploded. An orange glow blinded Talon as a ball of raging fire ripped through the room, decimating everything in its path. He heard Amber scream as the force of the explosion lifted him off his feet. He tumbled through the air, colliding painfully with numerous solid objects before slamming into the ground, a metallic thud echoing through his surroundings.

Talon's skull felt as though it had fractured. His ears rang, his eyesight fogging over. Stars speckled his blurred vision, and his breath caught in his chest as he tried to regain his wind. Talon rolled onto his side, his vision refocusing, throbbing aches swimming through his entire body. He clambered onto his knees and lifted his head, trying to make out his location.

Flaming debris lay everywhere. Piles of rubble, shattered glass, and splintered furniture littered his surroundings. He realized he was underground, staring up at the cold night sky. A pipe had burst, vomiting up murky water that spilled down the wreckage. He could hear the screams of a distant crowd, horrified at the event that had transpired.

Talon's chest spasmed as he came to a realization. Where was Amber… where was Castor?

Where was Orson?

With effort, he stumbled to his feet, still regaining his balance. He coughed and gagged into his sleeve, tasting bile on his tongue.

"C—Castor?" he croaked, his voice hoarse. "Amber?"

Talon limped through the area, scrambling up piles of crushed building, continuing to call out their names. Panic slipped its hood over his mind.

Through the ear-splitting sounds of the roaring fire, he heard one of them call out. He couldn't tell who, or what they were saying... just that it was one of them... at least *one* of them was alive. He slid down the debris pile, small pieces of stone rolling down behind him. Talon continued to yell for them as he sprinted through the maze of desolation.

"Guys?" he shouted. As he rounded a corner, someone crashed into him, sending both of them tumbling to the ground: Castor.

"Ow," Castor muttered, almost immediately stumbling to his feet. "You okay?"

He was covered in ash, his face almost unrecognizable in the flickering orange light. Talon nodded, relieved to see him unharmed. Castor held out his hand and pulled him to his feet before reaching inside his pocket and withdrawing a small metal cylinder. He clicked it, and it expanded into the spear Talon had knocked over on *The Independence*.

"What just happened?" he coughed.

"It had to be Zedah." Talon answered instantly. "I don't know how she found us."

"She might have tracked the ship." Castor said quickly, concern in his voice, then glanced around. "Where's Amber?"

Talon gasped, "I don't know."

He spun around, scanning the surroundings. A rumbling sound filled his ears, and a white searchlight illuminated the area.

"Get back," Castor whispered, pulling Talon along and diving behind a large piece of rubble.

The same aircraft he and Amber had seen earlier passed over them. A searchlight shining from underneath the ship scanned the area, white light spilling over the debris, before continuing on as though it hadn't spotted them.

A loud click suddenly echoed through the air, and bottle-like objects fell from the ship, a metallic ring resounding when they collided with the ground. The aircraft sped forward, disappearing from view as the cylinders began to shudder. They clicked again, vomiting up white smoke, making Talon realize the worst.

Tear gas.

The smoke draped the surroundings like a white blanket and obscured everything from view. It swam up Talon's nose and down his throat, burning his esophagus and making him gag. He could hear the rustle of Castor's jacket beside him as he pulled himself to his feet.

"I can't see anything," Castor managed through coughs, as if it wasn't already obvious. The gas stung Talon's eyes, but he barely noticed. All he wanted was to find a way out.

It suddenly dawned on him. That was what Zedah wanted. She was using the gas to force them out. This was her way of knowing if they were still alive.

"We have to find Amber?" Castor's voice was right beside him.

"How?" Talon doubted. "We can't see."

"I know, I know. But we can't leave her."

I didn't say I wanted to leave her, Talon thought, keeping his mouth shut. A sharp noise rang through his ears, making his head throb, and both he and Castor went silent.

Thump… thump… thump….

"What's that?" Castor whispered.

They echoed in tandem and sounded almost like… footsteps. No, they couldn't be footsteps. Talon knew that footsteps didn't sound like that. At least not *human* footsteps.

The thudding grew louder.

Two red lights flashed through the dark, dimmed by the fog, blinding them both. They shined directly at them, piercing them with the harsh scarlet light… almost like *eyes*. The lights moved closer, accompanied by a buzzing whir. Talon gripped his sword, and simultaneously heard Castor brace his spear.

The lights suddenly disappeared, and the sounds diminished.

There was silence everywhere, except for the crackling of the flames, and Talon and Castor's heavy breathing.

A metal hand rocketed out of the smoke, backhanding Castor out of the way, and grasping Talon by the neck with its cold, solid fingers. It lifted him off his feet, its grip clenching tighter around his throat, cutting off all means of oxygen. He kicked at it, but it was no use. The being didn't budge. The hand pressed painfully into his neck, and Talon's eyes bulged.

His vision fogged over, darkening like the sky does just before night sets in. He was losing consciousness, his limbs forfeiting their strength.

A girl's yell echoed in his ears and the hand released him, causing him to fall to his knees, coughing and spluttering. A ringing clang resounded through the air, and a shower of sparks burst forth like a firework. Whatever had a hold of him tumbled to the ground and didn't move again. Amber pulled her dagger from its shadowy form.

Amber's hand found Talon's arm, helping him to stand on his

aching legs.

"Are you okay? Where's Castor?" she asked breathlessly.

"I'm here," Castor grunted, his vague outline inching toward them. The fog thinned, allowing them to see each other more clearly than before. "What *was* that?"

Amber shook her head in exasperation. "I don't know."

Her dagger rested in her hand.

"Thanks," he expressed, when he had recovered his regular breathing pattern, rubbing his sore throat with his hand. "We *have* to find Orson."

The three of them sprinted through the maze of desolation as the fog continued to clear, calling out Orson's name. The flames grew larger as they searched, the glowing tendrils whipping around like a curtain in the wind. Minutes passed, and they found nothing to indicate that Orson was still alive. Talon stumbled to the crest of one of the debris piles, achieving a better view from the peak. The damage was much worse than he'd originally thought.

Multiple buildings had been destroyed in the bombing, their remains scattered across the streets and covering everything in a cloud of ash. The flames silhouetted the wreckage, contrasting the glow with the darkness. Fog poured over the destruction like low clouds on a cold winter day.

Zedah's ship had disappeared, he couldn't see it anywhere.

With a jolt of surprise, Talon spotted the silhouette of a man… *Orson*… and he wasn't alone.

Orson stood at the base of the mountain of debris, a sword gripped tightly in his hand. The firelight reflected off the blade, casting a metallic orange glow on whom his eyes were fixed. A wave of nausea moved through Talon's stomach.

Zedah...

She stood in front of Orson, fire in her eyes.

The same surge of hatred and rage that Talon felt when Zedah killed Alger coursed through his veins once again. Castor and Amber finally caught up with him, but before they could stop him, he'd already begun running toward Orson.

He practically tumbled down the pile, dust flying into the air and fragments of stone rolling after him. Castor and Amber yelled after him, following him down the debris, but he didn't listen... *wouldn't* listen.

Talon heard both Orson and Zedah exchanging conversation as he drew closer. Zedah lifted her head, tearing her eyes off the man in front of her, and stared directly at Talon. Her face was etched with conflict and almost... uncertainty.

Talon didn't care.

All he cared about was the pain she'd caused him, how she'd torn his life apart even further than it had already been. Orson turned, but before he could say anything, Talon was at his side, Castor and Amber hurrying along in his wake. There was a terrible beat of silence as Zedah stared daggers at the four of them.

"Hand him over," she ordered, her voice breathless. Orson inhaled deeply, then shook his head.

Zedah lifted her wrist and pressed a button on her wristband.

"Entities to me," she spoke into it.

The thumping sound they'd heard earlier echoed in Talon's ears. This time, it was accompanied by the source.

Four men, two on the left and two on the right, stalked toward them, cutting off their exits, making escape impossible. When they drew closer Talon saw, with a surge of terror, they weren't men at all.

They were made entirely out of metal, and mechanical joints provided movement. Their eyes were hollow, filled with red light, their gaze demon-like. Their faces were flat, lacking both noses and mouths… only a blank metal face with scarlet lights for eyes. The automatons moved in perfect tandem as they stepped further toward them.

Talon's breath caught in his chest, his blood going cold. He felt Castor and Amber shudder behind him. The three of them raised their weapons, bracing for a fight, but Orson didn't even seem to notice them. He still stared directly at Zedah, courage and defiance flickering across his face.

Talon stared at his parents' old friend. Was this the *real* him? Was this who Orson was when The Falcon's Nest still existed?

"Kresh hasn't told you, has he? He hasn't told you his true plan?" Orson asked her hastily. She lowered her sword an inch, her eyes darkening with evident confusion, but almost immediately lifted it up again.

"Hand him over… *now*…" she declared dangerously. Orson shook his head once again.

"*No*," he stated firmly, and a rush of sharp adrenaline pierced Talon's stomach.

Zedah raised her sword…

The androids attacked…

The sound of clashing metal resounded through the air as Orson and Zedah's blades connected. Talon slashed at an android's arm as it reached for him, and sparks flew into the air, but no damage was dealt.

He wanted to help Orson, but there was no escaping the mechanical men. Zedah parried Orson's strikes with ease, moving with the grace of a panther. Her sword slid across Orson's arm, drawing blood, and Talon heard him yell.

Minutes felt like hours. Talon's arms tired almost instantly and his sword grew heavy in his hands. One of the androids gripped Castor by his jacket collar and threw him against a block of stone, where he struggled to stand. Amber drove her dagger into another's chest, but it was like a tiny scrape to the lethal machine.

Orson thrust his foot out and kicked Zedah square in the stomach, sending her rolling to the ground. He rushed over to Talon, plunging his sword into an automaton's neck and slashing outward. Sparks rained and the headless automaton fell to the ground with a deafening crash.

"Listen to me," Orson said, urgency in his voice. "You have to go… get to your ship and fly out of here…"

Talon went nauseous at the very thought, his mind spiraling. He couldn't believe what had just come out of Orson's mouth.

"No! We—we're not leaving you here! You have to help us find the—"

Orson gripped Talon's shoulder as Zedah lifted herself to her feet. Talon saw something in his eyes he hadn't seen during their conversation earlier. The shadow of the man Orson once was.

"It's okay, Talon. You were right, I was a coward, but this is the way I can make amends…"

Tears stung Talon's eyes. He'd always sworn to himself that he wouldn't care about anyone… that he wouldn't risk the pain again.

But he couldn't stop it. The grief was already there.

Orson forced a small object into Talon's hand. The holo-device.

"Take it. You're your father's son… I know you can figure out the code. Remember what I told you about the Key," Orson said. "But, most importantly, remember that it's never the end… as long as you have hope… and as long as you maintain your love for others."

A cold stab of shock hit Talon like a poisoned knife. He'd heard someone say that before… but *who*? He didn't see anything else, not even Castor driving his spear through another automaton's head. All he saw was Orson, and all he felt was the pain… the same pain he'd felt when his parents died.

Zedah sprinted toward them, swinging her sword, going directly for Talon. Orson threw himself against her and they tumbled to the ground.

Amber slid her dagger against the third automaton's throat, severing the wires and causing it to crumple.

Orson grimaced as he restrained Zedah. Talon stumbled backward. He wanted to fall, wanted to pass out from the pain. He knew he couldn't… not *now*. This was their chance, and he would take it.

He spun around, temporarily wrenching the grief from his mind. With a yell, he plunged his sword through the final automaton's heart. Talon didn't wait for it to fall. He stumbled over Castor and Amber.

"We have to go!" he shouted.

"But—" Castor began. Talon shook his head, beckoning both of them to follow. Zedah broke through Orson's grip, snatched up her sword, and attempted to slash at him. Orson parried and their battle continued.

Talon met his eyes, and something passed between them. An understanding… hope… *care*.

He broke eye contact and sprinted through the maze of debris,

Castor and Amber directly behind him. Every instinct told him to stop, to turn around. He knew he couldn't.

They emerged onto the cobbled street, racing down the road, shoving past bewildered bystanders, trying to reach the ship.

The Independence sat still on the landing pad, and Castor slammed the button that lowered the boarding ramp. The three of them scrambled inside and, within seconds, the ship lifted off. It rocketed into the sky, toward the Laughing Highlands, Blackridge growing smaller and smaller behind them.

Amber buried her face in her hands and fell into the tattered leather seat. Talon's sword slid from his hand and landed on the floor with a clang. His entire body ached with pain, physical and mental.

Orson was still down there, still battling Zedah. Probably *failing*. He collapsed into a sitting position on the floor, his face stained with tears. The dull hum of the ship's engine echoed in his ears as the revelation sunk in over what had just happened.

BANG!

The ship suddenly jolted with the force of an earthquake, throwing him and Amber painfully onto the ground. Castor yelled a curse from the cockpit.

Talon leaped to one of the viewing ports, barely able to make out the vague outline of Zedah's ship, racing after them and launching strings of yellow bullets.

"Her ship's still on us!" Castor yelled from up front. "They've hit one of the thrusters!"

The engine groaned, and the ship trembled violently, alarms blaring. Talon stumbled into the cockpit and, through the viewing port, realized the snowy peaks of the Highlands were drawing closer and closer. Another crash threw him off his feet and Castor out of his chair. All the little trinkets flew off the shelves and thudded to the floor, vibrant red light flashing through the belly of the aircraft.

Glowing bullet strings whipped past as they broke through a cloud. Talon's heart stopped.

CRASH!

Amber screamed as the nose of the ship smashed into the tall pine trees, snapping them like twigs. They collided with the icy ground, the sudden inertia throwing Talon off his feet once again.

His head slammed into something hard and heavy, and everything went black and silent.

CHAPTER NINE

MAY 14TH, 2492

A searing knife felt like it was driving its way into Talon's skull as he came to. His eyes fluttered open, the morning light blinding him, his head ringing and spiking with pain. As his sense of touch returned, he noticed he was lying on something hard. After lifting himself into a sitting position and rubbing his splitting forehead, he saw Amber kneeling next to him. She breathed a sigh of relief.

"You okay?" she asked, rubbing her forehead.

"Yeah… yeah, I think so."

She nodded, then stood and made her way into the cockpit, breathlessly calling out Castor's name.

Talon was still in the belly of *The Independence*, and everything stood still and silent, though he noticed the aircraft seemed to be resting in a tilted fashion. A shower of bright sparks flew from a cracked rubber tube above his head.

We crashed, he struggled to remember, *are we stuck here?*

Amber helped Castor stand and exit the cockpit as he visibly shook off dizziness.

"You guys alright?" he asked in a drawling voice. Talon tried to nod, but the world spun out of control. He lay back down on the floor and shut his eyes, trying to quench the headache and maintain consciousness.

"Where are we?" Amber said.

"Somewhere in the Highlands," Castor responded. "I'm not sure where, though."

Talon noticed how cold it was, chilly mountain air drifting in through the gap left by the unhinged boarding ramp. He heard Castor make his way past him and push the ramp further open. It lowered choppily and with the most ear-piercing creak Talon had ever heard.

He opened his eyes. The dizziness subsided, and with it the pain in his head, but he knew he would have a bruise. Talon sat up again, using the leather seat to pull himself onto his feet, and offered his hand to Amber. She took it, and he helped her up.

The two of them followed Castor out of the ship and squinted in the harsh daylight. Talon realized they must've been out for most of the night. The sun was beginning to rise in the distance, scattering a pale glow across the sky.

The morning light reflected off the snow, causing it to sparkle as he stepped through it. They had landed in a large, snowy clearing. A massive wall of rock stood to the right, and at its base was a patch of berry bushes. To the left, the clearing ended where a sinister cliff dropped one hundred feet to a cluster of sharp rocks below.

Cantatonia stood strong in the distance, and the sight of it made Talon's stomach turn over. Everything from the night before came back to him in a rush of memory. Orson had stayed behind to give them a chance, and the thought of his sacrifice knotted Talon's chest. The thought that he'd left Orson there… the thought that Orson was probably dead because of him… his mind whirled with anger. Anger at himself. It pulsed through him as he tore the thoughts from his mind and continued through the snow, wrapping his overcoat tighter around his shivering shoulders.

The Independence was damaged, that much was clear, but Talon didn't know how long it would take to fix.

"The damage to the thruster isn't that bad," Castor explained, observing it with a mechanic's eye. He didn't look happy; his father's ship was left as an inoperable mess in the snow.

"Can we help with anything?" Amber asked.

Castor shrugged. "Yeah, the repairs will go a lot quicker with three. But it still might take a few days."

Talon suddenly felt the urge to help. He didn't want to be stuck up here longer than they needed to be.

"What do you need?" he asked, and Castor seemed startled to hear him speak.

"Um… there's a tool bag underneath the workbench. That would help. Could you guys bring the bench out too? I don't wanna lose anything in the snow."

Talon nodded, turned, and re-entered the ship, clearing off the workbench and placing the tool bag on top. He hooked his fingers underneath it and attempted to pull. It wasn't heavy, but it was awkward to maneuver.

Amber stepped inside quietly, watched him for a moment, then moved in to help.

She took the other side, and they carried the bench from the ship, setting it in the icy snow. Castor had climbed atop the thruster and was attempting to wrench something from its wiry depths. Sweat cascaded down his forehead as he pulled with all his might, scrunching up his face.

"What are you doing?" Amber asked with a small smile. With great force, Castor wrenched a gleaming item from the thruster.

"Got it!" he panted.

Amber said, "Got what?"

Talon squinted at the deformed triangular object in Castor's hand.

"This, my friend, is a point-fifty BMG bullet. It's what damaged the thruster."

Talon's mouth parted. "That's... a *bullet*?"

"Oh, you should see it with the shell. It's even bigger. Thank goodness they only hit us once. The thruster could've been damaged beyond repair."

"What are you gonna do with that thing?" Amber asked skeptically, peering at the massive bullet. He didn't understand how Castor could use it; it was half flattened because of the collision with the ship.

"I'm gonna keep it... just because," Castor responded, but Talon thought he saw a mischievous glint in his eye.

For hours, Castor directed them to different tasks as he himself worked on repairing the thruster. He gave them tools, explained how to use them, and showed how to fix some of the damage.

They oiled the boarding ramp after replacing the screws and rewiring the machinery, and it was soon in working order. Amber continuously found herself struggling throughout repairs. She'd been right; technology was *not* her thing.

Though the cold bit harshly at first, sweat dripped down Talon's forehead after just half an hour of work, and he was forced to remove his warm overcoat.

By the day's end they had gotten a lot accomplished, including repairing the ship's engine. When they crashed into their hammocks, late at night, Talon instantly fell asleep. Only later did he notice he hadn't awoken from a nightmare...

The next day, they continued repairs, working hard, but neither Talon nor Castor worked as hard as Amber. She was drenched in sweat from the beginning of the day; Talon knew she had a lot on her mind. He could understand that. He did, too. Orson's sacrifice kept cropping up in his mind, knots of regret forming in his stomach, rushes of painful adrenaline flushing through his veins.

"You okay," he asked Amber as she tightened a screw with visible difficulty. She placed her hands on her hips, wiped the sweat from her upper lip, and inhaled deeply.

"Yeah," she said quietly. "I'm just… thinking."

"About Orson?"

She hesitated before saying, "Yes… but also about… those *things*."

Talon instantly understood what she was talking about. The androids.

"Zedah called them something," he said. "Entities, I think."

Amber nodded. "I never knew robotics had advanced so far."

Her face remained somber. Silence passed between them, and there seemed to be more she wasn't telling him, but he didn't press the issue.

Later, Amber exhibited signs of exhaustion, her arms looking as though they were ready to fall off her body. Castor finally allowed himself to bring it to her attention.

"You take a break," he told her.

She protested, "What? But there's a lot to do and—"

He cut her off. "I know. Talon and I can handle it. You take a rest."

After a short while, Amber finally gave in. She pulled her cloak tightly around her shoulders and wandered away from the ship before taking a seat on a large rock, staring at the distant shape of Cantatonia.

"She seems upset," Talon said as he and Castor pieced together bits of detached machinery.

"Yeah," Castor confirmed. "She's gone through some hard times."

"What do you mean?" Talon asked. His curiosity was getting the better of him.

Castor shrugged and scratched at his chin. "Well, all I can say is that her dad wasn't exactly a *good* person. I found her alone when she was nine. She told me that she ran away from home. I think that's why she doesn't sleep well—she has bad dreams. But that's all she's agreed to tell me… even after five years."

Talon's mouth fell open, but he quickly closed it again. Amber had nightmares, *too*? He turned his head and fixed his eyes on her silhouette, sitting peacefully near the cliff's edge, not knowing what they were talking about. Once again, he allowed his curiosity to overtake.

"How old were you when… you lost them."

Castor set his screwdriver on the workbench and rubbed the back of his neck.

"My dad left to fight in the Jersian War when I was nine, and I never saw him again. I think he died during the Lithian Massacre, but I'm not sure."

A somber quiet fell between them as Castor stared blankly at the part he was supposed to be repairing.

"He gave me the spear… he had it as a sort of trophy for serving in the military, and he was the one who taught me how to fly."

There was a long pause.

"Your dad gave you a spear and taught you to fly when you were *nine*?" Talon said incredulously.

Castor laughed softly. "Eight, actually. He didn't exactly have a clean criminal record."

There was no stopping it… a short snicker escaped from Talon's mouth and… *wow*. It felt *amazing* to laugh. He couldn't even remember the last time he had *truly* laughed. It had to have been years. After a moment, they fell silent again, and all seriousness returned.

"And… your mom?" Talon asked cautiously. Castor stiffened, and Talon noticed he cleaned the part in his hand with much more vigor than before.

"Waver's Fever. She died a year after my dad left. We didn't have anyone else so… *I* was the only one who could care for her… and I—I didn't know how."

Castor's usually bright face darkened. He was angry at himself… Talon could see it in his eyes. A cold gust of wind whistled through the clearing, chilling his skin.

"I'm sorry…" he finally said. The words were out of his mouth before he knew it. But surprisingly, they didn't taste sour. He didn't even *know* what he was feeling.

"Well, everybody dies eventually," Castor said, glancing up at him. "But I guess that's why I like to fix things. Because… well, because I couldn't fix *her*. I was young, too. Only ten. But I always wonder what would've happened if I had known what to do."

Compassion. That's what he felt. Compassion for Castor. And for Amber. For what both of them had gone through.

"Wait," Castor paused, flashing a look of curiosity. "How old are *you*?"

"Fifteen."

"Same, but don't tell Amber... she's fourteen," Castor jested with a sly smirk.

Talon side-smiled before continuing the conversation. "When did you two meet?"

"Well," Castor said, "I found her living on the run soon after my mom died, a little over five years ago. She wasn't exactly in tip-top condition, but she still tries to deny that."

"And you offered for her to come with you?"

"That's right. She didn't want to at first, and I don't blame her. If my dad was as bad as she says *hers* was, I would have trouble trusting people, too. But she still won't tell me the details. Eventually she agreed, and we became friends."

Another pause followed, and Talon waited.

"But," Castor added hastily, "we're not like... a *thing*, or anything."

"I don't know," Talon said quietly. "Despite what you said, you seemed pretty protective back at the bar."

He thought he saw Castor's face go red. "Natural protective instinct, I guess. She feels more like a sibling."

"Mm-Hmm," Talon prodded.

Castor rolled his eyes, a mischievous smirk passing over his face. "I know what you're getting at, but currently it's just a friendship."

"Currently?"

Castor's sigh quickly turned into a laugh. "Seriously, she's like a sister to me. Not the other thing."

Talon laughed through his nose and continued tinkering with the machinery. He didn't even understand where this playful side of him came from, but he didn't care. He was *happy*... happy to talk... happy to laugh... happy to just *be* happy. And it felt wonderful.

A strange rustle snagged at Talon's ears, and he turned his attention toward the berry bushes. They shook gently, their leaves rustling. Amber sat near it, and she seemed to notice it, too.

"What's that?" Castor whispered, rotating his head.

The soft head of a beautiful young doe emerged from the leaves, and Talon felt his stomach flutter with shock.

The doe gradually made her way toward Amber, who sat in stunned silence for a moment before sliding off the rock and crouching low in the powdery snow.

"A—a deer?" Castor whispered breathlessly. "No one *ever* sees deer anymore."

Amber kindly outstretched her arm, and the doe gazed at her with its glistening dark eyes before slowly moving her head forward. She let her nose rest on Amber's hand and sniffed it affectionately.

Talon's mouth stretched upward, the wonderful sight momentarily taking away all sadness. All he felt was joy that he was seeing this, seeing a side of Amber he hadn't before.

Vulnerability.

She gently withdrew her hand, the doe staring at her for one more moment before whipping around and rocketing back into the bushes.

He saw Amber stand, lace her fingers together, and make her way back toward the rock. She sat alone, continuing to gaze at the city in the distance.

A couple of days later, Talon awoke feeling as stiff as a board of wood. He was exhausted, and his arms were trying to tell him that. He splashed cold water on his face, waking himself up enough to step outside. A clanging sound echoed through the air directly above him, and he searched for its source.

Castor lay on his stomach, atop of one of the thrusters, hammering something into place with a heavy black mallet. His face glistened with sweat, his hands covered in oily grease.

"Is it hot to you out here?" he asked breathlessly when he spotted Talon.

"No."

"It feels like it's ninety plus!"

"Well, you're wearing a jacket."

Castor shrugged. "Right. Well, I've been out here working since about five, so that'll do it too."

"Five in the *morning*?" Talon asked in disbelief.

"Yup," he answered as he hammered the last peg into place. "That should do it, we're done!"

"Done?"

"Done."

Castor slid from the thruster and landed clumsily in the snow. "I'll go wake Amber."

Talon nodded as Castor disappeared inside the ship. Though it had only been a few days, he'd gotten used to the mountain air, the sweet smell of the berry bushes, and the view of Cantatonia in the distance. It was almost as if he'd be sad to leave it, which directly contrasted how he'd felt about it when they first crashed, but he had absolutely no idea what was making him feel this way.

Talon wandered to the edge of the cliff, his hands resting in his pockets when his peaceful mind was suddenly infested by a horrific realization.

What am I doing? his mind shouted.

He'd done exactly what he'd told himself he wouldn't do; he was forming a bond with Castor and Amber… a *friendship*. And what was worse, he was beginning to *care* for them. He was relating to them, he was conversing with them, he was doing everything he'd sworn not to do.

I can't have happiness. It's already been taken from me. I can't go looking for it again… I'll only lose it. I can't have it.

Orson, in their last moments together, had told him that it was never the end as long as he maintained his love for others. Hadn't he heard someone say that before… who was it? It was a long time ago… he knew that much. But why couldn't he remember?

He didn't care.

Love was *exactly* what had caused his once happy life to end. Talon ran a hand through his hair, vigorously massaging his temples. He *wanted* to stop Kresh and save all those lives… he *truly* did.

He wasn't sure he could do that without furthering the friendship with Castor and Amber… and without losing *them*, too.

"Hey," came Amber's soft voice, "we're ready to leave."

Talon didn't turn to her, neither replying nor giving any indication that he'd heard her.

"You okay," she asked concernedly, noticing his restraint.

"Yeah," he finally answered. "I'm okay."

There was a short silence. Amber gave him one last soft glance and made her way back toward the ship.

Talon slipped his hand inside one of his pockets and withdrew the holo-device that Orson had given him. A rush of adrenaline surged through him when he remembered that his mother had once held this very same object. In his hand was the device that could start them on their journey to defeating the governor... to saving the lives of thousands.

He shoved it back in his pocket and re-entered the ship, where Castor and Amber sat waiting in the cockpit. Castor began flicking knobs, pulling tiny levers, and pressing buttons. The ship rumbled, breaking out of the icy snow and lifting itself into the chilly air as Talon took his seat.

The Independence rocketed toward Cantatonia. They flew right over the city, gliding farther and farther away until it was nothing but a silhouette in the distance.

"Where are we going?" Amber asked.

There was an awkward silence.

"You know," Castor rolled his eyes. "You're a *real* help sometimes."

"I'm just being realistic! We don't even have a plan!"

Talon said, "Shouldn't we talk about *this*?"

He pulled the holo-device out of his pocket and placed it on the console. Castor and Amber stared, their eyes widening in unmistakable shock.

"Waitwaitwait... Orson *gave* it to you?" Castor asked.

"Well, yeah..."

"*When?*" Amber asked, stunned.

"Um... right before we left."

"And you didn't tell us?" Castor said.

Talon felt guilty. "Sorry... I forgot about it."

He hadn't forgotten about it. He didn't understand his feelings, but he knew he'd wanted to avoid bringing it up...

A lengthy silence fell over the ship as they traveled over the Cantatonian landscape.

"Well," Castor said, "I guess we *should* talk about this."

After another moment's silence, Amber grabbed the holo-device, spinning it around in her hands.

"What are you doing?" Castor asked.

"Orson said there was a passcode, right?" she answered. She continued to roll it over in her hands, attempting to find some way to activate it, scrunching her face up in confusion.

Castor held out his hand. "Here, give it to me."

Amber sighed and handed the device over. Castor tinkered with it for a moment before placing his fingers on the lower section and twisting his wrist. A circular section rotated with a click, and the half-sphere began to glow, emanating a soft blue light. The light projected a flickering hologram into the air… a number pad.

"Great," Castor muttered, "How are we gonna get in?"

Talon remembered that Orson had said he would be able to figure it out. He'd said he believed in Talon. It only made the guilt worse.

Maybe he could figure it out. But how?

He didn't speak as Castor and Amber suggested random number combinations, typing them into the device, each attempt rejected.

A startling idea came to Talon's mind as the numbers continued to be kicked back. Orson said that Talon's father had invented the device. The code couldn't be random. It had to be something important… something important to *him*.

He guessed it almost immediately.

"Try two-nine-seven-seven," he suggested, and Castor shrugged. He swiped his fingers along the device, suggesting each of the four numbers.

2-9-7-7

Beep.

The hologram turned a brilliant shade of green as the passcode accessed the information. Castor laughed happily, his eyes widening, and Amber turned her gaze toward Talon, a smile stretching across her face.

"How did you *know* it?"

He waited a moment before mumbling, "It's my birthday."

A short pause followed as she stared at him, pursing her lips in a somewhat sad smile. Talon tore his eyes from hers as the gravity of the revelation sunk in.

The passcode was his birthday: February 9th, 2477. His insides turned as he continued to think.

He hadn't celebrated his birthday since the day he turned nine, over six years ago. His father had chosen his birthday as the passcode… and Talon knew that this knowledge would plague his thoughts forever.

He couldn't think any further when the device emitted a new image… an image of a *key*.

The Key, Talon realized. It didn't look like anything special. Just an ordinary, everyday key that someone would use to unlock a door. The image vanished before being replaced by a new one. A holographic map of the North American continent.

"What's going on?" Castor whispered. Amber shushed him even though there was no sound to listen to. A yellow dot appeared on the map, blinking with a fluid motion. The image increased in size, zooming toward the dot, and magnifying the location it indicated. The shapes of letters began to form, spelling out one word.

Shardsville.

"Danyor?" Amber said, a hint of contempt in her voice.

Castor blinked. "It says *Shardsville*."

"Shardsville is a city in Danyor."

"Oh… well, geography isn't one of my strengths."

Talon stuttered, "Why would it be showing a map of Danyor?"

They remained silent for a moment, trying to put their finger on it, when Amber suddenly gasped.

"It's the location of the first piece!" she exclaimed.

Talon stood from the chair and inched closer to the holographic map. Amber was right. Orson had said the device would lead them to the three pieces of the map to the Key. This had to be the location of the first one.

"The first piece," Talon began, annoyance seeping into his voice, "is in Shardsville?"

Amber grimaced. "Seems so."

"And," Castor said with mock politeness, "may I ask why we would even *consider* going there."

"I know," Amber sighed. "I hate it, too."

"Isn't it one of the most polluted places on Earth?" Talon asked.

"It won the 2483 Best Prize for *Most Polluted City*," Castor claimed.

"Is that a thing?"

"No, I made that up… but you're right; it's one of the most polluted cities."

Amber rolled her eyes. Talon had heard numerous stories of

how awful of a place Shardsville was, and the Empire of Danyor in general. It was common knowledge that, a few hundred years before, almost a third of America was conquered and taken over by a dictatorship, their empire destroying the economy, landscape, and nearly *everything* else. Shardsville itself had once been a great city, but it too had fallen under the hands of the empire.

Silence fell between the three of them as the ship's engine hummed deeply.

"Do we even want to do this? I mean… we're just kids, not an army," Castor said, his voice strained and hollow.

"We have to *try*," Amber declared. "If we don't… all those people…"

"Why can't we just warn them? They've got to have some sort of defense system or something."

Amber said, "Any defense system they might have would be under Kresh's control. He's too powerful for them to do anything about it."

Silence hung about the ship as they came to the realization. The realization that the only option *was* to try. To use whatever time they had left to stop Kresh. To finish what the Falcon's Nest started.

Amber stared right at Talon, who gazed back. His mind drifted to the realizations he'd had earlier. Would he be able to accomplish this without losing them? He had to believe he could. There *was* a way.

Talon nodded decidedly. Amber was right; they had to try. He still gazed into her green eyes. She turned to Castor, who waited a moment, then gently nodded.

"You might wanna get comfortable," he explained. "This is gonna take a while."

"You have autopilot, Castor," Amber stated.

"I know," he replied. "But I think I'd rather fly. I have some… stuff on my mind."

He glanced at Talon for a fraction of a second before turning to the console and lacing his fingers around the steering mechanism. Amber turned and departed from the cockpit, Talon following close behind. She spoke to him only when they were out of Castor's earshot.

"Did he tell you?" she whispered. He knew what she meant.

"Yeah, two days ago," he mumbled.

Amber smiled. "I'm happy for him… he doesn't like to talk about it."

They stood in silence, their eyes finding the ground. Talon had a sneaking suspicion she somehow knew they had been talking about her as a well.

"I… uh," Talon stumbled. "I just wanted to say that I'm sorry for how I've acted. I know that you guys have been through a lot, just like… *me*. But I guess that I didn't want to believe that."

"It's okay," Amber said immediately. "I understand. After my mother died, it took me a long time to start trusting people again. He probably doesn't think I'd admit this to him, but Castor taught me what trust can bring. Happiness… a family."

"I think he already knows that. He's smarter than he lets on," Talon reasoned. Amber laughed—it was a beautiful sound that made Talon's heart flutter.

"I should probably get to work," she said after a short moment. Talon nodded before sinking into one of the leather chairs, watching her ascend the ladder into the gunner's position.

Finally, he admitted it to himself. He cared for them—for *both* of them—and it scared him. If he lost them…

That thought made his heart race horribly… painfully. He didn't know how much more pain he could take.

There *was* a way to save them, and to stop the pain. The idea already whirled through his head. A plan. A plan to stop the governor. What if he didn't need them? What if he could stop the governor on his own, without Castor and Amber?

No, that was a terrible idea. He was annoyed at himself for even thinking about it. But something in it continued to nag at him. What if the only way to protect Castor and Amber… was to be without them entirely?

The Independence's engine hummed in Talon's ears as the hours passed by. Soon after they departed from the Highlands, he noticed an impressive change in scenery.

Towering cliffs dwarfed the aircraft, casting a long grim shadow on the ship. Occasional towns and minute cities patched the landscape, and they only stopped once to refuel and empty the sewage tank. Castor found a small money bag hiding behind his hammock, so they could pay for the fuel.

Hours passed and stunning scenery with it. The most amazing landscapes Talon had ever seen made the long ride worth it. Vibrant forests reached at them with their branches, rivers of sparkling water slithering in and out of the trees. A mountain range, much more beautiful than the Highlands, sat in the distance, their snow-capped peaks shimmering in the sunlight. The sight reminded Talon that not *all* of the world had been tormented by the Quake and tyrannical leadership. Once all this was over, he knew he wanted to come back here, even if his chances of surviving their escapades were slim.

By midday, they had reached Kansas, one of the four states that still bore its original name, besides Virginia, New Jersey, and New York. The sight was *breathtaking*.

A sea of hills passed beneath them, appearing like an angry ocean whose waves rose and fell with formidable strength. Rivers of glowing magma ran through the crevices, vomiting up molten bubbles and smoke. However, the most shocking thing about this sea of hills was that they were entirely gray. Hundreds of years of being exposed to the elements had turned this place into an extraordinary volcanic wasteland, laid bare by the numerous firestorms and eruptions. Though it bore the marks of decimation, there was something strangely beautiful about it. Talon wondered how long it had taken for it to become like this, keeping his eyes out the window for over an hour. He didn't remember ever reading about *this*.

Throughout the next few hours, they sped over the Plains of Tegrirath, a long expanse of yellow grass where many settlements, large and small, had made their home over the years.

The Sea of Stone was, perhaps, the most intimidating to behold; giant petrified rock formations almost identical to cresting ocean waves, made entirely out of stone.

The Harcourt Mountains arched over them like overgrown grass, forming a kind of cragged tunnel for them to fly through.

The sunlight soon turned soft and orange as Talon's eyelids grew heavy. He fought off the sleepiness, knowing they would arrive soon. Castor ambled out of the cockpit, dark bags hanging under his eyes as he gently rubbed the back of his neck.

"We just crossed the Danyorian borderline. It'll be about an hour until we arrive," he said. Talon nodded.

Amber had been messing around on the various touchscreens, trying to uncover some more helpful information.

"So," she began, turning to Castor, "where are the respirators?"

"Why?"

"We need them."

"Why?"

Amber sighed. "The air in Shardsville is too dangerous to breathe. It's full of toxic chemicals that can kill you if you don't wear a respirator."

"Then how do the citizens survive?" Talon asked quietly.

"They wear them… but I guess most stay inside because they don't want to go out in the first place."

Castor rummaged behind his hammock and withdrew three respirators. Serrated tubes ran from the tip of a cylindrical breathing apparatus, connecting to the top of the headset

How much space is behind that hammock? Talon wondered, knowing that Castor kept most of his stuff behind it. He handed two of the three to Talon and Amber before making his way back into the cockpit.

An hour later, he called to them. "Guys… we're here."

Castor's voice was deep and shallow, and Talon understood why when he laid eyes on the sight before them. It would haunt him forever.

Shardsville was like a city from hell, and the first instinct Talon had was to run to the back of the aircraft and curl up behind the hammocks. The ghostly silhouettes of towering skyscrapers stretched into the thick green clouds that flickered with lightning, casting a sinister illumination over the entire city. The glowing lights of countless fires dotted the landscape, sandwiched between buildings or behind factories that vomited up sickening black smoke.

Hundreds of years of pollution and lawlessness flashed its hideous scars everywhere they turned. The city was ridden with toxicity of all kinds. The ocean sat in the distance, gray and covered in an unnatural fog. Massive smoke plumes curled into the sky, conjuring up sporadic lightning storms of their own. Rusty, crooked cell towers stood lopsided on the rooftops like aged gravestones for giants. Though he stood within the walls of the ship, Talon could faintly smell the sharp stench that was the air outside. Bitter, thick, strong, and disgusting.

Talon pulled his eyes away from the desolation and focused on Castor and Amber, whose faces were pale and stoic, their bodies rigid and stiff.

"It's so much worse than I thought it would be," Amber whispered, her voice choking, her eyes shining with tears.

Castor sat in silence, though Talon could hear him breathing heavily and angrily. He knew how he felt. Anger seeped into his heart as he thought of what this place's evil leadership had done to the landscape... to the people. He remembered that several previous states made up Danyor, all of them ruled by the same clique of corrupt dictators basking in the joys of wealth, power, and luxury. All as their own people suffered under them.

Danyor used to be a wonderful place; Talon had read about the prosperity it once held, seen old photos of its shining beaches, snow-capped peaks, grand canyons, and red-rocked deserts. It used to be a place of prosperity, culture, and riches. The people used to thrive. They used to *live*.

Everywhere Talon looked, he saw flashes of the pride this place had once held. Glimpses of a past long dead, but not forgotten, like a ghostly memory of a loved one who had fallen down the wrong path.

The Independence descended toward the buildings—the damage was even worse up close. Flat-roofed buildings stood like ancient ruins, their walls charred and blackened as if they had been blitzed. Abandoned shops lined the roads they cruised over, their windows long shattered, their contents never bought, never sold, never used. The few people they could see moved like snails, their bodies covered by thick coats and ponchos, their faces shrouded beneath different types of breathing apparatuses.

Talon was so focused on the hell-scape that he didn't even notice Castor set the ship down on the uneven street. He saw a few citizens peer toward *The Independence* from behind curtained windows, his thoughts overwhelmed with grief and sorrow. He wanted to help these people, wanted to help restore this place to the thriving metropolis it once was. But he forced himself to snap out of his trance and focus.

We're here for the piece of the map, he told himself. *Pull yourself together*.

They stood for a good five minutes in silence as the sky darkened, the sun dipping below the grisly horizon. Rain began to fall, making citizens rush inside as if their lives depended on it.

What is going on? Talon wondered, his thoughts in a whirlwind. Even through the walls of the aircraft, he could hear people screaming; it was as though the rain was harming them. But Talon noticed something strange about the sudden drizzle. When the droplets hit the viewing port, they sizzled, and then vanished.

"Acid rain," Amber realized, pressing her lips together. "We'll have to wait it out."

"I'm not going *anywhere* tonight," Castor declared, contempt woven into his tone as he stared out the window.

Amber nodded. "We should try to get some sleep. Tomorrow's going to be a long day."

I don't know how I'm ever gonna be able to sleep, Talon doubted. He took several deep breaths and sauntered over to his hammock, gently lying down on the swaying piece of tattered fabric.

He rested his hand behind his head as numerous thoughts pierced his mind. How had this place ever gotten like this? How had it toppled from its once glamorous pedestal? He knew the answer to that. The invasion of a pestilent corruption had shattered Danyor's previous pride.

But one question still lingered: could it ever be remedied? If it could, Talon knew he wanted to help in *any* way he could…

But he needed to focus on why they had come, and on what they needed. He wanted to save all those people in Borough III, and he knew he had to succeed. But he didn't know how he could do that without the possibility of further pain. The plan continued to form in his mind, becoming stronger and clearer as the minutes passed. He'd finally accepted that he cared for both Castor and Amber. If you cared for something, didn't that mean that you did what you could to protect it?

He knew that's what he had to do. He had to protect them… both of them. Even if it meant leaving them behind.

CHAPTER TEN

MAY 18TH, 2492

The warden's whip flashed against Zedah's arm, and she let a harrowing scream shoot from her mouth. She fell face-first in the mud, gashing her hand on a piece of brick.

"*Stay on task!*" the warden shouted in a terrible voice. Zedah could hear the other children sobbing, their gray uniforms covered in soil, sweat, and vomit. Her arm seared with pain as she attempted to push herself to her knees, her feeble arms shaking horribly. She could feel the hot blood running down her shoulder, tears spilling from her eyes.

Daddy's dead… Daddy's dead…

He'd died last night. Before he'd even taken his last breath, they'd thrown him into the pile of other dead prisoners, unidentifiable in their identical uniforms, and carted him off for disposal.

The warden yelled again, raising his whip. "You want another?"

More tears fell down Zedah's face, and she shut her eyes hard. A yell echoed in her ears, and she allowed herself to look.

"*Mommy!*"

Her mother pulled at the warden's arm, attempting to force him away from Zedah. He overpowered her easily.

"Mommy, Mommy don't!"

The warden threw her mother to the ground, a wicked smile stretching across his face. "Oh, you want to play, huh?"

Zedah stared in horror as he raised his whip, and her mother's scream rent the air.

■

Zedah shot awake, clutching at the soft sheets of her large mattress. The sun was barely rising, a cold air seeping into the room, her body drenched in a hot sweat. She heaved in breaths, gulping down whatever air her lungs could find before pulling the sheets closer to her chest.

She allowed herself a few moments to focus, then pulled at the hem of her sleeve and gazed at her shoulder. The scar was still there, a straight line of faded white. She could still remember the pain… had felt it in her nightmare.

She stepped out of bed and walked to the mirror that reflected the incoming sunlight. More scars dotted her body. A long one on her forearm, where another warden had whipped her. One just above her left collar bone, where the female camp captain had hit her with a truncheon. Five others on her back, where she'd received numerous deep lashes.

Zedah thought they would go away one day, thought that over time the scars would disappear. They'd only faded, and she knew they were there to stay.

But she couldn't think about that now. She had to focus. It was May 18th… today was a holiday. Today was the celebration.

■

The elegant hovercar drifted through the streets of Manhattan, dwarfed by the colossal, glistening skyscrapers. Zedah sat with her legs crossed in the backseat, resting against a blue pillow propped against the black leather cushions. Wealthy pedestrians in luxurious clothes whipped in and out of vision as she stared out the spotless window.

May 18th... Bluebook Day.

It was one of the only days out of the year she had an excuse to dress up, and one of the only days she was *willing* to. She had decided to wear a green, form-fitting dress, since it matched her eyes. Her hair was meticulously curled, and she had applied a thin coat of red gloss over her lips. In her own opinion, she looked beautiful, but she would never admit that to anyone else.

The bony, stoic driver kept silent as they twisted and turned through the streets. She couldn't remember his name. William? No, Winston.

They passed directly beneath Prime Tower, and Zedah noticed the shape of the Empire State Building as it flashed and then vanished between the gaps separating buildings.

She checked inside her little black bag to make sure her copy of the Bluebook still sat inside. The sky-colored spine peered at her from the darkness of the pouch.

As the minutes passed, other thoughts filled her mind. She wondered how crowded it would be, since only First-Class citizens were allowed to live in Borough I. Would the lesser classes be visiting from the other Boroughs? She assumed so, since they *always* were.

However, the citizens had been getting even more confident in themselves. Riotous protests were becoming much more frequent. Kresh had been so focused on completing the cargo fleet that he'd brushed these issues aside. He would always say the protests would be dealt with soon, but when *was* soon?

A week? A month? A year?

It wasn't her concern. Not *yet*. She had a job to do.

The boy may have escaped... *again*... but at least there was a chance he and his accomplices hadn't survived the crash of their ship. Besides, Zedah had brought back a valuable prisoner, and Kresh had been well pleased.

But the search for the boy weighed on her more than she had been prepared for. He had such a strong connection to the past... *too* strong.

Thinking about it haunted her. It always did. She had a stronger connection to him than he knew, and she almost wasn't proud of it. But she knew she was lying to herself—Kresh's way was *always* the way, and her past deeds had been in his service.

The crowds grew heavier, and the sight of people whose garments reflected their economic stature captured Zedah's attention. A red carpet surrounded by various news vans and reporters lined the street, leading to a small, white building, on which a balcony protruded from the exterior of the second floor.

Zedah could faintly see the aged symbol perched at the pinnacle of the building. It used to be a symbol of freedom. Now, it was a symbol of strength... of power.

The hovercar slowed and halted beside the blood-colored carpet, next to which many colorful people stood, anxiously awaiting the arrival of their leaders.

Zedah exited the vehicle, black bag in hand, and confidently strode down the carpet, making her way toward the structure. She could feel the bystander's eyes on her as she drew closer and closer to the building.

Two bellmen pulled open the glass doors, and she stepped inside.

The lobby was quite elegant, and she recognized it from the previous seven Bluebook Days. Leather seats were arranged in a circle, where they faintly reflected the golden light cast by the crystalline chandelier hanging above. Two marble staircases, one on each side of the room, curved upward toward the second floor, where symmetrical windows allowed daylight to pour through.

As time went on, the four members of the Bluehouse Prime, Mayor Xian, Raul Barrios, Tykeim Mills, and Davith Coronil arrived, an air of confident pride emanating from their shoulders.

"Officer Kahzak," Barrios crooned when he entered the building, an arrogant smile crossing his thin lips.

Zedah knew that Kresh despised this man. Whenever his name came up, the governor let a rare shadow of irritation mar his stony features.

"Ah, you're all here," came a voice from the other side of the room, and Zedah turned. Kresh was descending one of the marble staircases, dressed in a navy-blue suit with a matching tie.

"Governor Kresh," Coronil acknowledged.

"Members of Prime. Zedah."

Kresh acknowledged each of them by nodding his head.

Soon, he had joined them, and elegantly dressed waiters and waitresses emerged carrying trays of drinks. Kresh passed a glass of champagne to Zedah. It was the most mind-numbing substance she had tasted in a while.

"Where have you been commissioned lately, Officer Kahzak?" Coronil inquired, "I haven't heard much."

The remainder of the Prime nodded in agreement. For a fraction of a second, Zedah glanced at Kresh. His face told her he hadn't revealed any of their current exploits to the Prime.

"Nothing much, sir. I've been laying low."

Coronil nodded, turning his attention back to his refreshment.

Later, when Kresh and Zedah had a private moment, the governor said, "I trust that you will continue your search after today."

She immediately nodded. "Yes, sir, I will be back on the job tomorrow."

"Good. The prisoner you brought back has been of no use to me. He refuses to speak."

"I don't doubt it, sir."

"And I wouldn't expect you to," Kresh declared. "He, especially, is not an easy shell to break. I don't believe we will get any further with him."

The governor smiled cruelly, and the look in his eyes startled Zedah. He seemed to be anticipating something sinister, with *joy* instead of worry. That wasn't like him. Kresh wasn't a cruel man. At least... not that *she'd* ever noticed.

Zedah decided to change the subject. "The Entity Project worked perfectly, sir."

"Yes, I would expect so. But the boy still escaped, so there is obviously room for improvement."

Mills strode over to them. "Governor Kresh... it is time."

Kresh nodded as the members of Prime made their way toward the left staircase. Zedah motioned for the governor to go before her, but he shook his head.

"I'd prefer to see everyone. It is unsettling when something with a conscience is behind me."

Some*thing*?

He offered her his arm, and after a stunned moment, she gently accepted. They ascended the stairs and emerged onto the second floor, where they traveled down a long hallway before arriving at two, tall glass doors which swung open automatically. Zedah could feel the warm air as she, Kresh, and the Prime stepped outside and onto the balcony.

She turned her attention upward, staring at the tall symbol, placed on the top of the building.

There stood all that was left of the statue that was once called Lady Liberty; a shimmering green hand, gripping a beautiful torch, pointing it skyward. None of the rest of the statue had survived the Quake, being lost somewhere at the bottom of the harbor. All that could be retrieved was her hand, grasping the torch that once symbolized freedom.

Kresh had taken it and placed it atop this building as a reminder. A reminder that the chaos of freedom was gone, and that order and control now reigned.

What a brilliant idea, Zedah thought every time she laid eyes on the fragment of the statue. The governor was a brilliant man, dedicated to stopping chaos. Stopping freedom.

The people hated all the rules and laws and restrictions and class separations, but they just didn't *understand*. They wanted their freedoms, but they didn't see that freedom was what caused everything to descend deeper into destruction.

Zedah tore her eyes away from the magnificent symbol and stared down at the crowd below. A blanket of people stretched down the street as far as she could see. Thousands of people had to be there.

Only three of the five classes were taking part in the celebration, and each class was separated into their own individual columns; Zedah could tell by the quality of their clothing. On the left stood the citizens of First Class, dressed in tuxedos and glamorous dresses. Second Class of Borough II stood in the direct middle, and Third Class of Borough III to the right of them. Each of the lesser two classes reflected their rank in their simpler clothing. Still, Fourth and Fifth Class were absent, and that was probably for the better; they would've ruined the image of elegance with their appearances.

The sight of the crowd was a beautiful display of controlled order, separating each class into groups of their own based on their social stature. Zedah loved the view, a feeling of elation fluttering through her stomach as she stood over them. It had taken *so* much for her to get to where she was now, even if Kresh was generous after he helped abolish the Danyorian concentration camps.

No, she told herself, *shut it out of your mind. Don't think about it.*

As she told herself these things, Kresh strode confidently up to the lectern placed on the balcony. A static clicking sound resounded through the air as Kresh tapped the microphone protruding from the stand.

"My fellow New Yorkers," he announced, his voice greatly magnified. "Today marks the seventh annual Bluebook Day."

There was an eruption of applause from the crowd, but Zedah noticed the upper two classes clapped much more readily than the third.

Kresh continued, "This celebration commemorates the day the policy to carry the Bluebook was enforced… and look at where it has gotten us."

Another round of applause.

"Over the last seven years, crime rate has decreased, and those of you who remain faithful have been rewarded with a safer city."

There was a third round of applause, but Zedah noticed that it seemed a little uncertain… a little disagreeing. Kresh pretended not to notice.

"Please, everyone withdraw your Bluebooks, and let us have a moment of silence."

As Zedah pulled her copy of the little book from her black bag, she noticed a blanket of blue appear over the crowd as they did the same. Every single person, whether it was Kresh, the Prime, or the citizens, held their Bluebooks high above their heads and closed their eyes. Silence fell over the crowd as Zedah copied them, taking to heart all the laws and regulations written inside, promising to follow them like everyone who was faithful to the government did.

After a short minute, Kresh lowered his Bluebook and began to speak. "Now, I desire to bring to light some of the current problems facing our city."

The crowd, the Prime, and Zedah waited for him to continue.

"Radicals," he stated. "Protestors. Rioters. These three classifications of people all violate our regulations and fall under the same class: terrorists. They are infiltrating our city by the number. More sprout up like weeds every day."

Zedah was stunned. Kresh was truly speaking about this serious issue now. He had been so focused on the cargo fleet he'd not truly acknowledged the importance of this problem. Had he been forming a plan in his mind all along? Had he truly been worried about it?

"I want to demonstrate to all of you," Kresh said, "the punishment that will now be inflicted upon those who are caught participating in *any* of these felonies."

Zedah stole a glance at the rest of the Prime, who seemed just as confused as she was, but no one spoke. There was no mistaking the hatred in Kresh's voice.

The governor turned and waved at the transparent doors that stood behind them. Zedah and the Prime stared as they swung open, and the horror of what emerged would haunt Zedah for as long as she lived.

Two soldiers stepped onto the balcony, each pulling a separate chain attached to the scarred wrists of a middle-aged man. The soldiers dragged him out, his features becoming much more evident in the harsh light. His white beard dripped red with blood, and a horrible bruise swelled on his right cheek. Shining tears rimmed his deep, dark eyes.

Horror rushed through Zedah like a tidal wave as they continued to pull the prisoner… *her* prisoner into the light. Was *this* what Kresh had done to him? Torture?

In a flash of harrowing memory, she was brought back into the past. This was what she'd had to see every day for almost a year. Every day, even after her parents had died in the camps, this sight invaded her eyes.

Every day until Kresh had rescued her from it. And now… now he was the one facilitating it.

The governor announced to the crowd, "Orson Rye. A known conspirator against our government who has escaped capture for nearly seven years. And now, thanks to Officer Kahzak, we have finally intercepted him."

Zedah didn't *want* the credit. She didn't *want* to be a part of this.

She could hear the Prime's stunned voices, whispering to each other, recollecting that she had told them no new developments had sprung up... that she was laying low.

"Governor Kresh," Barrios seethed. "What is the *meaning* of this? What are you *doing*?"

"The people need to learn a lesson," Kresh explained.

"What has gotten into you? They do not need to see this!"

"On the contrary, Barrios, they *do* need to see this. This man needs to be made an example of, and this is the only way to do it."

Barrios couldn't speak; he only stared with fiery hate.

Orson fixed his eyes on Zedah, whose face remained frozen in shock, and stared at her with an expression she'd almost forgotten. Compassion.

Kresh stepped toward the prisoner, looming over him, both hands behind his back.

"Give me the location of the boy, and I will call this off," Kresh ordered.

"I've told you already," Orson said, a raw, sly smile stretching across his bruised face. "I don't know where he is. Even if I did, I wouldn't tell you. Talon is *twice* the person you'll ever be."

Kresh's face flushed with rage, and he waved his hand. Another cruel sight plagued Zedah's vision. Three Entities stalked from the building and onto the balcony. The one in the center violently grasped the back of Orson's collar and lifted him off his feet. The governor moved in, getting dangerously close to Orson's face.

Zedah finally snapped out of her trance and placed a hand on Kresh's shoulder.

"Please... sir, is this..." she stuttered with a cracked voice. Kresh shot a glare at her so terrible it made her recoil in fear. It was an expression that she had never seen from him before... one that told her he was willing to do *anything* to remain in power. He turned his attention back to Orson.

"Give me his location," the governor ordered, with murderous contempt.

"*No*," Orson declared without a hint of fear in his broken voice.

Kresh immediately stepped back and nodded his head.

The Entity drew its razor-sharp claws...

Orson closed his eyes...

Zedah's heart stopped.

As the Entity plunged its claws into Orson's back, blood spurted onto its metal fingers. The prisoner fell from the android's grip and to his knees. He teetered before falling onto his side with a dull thud. His eyes fluttered closed... he didn't move again.

There was silence, but Zedah wanted to scream. Her mind shouted at her, trying to cast out what she had just witnessed, but to no avail.

She clenched her eyes shut as Kresh finished his speech in triumph, but she didn't hear a word of it.

All Zedah could hear were the sounds of a dying man, whose last breath seemed to scatter itself across the sky. She heard the Entities stalk off the balcony, heard the crowd's terrified whispers, heard the soldiers drag the body away.

When she allowed her eyes to open, she saw the governor standing before her. The Prime was frozen in horrified shock at what Kresh had done.

"Come with me, Zedah," he crooned, out of earshot of the Prime. "It is time that I told you what we are *truly* building."

CHAPTER ELEVEN

MAY 18TH, 2492

A deafening clap of thunder split the silence, startling Talon awake. Castor gasped and tumbled out of his hammock with a loud thud.

Talon rubbed his eyes, a wave of dread overcoming him when he realized they were still in Shardsville. That they wouldn't be leaving until they'd obtained the piece of the map.

He could see Amber's vague outline sitting upright in the cockpit, staring at the street outside as lightning flickered through the clouds like neon lights. He climbed out of the hammock, a bit discombobulated, and sauntered into the cockpit.

"I hate this," she stated with grief. "It reminds me…"

She paused, and Talon waited. Amber seemed to be talking more to herself, but when she fully realized he stood there, she sighed.

"Sorry."

Talon said, "No, it's fine… I hate it, too."

A small, strained smile appeared on her lips, but it didn't go any further. Castor stumbled over to them, his eyes bloodshot.

He made a feeble attempt at a joke. "I guess people don't need to buy alarm clocks here."

Amber half-laughed, and so did Talon, but the fleeting joy didn't feel as comforting as it had back in the Highlands. The three of them lingered for a moment, gazing out the window at the hellish landscape. At the ghost of a once prosperous city.

"Well," Castor finally spoke, "I guess we should do this."

Amber nodded. "Yes…"

It wasn't so simple to Talon. They were forgetting something.

"Um… where are we supposed to start?"

Amber and Castor stopped before sinking a few inches.

"Well… maybe we should ask around," Amber suggested skeptically.

"In this place?" Castor said. "No way. Look, I tolerated it in Blackridge, but I will *not* tolerate it here. I don't wanna be clubbed on the head with another bottle… or worse."

They stood for another silent moment, each trying to form a plan, when a new idea popped into Talon's head.

"The holo-device," he said quietly.

Amber asked, "What about it?"

"Maybe it has directions… just a thought."

Castor and Amber glanced at each other, before Castor retrieved the device from the console and flicked it on. Its luminous glow cast a cold light around the cockpit and the map of America projected itself into the air. The area indicated by the flashing yellow dot grew, forming a *new* kind of map.

Instead of the indicated location of Shardsville, they saw grids, outlines of buildings and, sure enough, the highlighted path to the map's location. Talon sighed in relief, and Amber slumped in her chair, clearly relieved they didn't have to search blindly.

Castor moved his fingers along the device's smooth surface, and the map responded to his touch, swiveling around as he followed the highlighted roads until finally reaching the location.

Words formed, and he zoomed in on the image.

"*Capital Tower*," he read slowly.

They all stared at each other for a moment, before realizing the haunting fact they were going to have to travel through the desolate city.

Talon pulled on his overcoat and grabbed his sword before placing a respirator over his nose and mouth. It was a confusing feeling, breathing through a mechanical apparatus that hummed whenever he inhaled. Both Castor and Amber gathered their weapons and donned respirators of their own.

"Be on guard," Amber said, her voice muffled by the contraption over her face. "This place is… well, let's just say that I don't want to see the worst of this city."

"How are we gonna get around?" Talon asked. "Downtown is too far to walk, and we can't just land the ship there."

"That's easy," Castor said confidently, and they turned to him. "We'll rent a hovercar."

There was an awkward beat of silence.

"What?" Castor said incredulously when he glanced at Amber and saw her face.

"Do you even know how to drive?" she asked

"It's been a while," he replied, "but I think I remember some of it."

"How long has it been?"

"Five or six years, but I'll be fine. The things that you're taught when you're young stick with you, am I right… *right*?"

Amber didn't look convinced, apparently taking into consideration that Castor probably learned illegally and while underage.

Castor yanked the lever, and the boarding ramp lowered. An incredible and heavy wave of humidity caused sweat to break out on Talon's forehead almost immediately. It was still early morning, but he realized the pollution in the air had affected the climate dramatically, making it hot when it shouldn't have been. An unnatural blanket of heat.

Even through the respirator, he detected the faint smell of sulfur and wondered how much of it hung in the surrounding air. His eyes began to water, leading him to think they should've brought goggles as well, but he realized that it wasn't going to get any better.

The three of them crept down the thin sidewalks, past pedestrians who acted frightened at the very sight of them. A wave of grief struck Talon like a bullet of sorrow. These people had suffered so long and so *hard*. Their clothes were rags, their respirators were made of deteriorating plastic, and their eyes glistened with a reflective gloss. His sadness only increased as they journeyed deeper into the city.

Talon noticed the colors of the place were too dull, not at all what they would appear as in the sunlight. The blues were too gray, the reds too purple, the oranges too brown. They sauntered past a line of old shops and corner stores, all deserted, their abandoned products still resting in the window displays. Moldy feather boas, torn headdresses, and the rags of sequined outfits flashed at them from inside some of the buildings. Grocery stores sat long looted, and a robbed jewelry outlet had collapsed in on itself. Talon tore his eyes away from his surroundings and directed them downward.

He didn't want to look at this place anymore. This experience almost made the pain worse; he could feel the people's loss just as much as he could feel his own. He could feel their broken pride, feel their anger at what this place's leadership had done—was *still* doing.

The three of them turned toward a back alley, lined with tangled wires, crumbled brick, and obscene graffiti, when an alarming sight stopped them in their tracks. A group of three people, men by the looks of them, stood a short way down the uneven sidewalk, and their attire was one of the most haunting things that Talon had ever seen. They wore flowing black robes and atop each of their heads was a plague mask. Their leathery, crow-like faces glistened softly in the green light. Their beady black eyes gazed at them, and the long, crooked beaks shot outward like a singular tentacle.

Castor stepped in front of Amber before saying, "Just keep walking."

They backed out of the alley, and out of his peripherals, Talon could see the horrible trio's gaze following them with their devilish eyes. When they had turned a corner, they breathed a sigh of relief, and continued down the road until they found a large junkyard filled with rusty metal and wrecked pieces of equipment.

A few old hovercars were parked out front, and a man about the height of Talon's waist shuffled out of the grungy building that stood beside the junkyard. He wore an oil-stained shirt and torn black pants, his face covered by a respirator.

"Can I help you?" he said in a raspy, condescending sort of voice.

"Do you rent out hovercars?" Castor asked.

"Depends. How much you got?"

Castor slipped his hand inside his pocket and withdrew the tattered pouch of money he'd found back on *The Independence*. He withdrew three silver tokens and handed them to the man, who bit each one before beckoning them into the junkyard.

"These keys work on all three that I've got," the man stated, handing them a scratched key on a chain. "Take your pick, but bring it back before tonight, or it'll be an extra three tokens."

He disappeared into the tiny building and slammed the splintered door behind him. Even *he* had a demeanor of hopelessness.

Castor shrugged. "Well, I guess we can choose. Which one looks the coolest?"

"None of them," Amber said, pursing her lips.

They selected randomly: gray, with two modest engines at the rear that glowed red when activated, and four solid seats.

It took Castor a moment to remember the positioning of all the controls and how to use them, but once he got the hang of it, they were on the road.

As they drove down the streets, the buildings became taller and wider, and Talon realized they were drawing closer to the downtown area. He could feel the humid, miserable wind rustling his hair as they sped through the horrible city, his eyes stinging even worse than before. His shirt clung to him underneath his overcoat as sweat continued to perspire on his forehead.

They passed factories engulfed in a flaming inferno. Sparks showered down from broken streetlamps and shining glass littered the streets. Several billboards, covered in multiple layers of rust, stood lopsided along the road, the images upon them in tatters. The immortal thunderstorm flashed above as if an endless supernatural battle was taking place. Skeletons of buildings towered over them like elderly giants seeking their prey. Talon clutched the holo-device tightly in his hand and stared at the map, guiding Castor who kept his eyes on the road.

"To the left… oh, I mean, *right*… turn around and go back down that street."

This is humiliating, he thought, and cringed at how terrible of a job he was doing as navigator. They drove for over half an hour, even though there wasn't a single other hovercar on the road. Talon kept his eyes fixed on the device, determined not to slip up again, until…

Amber said softly, "There it is."

Capital Tower stood a few streets down, the illuminations from the lightning reflecting off its glass surface.

The building oozed a lost elegance. Its build was broad and dominating, easily the most impressive building in the city. Many of its windows had shattered over the years, its spire bent like an upside-down L. The three of them gazed up at it in awe until a rush of dread overcame Talon. The first piece of the map was somewhere in there, but how were they going to find it in that massive of a space?

Castor parked the hovercar right next to the sidewalk and they stepped out, cautiously making their way toward the horrifying building. Talon stepped cautiously up the cracked stairs leading toward the glass entrance to the skyscraper. He couldn't look up—it was too intimidating, too terrifying. When they arrived, they noticed the entrance was boarded off by rotting slabs of wood, yellow tape blocking the opening. A rusted metal sign hung from a red chain over the doorway.

NO TRESPASSING

Amber sighed in defeat. "How are we going to get in?"

"Like this," Castor said with a mischievous smirk. He placed his hands on the wooden boards and began to tug. Amber rolled her eyes but allowed him to proceed.

The board broke with a dull crunch after just a few pulls, and

Castor swiped aside the caution tape as if they were cobwebs. He stepped inside the building, acting as though there was nothing to worry about. Talon glanced at Amber, who glanced around to make sure no one was watching, then frowned.

Talon shrugged and followed Castor inside before taking in the surroundings. They stood in what he assumed to be a once-beautiful lobby. A towering glass pane stood to their left, designed to look like a transparent, wavy curtain, reflecting sharp light into Talon's eyes. Pieces of it had broken off and shattered, the glass crunching under his feet. White columns stood in a symmetrical pattern along the tile walkway that led to the stairs, though many of the marble squares had broken in half, their remains strewn across the floor. Talon could faintly smell rotting wood through his respirator.

Castor whistled. "Looks like this place has seen better days."

Talon agreed. He could tell the building had once been a luxurious work of art. Now, it seemed like a place where phantoms might've lived.

A sharp noise startled him, and he gazed around for the source. The piercing ring resounded through the lobby, echoing off the walls and floor.

"What's that?" Castor asked, and they gazed around the area. After a moment, Talon realized it was coming from his pocket. Reaching inside, he pulled out the holo-device.

"What's it doing?" Amber said from behind.

"I don't know."

The device beeped slowly, about once every two seconds, but when it did the blue light turned a pale red. Talon stepped toward the ruins of the staircase, holding the device out in front of him. As he began to ascend the stairs, the beeping grew both faster and louder, and he suddenly understood.

"It's guiding us," he said, a relieved smile stretching across his face. Castor and Amber climbed the stairs and gazed at the device.

The Nest thought of everything, Talon realized.

As they ascended, the pace of the beeping continued to increase.

"Is it telling us to go up?" Castor queried, and Talon nodded.

It was as if the piece of the map was a beacon, trying to guide the holo-device to itself. They followed it further up the staircase and down an extensive white hallway, leading to another flight of stairs. The pace of the ringing continued to grow faster as they traversed through the building, passing floor after floor. It became much more difficult to climb the stairs after the fifth and sixth flight. They could see the hideous city shrinking out the window.

Talon glanced up, his heart sinking. They had reached a workspace, complete with decaying desks, shattered monitors, and cracked lamps. Amber sighed and Talon glanced at her. Her face was twisted with pain and sorrow as she stared at the ruins of the old room.

"People used to have *lives* in this city…"

She didn't need to finish for Talon to understand what she was getting at. He'd been thinking about Shardsville's long-lost glamor ever since they had arrived. But he had to maintain the hope that the city could one day be better. That it could one day heal.

They slowly followed the ever-beeping holo-device to yet another flight of stairs that spiraled upward like a tornado. Talon kept his eyes on the mechanism in his hand as it flashed red and blue until… it stopped.

"Um…" he whispered to himself, lightly tapping it.

"We're here. It has to be here," Amber said.

Talon lifted his eyes from the device and took in the surroundings. It was an expansive, empty room with a few metal columns here and there, their footsteps echoing off the stone floor. As they stepped inside, Talon could feel that this was the place. The place where the Nest must've hidden the piece.

"Look around," he said, and they split up, inspecting the floor and the columns, the walls and the windows. They searched for over twenty minutes, until Talon was sure they had inspected every inch of the place.

None of them had found anything to indicate the piece of the map was here. Talon took a step back, shoved both hands through his hair, and leaned against one of the columns, an exasperated breath escaping from his mouth.

"Hey, guys," Amber called from the opposite end of the room, and Talon snapped his head toward her. "You may want to check this out."

They rushed over and inspected the piece of wall she'd been staring at curiously. Carved into the stone was a circular symbol, no bigger than a token, but its design was what caught Talon's eye.

A wing… a bird's wing… but much bigger… almost like a *falcon's* wing. It was encased in a ring that provided the symbol's circular shape, its feathers flared boldly as though it were in flight.

"The Falcon's Nest… it's their symbol!" Castor exclaimed.

Amber smiled, then nodded enthusiastically.

Talon placed his thumb on the symbol and attempted to push at it, trying to discover whether it was some sort of button. Nothing happened, and he rubbed the back of his neck.

They're not gonna make it that easy, he told himself.

A low beep sounded from inside his pocket, and he withdrew

the holo-device. It shone with light, but not red or blue. It was deep gold. The device continued to ding softly, and Talon glanced from it to the symbol.

"What are you doing?" Castor asked.

"Just trying something."

He inched the device closer to the wall, attempting to see if it would act as... *something*. Maybe some sort of password or key.

Ding!

The noise emanated from the device, startling Talon and making him jump. The hoop that encased the falcon's wing began to glow a brilliant blue, the same color as the light emanating from the holo-device, and a small, square section of the wall broke away, acting like a minute drawer. Amber gasped happily as Talon pulled the drawer open, and they peered inside.

Lying on a small, scarlet rag was a connection drive, its metal plug glinting in the greenish light of the room, and its simple black handle resting peacefully inside. Talon grinned as he reached inside and withdrew the drive, smiling even wider when it left the drawer.

Castor laughed and clapped him on the back as he turned back toward them, and they all glanced around at each other in triumph.

"One down," Castor said. "Two to go."

Talon breathed and repeated, "Two to go."

He gripped the drive and plugged it easily into one of the connection ports on the holo-device. A hologram immediately shot up and into the air, forming the same map of the North American continent as before. But this time, the blinking yellow dot indicated a *different* location... New York. Words formed in mid-air, and the three of them read them closely.

Ledger's Lair, Upstate New York.

Castor's face went pale, morphing into a sickly shade of milky white.

"Oh no," he said immediately. "Never... no way."

"What is it?" Talon asked incredulously.

"We're not going *there*!"

"Why not?"

Talon noticed Amber roll her eyes.

"The Children of Ledger," Castor claimed. "That's where they live!"

"Castor," Amber began, annoyance in her voice, "when are you going to accept that they *don't* exist."

"They *do* exist! There have been sightings, and people have literally vanished around those parts."

Talon watched them like a tennis match, remembering that Amber had said the Children of Ledger were legends... *fake* legends.

"It doesn't matter," Amber said. "Besides, if we're careful, what could go wrong?"

"*Hey!*" a gruff voice shouted from behind, and they spun around, nearly jumping out of their skins. Three men, each dressed in white with pistols strapped to their belts, stood behind them, their faces contorted in anger behind their respirators.

Security, Talon realized with dread, *apparently, they have security*.

"You can't be in here! How did you get in here?!" one of them spat.

"Run," Castor squeaked. The three of them sprinted back toward the staircase, the security guards pursuing them furiously. Talon felt like he was flying as fast as humanly possible down numerous flights of stairs and long hallways. The guards were right on top of them until...

"Split up!" Amber yelled, and they immediately heeded her words. Talon veered left and found himself in a dimly lit loft with a spiral staircase leading downward. No footsteps echoed behind him, and he had no idea where he was.

"Guys?"

His voice echoed through the empty space, and a rageful shout came from one of the corridors. Talon bolted down the stairs and through a door. He found himself back in the lobby, where he, Castor, and Amber all crashed painfully into each other, tumbling to the floor.

"The hovercar is just outside!" Castor exclaimed, not even stopping to see if they were okay. The three of them scrambled up, sprinting through the shattered doors and down the sidewalk. They leaped into their seats and Castor stabbed the keys into the console. The hovercar revved to life as he slammed his foot on the gas, causing them to rocket down the street. Amber yelled as the inertia threw her against the side of the door. Talon could see the security guards stop as they exited the building, watching helplessly as they raced down the street and weaved through the buildings. He knew what they were thinking.

Just a few dumb kids breaking into an abandoned building for the fun of it.

After a short moment, the three of them burst out laughing, the noise distorted by the respirators. Amber's face looked like a mixture of amusement and guilt.

"That really... *wasn't* funny," she claimed, but still couldn't contain her laughter.

"Well, we got away, didn't we?" Castor replied happily. Talon snickered and gazed at the first piece of the map, connected to the holo-device. After an extensive couple of hours, they finally found the street that would lead them back to *The Independence*.

They returned the hovercar to the small man at the junkyard and cautiously made their way back toward the ship, careful to avoid the street where they had run into the trio donning the plague masks. They entered the aircraft and finally removed their respirators, making Talon appreciate natural breathing more than anything in the world. Before they spoke any further, they crashed into their seats in the cockpit, gathering their thoughts.

"I really don't like this," Castor said.

Talon cocked his head. "Don't like what?"

"Where the device is leading us next."

"Come *on*, Castor," Amber said exasperatedly. "We *have* to go. If going in there makes you uncomfortable, you're welcome to stay on the ship."

Castor squinted, evidently offended. "I *won't* be staying on the ship, but just know that you *can't* change my mind."

He immediately turned to the console, flipping switches and pressing buttons until the ship rose into the air, and they shot into the sky. Talon stared at the city as it shrank behind them, and a wave of guilt covered him like a cloud as thick as the ones over Shardsville.

He felt guilt for leaving all the citizens to fend for themselves. Guilt for not seeking to do anything about it. Guilt for standing by and only observing what the place's cruel leadership had done.

The hopelessness of the place infested his thoughts, and he tore his eyes away, unable to stare at it any longer. But he knew they needed to help New York. They needed to help them before they could even think about helping anyone else. And he knew that a place like Shardsville was beyond help. It was beyond saving.

Maybe the *people* could be saved. He didn't know. But the Empire that now ruled a once thriving side of America had destroyed all the prosperity. It had destroyed itself.

Shardsville was dead.

CHAPTER TWELVE

MAY 18TH, 2492

Talon rubbed his heavy eyes, yawning widely. It was past ten, the sun long gone, when they crossed into New York. The blackness of night stretched over *The Independence*, making it impossible to see out any of the viewing ports except the one in the cockpit. Amber slept soundly, sitting upright in one of the leather seats, her hand pressed hard against her face.

Castor seemed exhausted. He'd been at the helm of the ship since they left Shardsville; he seemed ready to pass out. Talon could understand, he'd made two ten-hour flights in the last two days.

"I'll set us down somewhere in the trees," he said.

The Independence descended toward the dusty ground and set itself on the soft earth. Castor flipped the engine off, stood from his seat, and stretched his arms.

"I'm gonna get some sleep," he drawled. "You should, too."

"Before you do," Talon said, "can you explain to me why you're so… *scared* of this place."

Castor looked relieved to have a chance to talk about it without Amber telling him off.

"Well," he explained, "about fifty years ago, a man named William Ledger wanted to create some sort of armored android that could help the New York military in its wars and stuff. He invented the first power source strong enough to where they never had to recharge or anything."

Talon said, "So, what happened?"

Castor frowned.

"Once he completed his first full army, they went… haywire. No one knows why, but he obviously made a mistake. They killed him and his entire team, and then disappeared into Upstate."

A short pause followed.

"A lot of people don't believe that Ledger existed," Castor continued, "but there have been sightings of the androids, and a lot of people have disappeared up here."

"Where would they be, though, if no one has ever found them all?" Talon asked.

"People say that they live in the abandoned sewer systems beneath Upstate. They call it Ledger's Lair, and they call the androids the Children of Ledger, since he created them. If you ask me, it's the perfect place to hide a piece of the map—no one wants to go there."

Talon turned the idea over in his head. It sounded quite plausible. What if the androids were still down there, since they never had to recharge? But, if they existed, how had the Nest gotten the piece down there without being found? He understood he might never know the answer.

"Amber doesn't believe in them, but I do," Castor said.

Talon nodded and Castor shrugged before beginning to make his way toward his hammock.

Before he could get too far, Talon asked, "What—exactly—*are* the androids?"

Castor turned and shuddered before responding. "They're basically spiders… *giant* spiders."

Talon recoiled a few inches. Of *all* the possible designs, Ledger *had* to choose spiders.

Perfect.

Castor turned and glanced at Amber, who still sat in a deep sleep. He smiled softly and walked groggily to his hammock.

Talon gazed out the viewing port, barely able to see the outline of the dead trees through the darkness. Soon, he crashed into his hammock, and fell fast asleep.

A scream pierced the air as the blazing inferno rolled across the room, the putrid smell of gas swarming like a storm cloud. A terrible ring resounded through Talon's ears as he struggled to push himself to his knees.

He was covered in ash, and the debris from the explosion had ripped his clothes to tattered shreds. The firelight danced within his vision, but it was anything but a happy dance.

"M-mom? Dad?" he choked through raspy coughs. No reply.

A column fell with a crash, missing him by less than a foot. Tears streamed down his face, slicing through the coat of soot plastering his face. Blood trickled from his nose and onto his lips, staining his torn clothes and filling his mouth with the taste of iron.

"Mom? Dad?" he sobbed. He couldn't hear anything; the ringing swam through his head as he heaved himself onto his forearms, trying to reach anything he could… *anything*.

CRACK!

The floor gave way, becoming a sinkhole as it crumbled into ruin, crashing to the floor below, carrying Talon with it. He smashed his head against a chunk of rubble, and everything went black.

A white light stung his eyes as he came to, realizing he was lying on something hard and rough, blustery clouds casting snowflakes to the ground. A crowd yelled in horror. A person's dark-skinned face flickered within his line of sight.

Whether the doctor was a man or a woman, he couldn't tell. Everything was so blurry... so *dark*.

The doctor was telling him something... but *what*? Were they trying to comfort him? To tell him that everything was going to be okay?

As his sense of touch returned, he realized he was lying on the sidewalk, the fresh ruins of the Guntheon Building crumbling just a few yards away.

The yells of the bystanders shattered the silence.

Talon shot up in his hammock, sweat drenching his body as if it had been poured on with a bucket. It was still dark outside, raindrops splattering against the viewing ports.

"You okay?" said a voice. It was Castor, lying in his hammock. For a moment he nearly resolved to tell Castor what was wrong. But he settled on avoiding eye contact.

"Yeah," he whispered quietly.

Castor didn't seem convinced. "You sure?"

"I'm fine."

He *wasn't* fine. He pulled off his sopping shirt, then rolled over in the hammock, pretending to fall back asleep. He could feel Castor's skeptical eyes on him, wondering what was up, wondering what was bothering him.

Morning arrived, daylight streaming through the raindrops that rested on the glass of the viewing ports, casting a crystalline glow across the ship's interior. Amber still slept in the same position on the leather seat, her hand pressing hard against her face.

Talon slid from his hammock, rubbing his eyes, still drowsy from being up so late. He chose an apple from the food cupboard and bit into it. He nearly choked when Amber shot awake with a massive gasp.

"You okay?" he asked quickly, once he'd recovered his senses. Her eyes remained wide for a brief, tense moment before she buried them in her hands. He knelt and placed a hand on her shoulder, gripping it tightly, hearing her cry softly.

"What's the matter?" he repeated.

"Worst one…" she muttered to herself

"Worst what?" Talon asked, "Were you dreaming?"

Amber breathed deeply, wiping her face with her hands and pressing her lips together tightly, avoiding Talon's gaze.

"I'm sorry," she said.

"Are you okay?"

She nodded vigorously, as if that made it true. Talon could see that it wasn't. But one thing was for sure; Amber had been dreaming about something terrible.

"I didn't sleep well either… I have dreams, too," Talon consoled, his mind refilling with the contents of his own nightmares.

Amber half smiled, but it didn't seem genuine. "About what?"

Talon's face dropped, and Amber seemed to realize what she was asking.

"Oh, I'm sorry, I didn't mean to—"

"No, it's… fine," he said, and he meant it. Amber dried the last of her tears and stood from the seat before putting on her regular serious face.

"I'll go wake Castor," she stated quietly, and he nodded. Talon made his way into the cockpit and retrieved the holo-device from one of the shelves before switching it on and typing in the passcode. The map appeared, guiding him with a yellow path. This time there were no roads, so they would have to trudge through the dirt on foot.

He knew that wasn't what was bothering him.

The truth was that he was just distracting himself. Amber's sudden behavior had disturbed him and thinking about it made his stomach cramp. Now, it had been proven she had nightmares as well, and he didn't have to think long to guess what they were about. She was dreaming about her past, he could see it in her eyes.

And he actually felt sorry for her.

His care for them was growing stronger by the day, and he tried to fight it… to make it stop. It was dangerous… he *couldn't* care… *wouldn't* care…not for *anyone*… not unless he wanted to feel the pain again. But he had a plan… and he *would* carry it out. He couldn't tell Castor and Amber about it. Not yet.

Castor poked his head into the cockpit, dark bags hanging under his eyes. "We should figure out what we're gonna do."

He and Talon made their way into the body of the ship where the three of them sat down on the ground in a circle. Talon swiped through the holographic map, following the yellow path until…

"There it is," Amber said. Talon noticed her voice sounded a little hoarse. The map had landed on a blinking yellow dot. The end of the path, their destination.

"That's where the entrance is?" Castor asked, scratching his head. "There's nothing around here but dirt and trees."

Amber tilted her head, evidently pondering this, then stated, "It's only twenty-three miles away. Can you fly us there?"

Talon handed Castor the holo-device and he disappeared back into the cockpit, revving the ship's engine. As they lifted off, Talon glanced at Amber, who seemed deep in contemplation. He opened his mouth to speak but shut it quickly, forcing himself not to ask.

As the minutes passed, the silence grew even more unbearable. Talon noticed Amber running her hands through her long, thin hair. Her face looked even more beautiful when her gold locks fell in front of it.

"Woah!" Castor called from inside the cockpit, and Talon and Amber stumbled inside.

"What is it?" Amber inquired, but Castor didn't have to answer. A massive crater stood before them, as if a meteorite had stopped by for a visit and then left. It was like a bowl made of pumice and dirt.

"The entrance is at the bottom," Castor explained, peering at the map, then shaking his head. "I can't land in there without a flat surface."

The Independence descended toward the ground, landing near the edge of the crater before Castor shut the engines off.

"How far down is it?" Amber asked.

Castor said, "The map says about half a mile."

They were silent for a moment before they turned and walked to the back of the ship, gathering their things. Talon pulled on his overcoat before grabbing his sword and noticed Castor slip a flashlight into his jacket pocket. They obtained the holo-device and exited the ship, the smell of dust swirling through their nostrils.

"How are we gonna get down?" Castor said as he stared over the edge.

"That's the easy part," Amber explained. "Getting back up will be a problem."

"It's too steep to climb back up," Talon said.

Castor shrugged. "Not impossible. We can do it if we try."

He clumsily stepped into the crater and stumbled, his foot sinking a few inches into the pumice. As he continued down, using his arms to balance, dirt and sand trailed down the slope like water.

Talon and Amber stepped in after him; it was harder than Talon thought it would be. Soon, his legs ached from constantly having to yank his feet from the dirt and step forward. After a few short minutes, he got the hang of it, breathing hard, and he noticed that Castor and Amber were tiring as well.

Castor slipped, falling onto his back and sliding a good ten feet before stumbling back up and attempting to brush the dusty pumice off his back.

Amber stopped. Castor's fall seemed to have given her an idea.

She sat down in the pumice, used her arms to push against the dirt, and slid clumsily down the slope. Talon and Castor watched until she reached the bottom, stood up, and glanced back up at them.

"We don't have all day," she called, her voice echoing through the air.

Castor mumbled, "Who said that we didn't?"

The two of them followed suit, and soon all three of them stood at the bottom of the massive crater.

They dusted each other off and Talon withdrew the holo-device.

He flipped it on and muttered to himself, "Okay, where are we?"

The answer surprised him. They were standing at the floor of the crater, and the map's blinking dot indicated that the entrance to Ledger's Lair... stood right *beside* them.

"I don't get it," Castor said, looking around. "There's nothing here."

They stood for a moment, gazing around in confusion before Amber dropped to her knees and began to dig.

"You're not shy about getting dirty today, are you?" Castor teased.

"Just help me look," Amber snapped.

Talon cocked his head. "For what?"

"Anything, maybe there's—"

She didn't have to finish—her hand landed on something hard and hollow. A section of a large metal object protruded from the dirt, and Amber dug around it as if there was no tomorrow. Talon and Castor dropped to their knees and helped. It took over five minutes to uncover the entire object, and when they did, they stepped back to observe.

It was a large cylindrical trapdoor, on top of which was a rusted turn wheel.

Talon bent down, gripped the turn wheel and began to pull. It didn't budge. After a short moment, Castor looped in to assist, throwing his weight against the hoop of metal with a loud grunt.

Amber watched, an amused smile flickering across her face.

CREAK!

The rust gave way, crumbling into little flakes as the turn wheel rotated and they forced the heavy trapdoor open. A deep, drawling whoosh emanated from the space beneath.

The three of them peered through the circular door, trying to make out some sort of room or… *anything*.

All they could see was a vertical tunnel that led deep underground. Hollow metal bars implanted in the curved wall acted like a ladder.

It was so dark they couldn't see the bottom; the tunnel and ladder descended until they disappeared into the blackness below.

Castor gulped and Amber glanced at him with a quizzical expression.

"You're not going to stop here, are you?" she asked with a light chuckle.

"No!" he slung back. "I didn't say I was!"

Castor, to Amber's surprise, took the lead and stepped onto the ladder, beginning to descend. Talon followed, and he noticed that Amber had dropped in when a shape blotted out the sun.

The first thing that hit him was the smell… It was *awful*.

"Ugh," Castor muttered, holding a hand over his nose.

"This *did* used to be an active sewer system," Amber explained, her voice echoing eerily through the tube.

"Yeah… but it's not just sewage… it also smells like… something died."

Talon agreed. Something dead was rotting down here and he didn't want to know what it was. The holo-device began to beep in his pocket, pacing itself quicker as they continued to descend the ladder. He couldn't check it yet; he needed to focus on getting to level ground.

Minutes passed and Talon assumed their pace could've been a

lot quicker if they had some light. His arms grew weary as they traveled further underground until…

"Guys," Castor called up to them. "Just a few more rungs and you'll be at the bottom."

Talon's feet met air and he dropped, landing clumsily in ankle deep sewage water before grunting in disgust.

"I know," Castor's voice whispered beside him. "It's gross."

He flipped on a flashlight, illuminating their surroundings as Amber reached their location. They stood in a wide metal pipe situated horizontally. It ran in both directions, but the problem was which way they needed to go. Talon withdrew the holo-device and began to walk left. The beeping slowed so he turned to the right, and its pace quickened.

"This way," he said quietly. They stepped down the pipe cautiously, the trickling sound of sewage echoing off the metal walls.

Castor was muttering to himself, "We're actually *in* Ledger's Lair…"

Talon gripped his sword tightly. Even if the Children of Ledger *didn't* exist, there was still something terribly unnerving about this place. Castor had been right. This was the perfect place to hide a piece of the map.

Ten minutes later they came to a left turn sprouting off the existing pipe. Without a word to each other, they turned down it and continued to make their way through the maze of tunnels and corridors.

After the fifth turn, Castor shined the flashlight down one of the passageways, and all three of them gasped in horror. They had found the source of the smell.

Rats lined the pipe as far as they could see… and all of them were dead. Every single one of them lay on either its side or stomach, shriveled and unmoving. Some of them were partially decayed, yellowish skulls poking through their hairy skin.

The odor of dead rodents and sewage concocted an almost unbearable stench, causing the three of them to cover their noses with their hands.

"Maybe an animal?" Amber suggested skeptically.

"They're not eaten. And what kind of animal would live in the sewers and kill rats for fun?" Castor challenged, raising an eyebrow. Amber rolled her eyes and sighed.

"I know what you're going to say, Castor, but they *don't* exist," she declared with finality. Castor shook his head but seemed to decide not to challenge her further.

Instead, he asked, "Do we have to go this way?"

Talon glanced at the device and stepped forward.

"Yes," he affirmed with dread. The other two sank a few feet before slowly following Talon down the pipe, careful to avoid stepping on the hairy carcasses.

"What was that?" Castor gasped, spinning around.

"Stop it, Castor," Amber said.

He shook his head. "I *mean* it!"

They listened. For a moment, nothing happened. Then, Talon heard it.

Through a separate pipe, a loud metallic clanking noise echoed off the tubular walls. It was followed by a buzzing whir and a repetitive clicking that sounded suspiciously like claws. A painful rush of terror flickered through Talon's nerves, his stomach fluttered, and he finally decided he believed in the legend.

"I—I guess it's a good thing that we're not going that way," he whispered, and they continued down their current tunnel, the terrifying sounds shrinking in volume as they moved further away.

They turned down more tunnels filled with rat cadavers as the beeping grew faster and faster. Talon stared at the device until they were suddenly surrounded by silence.

The beeping had stopped.

He lifted his head and fixed his eyes on what lay before them.

It was a dead end; the pipe continued forward for only a few more paces before ending at a thick black wall of aging bricks. A moment of silence hung over them before they rushed toward it in earnest, moving their hands along the structure, feeling for anything.

"Here!" Castor exclaimed, his beaming face illuminated by the flashlight. He'd found the small symbol, running his index finger along the wing carved into the stone. Talon gripped the holo-device and moved it toward the symbol, waiting for it to unlock.

Ding!

The symbol began to glow, its pale illuminations reflecting off the ankle-deep water. The single brick bearing the symbol broke away from the wall, moving outward as a thick layer of dust curled into the air. Castor wrapped his finger around the brick and pulled it free, aged cobwebs hanging off it like miniature vines. There was a hole in the wall where the brick had been removed, and Talon took the flashlight from Castor before shining it inside.

He plunged his hand through the hole, feeling around until… he felt his fingers close around something small, and a grin spread across his face. Talon withdrew the second piece of the map and glanced at Castor and Amber, their faces lighting up with joy.

"One more to go," Castor said earnestly as Talon slipped the connection drive into his overcoat pocket, along with the holo-device.

A sudden realization struck him as soon as he got to his feet.

"How are we gonna get out?" he asked, and Amber's face fell.

"Use the holo-device," Castor resolved.

Talon shook his head. "It leads us to the pieces of the map, not back to the ship."

They stood in terrified silence before Castor made his way into the tunnel again, avoiding the dead rats.

"What are you doing?" Amber inquired.

"It can't be that hard to find our way back," he reasoned. "We didn't take too many turns. We'll probably remember which way we came—"

But Castor suddenly stopped speaking. The same horrible clicking noise met Talon's ears once again, and his breath caught in his chest as he beheld what lay before them.

Five red lights gazed at them through the darkness… like *eyes*. They were lined symmetrically—three on top, two on bottom—but the sight was almost enough to make Talon collapse in terror. A second set appeared… then a third… then a fourth… a fifth… a sixth…

All they could see were the eyes… the flickering eyes of the Children of Ledger… illuminating everything with a violent red light.

Talon shook uncontrollably, horror spreading through his entire body. This wasn't real. This was all a dream. He almost crouched down to splash his face in the murky water, wanting nothing more than to wake up from this nightmare.

Eight metal legs sprouted from the shapes of the arachnids, curling from their bodies to the ground below, round joints providing movement. At the end of each leg was a serrated claw, circular openings lining each of their limbs. They were covered in coats of rust, making them clank and creak as they moved. Harsh, chiseled features protruded from their already nightmarish faces, and two steel pincers clicked together like giant teeth.

Talon, Castor, and Amber stood paralyzed, raw fear swimming through their veins as the scarlet light pulsed through the tunnel. They were unable to move… unable to think.

Castor's grip on the flashlight slackened and it fell from his hand, splashing into the sewage with a voluminous echo.

A deafening screech shattered Talon's eardrums. Amber screamed as the lights rushed forward with the speed of a leopard, their legs sweeping their bodies up walls of the tunnel. Castor yanked both Talon and Amber from their trance, and the three of them raced down the tunnel, the ear-splitting sounds of the Children ringing in Talon's ears.

The androids continued to pursue, the screeching growing louder through the pipes. Through separate tunnels, Talon could see multiple groups of metal spiders, racing toward them with the rage of a cyclone. There were hundreds, countless red lights toppling over each other.

The connection drive slid around in Talon's pocket, but he didn't even notice. He didn't even care that he was trampling the rat carcasses. All he wanted was to get *out*…

The only light came from the flickering illuminations provided by the spiders' eyes, the scarlet, demonic glow lighting their path through the tunnel. Amber yelled something over the noise, but it was barely audible. Talon's mind spiraled with terror as the Children drew closer, as though hungry for a bloody meal.

They whirled around a corner, Talon's feet met air, and before he knew it, he was falling. He landed on his back, his wind leaving him, and the world went black.

Blurred images flickered within Talon's vision as his eyes fluttered open. He could feel someone's hand gripping his arm, attempting to drag him across the soft, wet ground. He shook off the dizziness and the headache, climbing to his knees, a person's voice whispering in his ear.

As his vision refocused, he realized the one pulling him was Castor. But before he could speak, Castor outstretched his hand and clamped it hard over Talon's mouth. A ringing clank resounded above him, and he slowly lifted his head, shifting his eyes upward.

He saw the vague shapes of the Children, their devilish eyes sweeping the surroundings but, strangely, with an almost oblivious gaze.

Castor mouthed two words. *They're blind*.

How? How were the Children blind if they had been chasing them? The answer came to Talon almost immediately. They could *hear*. They had heard Castor drop the flashlight… heard them sprinting through the tunnel.

Talon flipped onto his stomach, crawling silently through the dirt, Castor right beside him. They reached the other side of the cavern, where a cluster of boulders hid them from the Children.

Talon placed a hand on his forehead and massaged the pain out of it. Amber's shoulder brushed against his. He could barely see her pale face in the harsh red light, but allowed himself to focus on their surroundings.

The ground was soft soil, the wall made of rock. He could see where they had fallen from, ten feet above; the tunnel had ended when it reached the cave. The Children descended from the rocky ceiling and onto the ground, their spindly legs moving them across the wet earth.

Castor pointed to the other side of the cave. A crack wove its way down the wall of rock, large enough to squeeze through. But the thing that caught Talon's eye was the amount of golden light creeping through

Daylight.

They were so close… they just had to get past the Children.

Sheer horror curdled Talon's blood as he watched the spiders, crawling around like gnats just before they're disturbed. Castor turned and peered at the two of them before the lines in his forehead deepened. He pressed a finger to his lips and beckoned them to follow.

Talon grabbed Castor's sleeve and yanked him back, violently shaking his head. They locked eyes, and one look told Talon everything.

It's the only way.

Talon forced himself to withdraw his hand as Castor stood, drew a deep breath, and crept into the midst of the spiders.

He watched him go as the androids swirled around, searching only by ear. Castor inched closer toward the opening, and Amber caught her breath when one of the Children sped right past him, nearly knocking him off his feet.

Talon's body was rigid and frozen, beads of cold sweat rolling down his forehead as Castor continued to move forward. The spiders were swarming even faster now, and Talon knew they could sense a presence among them. Their eyes continued to flicker menacingly, reflecting off the stone walls.

Castor crouched onto his hands and knees and slid through the opening before whirling around and fixing his gaze toward Talon and Amber. Relief swept over Talon like a warm blanket when he realized that Castor was through. He turned to Amber, beckoning her to go.

She shook her head adamantly.

In the lightest whisper he could muster, Talon said, "I don't want you stuck back here… if something goes wrong."

Amber pressed her lips together tightly and swiped a strand of hair from her dirty face. She crawled past Talon and into the cloud of stirring automatons.

Talon saw her shaking with terror as she crept through their midst. A spider's claw nearly landed on her foot as she ever so slowly made her way toward Castor, who extended a hand and helped her through the crevice.

Finally, Talon stood, inhaled deeply, and stepped toward the spiders. They swarmed as he moved through their ranks, careful to avoid touching them. Sweat dripped from his face as he inched through the hoard. He dropped to his hands and knees when they began to slowly disperse.

Something dripped onto his head, making his hair cling to his skull. He craned his neck upward, more drops of it falling onto his face.

Oil, he realized. The spiders on the ceiling were dripping oil. He turned to continue toward the opening and nearly yelled in shock.

He was blinded by flickering red lights, inches from his face.

One of the Children had made its way up to him, sensing something there, sensing that something was amiss. It moved forward, and Talon lay on his stomach. He could feel the heat emanating from the spider's body as it crawled over him, its legs landing inches from his arms.

When it had gone, Talon took in a large but silent breath and moved even further toward the opening.

Almost there... almost there...

Amber reached for him. He clasped her hand, a relieved smile coming to his face.

The joy didn't last long.

His elbow collided with the side of the wall and a chunk of rock crumbled to the floor, scattering across the dirt with an echo. It felt as if life itself had drained from his entire body.

The spiders screeched and charged toward. A metal leg reached toward Talon, and he scrambled backward with a yell. The arachnids tried to press their way through the opening but to no avail, their metal legs clawing at them with ferocious violence.

"Come on!" Castor exclaimed, and they raced down the narrow passage. They hadn't gone far when they found a long rock tunnel leading upward, the sun beaming down at them. Talon could still hear the echoing roars of the Children.

Castor planted his hands and feet on the rock and hoisted himself upward. Talon's muscles ached as he and Amber followed, climbing for nearly five minutes before emerging out and into the blazing sun.

Talon lay painfully on his back as he gulped down the fresh air, knowing he would never be more thankful for oxygen ever again.

"They—they couldn't see us?" Amber panted, her voice hoarse.

Castor affirmed her question with a nod. "They were blind. Their vision must've stopped working a long time ago. Or maybe their eyes needed to be controlled manually."

He helped Amber to her feet as Talon stood from the ground, brushing himself off. Castor's sly face said everything as he kept his eyes fixed on Amber.

"I *did* tell you."

An expression of guilt passed over her face. "I'm sorry…"

Castor laughed. "Well, now we know that you're not *always* right."

Amber side-smiled, but it didn't look real. They were all rattled, and their bodies ached from the climb. They stood a short way from the edge of the crater, and Talon could see the silver glint of *The Independence* lying in wait for them, less than half a mile away.

"You still have the piece of the map, right?" Castor asked. Talon nodded and withdrew the connection drive from his pocket, gripping it tightly. He also retrieved the holo-device and held both objects side by side.

The first connection drive was still plugged into the device, leaving two ports open for use. Talon inserted the second drive, and a hologram immediately sprang up, the yellow dot indicating a location not far from New York.

Headquarters, New Jersey.

"Headquarters?" Castor said, confused. "What's headquarters?"

Talon shrugged. "I don't know."

After a brief pause, Amber said, "Let's find out."

She inclined her head toward the ship, and they began their journey back, trudging through the sandy pumice.

"At least we don't have to hike back up the crater," Castor said optimistically, and Talon smirked.

Yeah, he thought, *and we got a slippery rock wall in its place.*

He realized how their time in the sewers had left a lasting odor on them, their shoes still wet and disgusting from the murky water.

When they reached the ship, they climbed inside, setting their things near the hammocks.

"Showers before we leave?" Castor suggested, and both Talon and Amber agreed.

Talon let Amber go first. He let his mind wander, trying to take his thoughts off the Children as the hot water ran down his skin. They had retrieved two of the pieces. One more to go. They were so close, so close to completing the map.

He shut off the water and dried himself. As he dressed, he could hear Castor and Amber's muffled voices through the walls.

"—whole thing is terrifying," Amber was saying.

"I know," Castor replied. "Ledger really had a screw loose."

Talon laughed quietly. Amber had finally let Castor tell her the whole story of Ledger, even though she'd probably heard it before. Maybe she felt like she owed it to him for previously giving him such a hard time about it.

"I can't believe New York hasn't investigated it yet," she said.

"Yeah… maybe they think a lot of it was a myth. But that would be weird, since Ledger created the Children *for* them."

"Well, we have to focus. One more piece, then the Key."

There was a moment of silence before Castor, quite suddenly, said, "I wish my dad was here."

Another quiet moment.

"He'd be proud of you, Castor," Amber responded. "So would

your mom. You've been very strong."

"Really?"

Amber laughed. "Yes… you take care of the ship *and* put up with me. It's a lot to handle."

Talon heard Castor laugh, too. He smiled, but a nagging pain accompanied the sudden vulnerability he'd heard from Castor. He couldn't see him, but he could hear the longing in his voice. The longing for his dad, the longing for someone to run to. The longing to not always have to be the one to run things, handle things, oversee things.

After a long moment of silence, Talon finally opened the door and stepped into the belly of the ship. When Castor exited the bathroom after his shift, he immediately went to the cockpit, flipped on the holo-device, and *The Independence* lifted into the air, bound for the location of the final piece of the map.

CHAPTER THIRTEEN

MAY 19TH, 2492

A dark shadow crept over Prime Tower as the sun passed behind the Empire State Building. Kresh stood at the window in the council chamber, gazing through the glass at his massive domain, a sense of immense pride swimming through his blood. The clock ticked away, a sharp *click, click, click* repeating itself over and over like a distant echo.

An impatience nagged at him. The Third Borough Project would be completed soon, but it wouldn't come soon enough. His victory wouldn't be achieved until the fleet was finished. Peace wouldn't be accomplished until Borough III was gone. Until the city bowed down to him. Until *everyone* bowed down to him.

When they did, there would be no more rebellion. There would be no more unrest. No more riots like the one that had destroyed his unit. Destroyed *him*.

Zedah stood against the wall nearby, her head bowed. Ever since he had told her, just the day before, what the true purpose of the Third Borough Project was, she had changed. Her whole demeanor was different. She barely spoke, keeping her head low. Dark bags hung under her eyes, proving to Kresh that she hadn't gotten any sleep.

He had told her everything. Everything there was to know. About the boy's parents and Orson, and what they had discovered. About his invention of the Key, and where it had been hidden until…

He couldn't let his mind go there, but he knew the boy and his colleagues would fail at retrieving the Key. Kresh had a card to play the boy didn't know about, but it would only work if he stayed ignorant of its existence.

Perhaps it had been a mistake informing Zedah of his true intent; she seemed like a different person... a person truly conflicted. If she tried anything, Kresh knew he would have to stop her, and it was something he was willing to do for the greater good.

The governor paced the room, barely aware that Zedah's gaze followed him before settling on the soldiers positioned against the walls. Six of them, four more than usual, and Kresh was sure that it would get a reaction out of the Prime when they arrived.

Almost as soon as this thought entered his mind, the wooden doors swung open and the four members of Prime strode into the room, an air of condescending confidence about them that Kresh knew would be crushed within the hour.

"Kresh," Barrios stated immediately. "Sit."

"Excuse me?" the governor said, almost unable to hide the hatred pleading to burst forth.

Barrios' nostrils flared. "Sit."

A murderous surge of rage imploded inside of Kresh; he wanted to lash out, he wanted to see this man suffer, wanted to see him in torment. Who did Barrios think he was, ordering him to sit... as if he were an *animal*.

He nodded politely and took his seat at the table before stealing a glance at Zedah, who surveyed them in tense silence.

"You requested this meeting, gentlemen?" Kresh began.

"Yes," Mills stated, but didn't go further.

Kresh prompted, "Well? What is it that you would like to

discuss?"

It amused him to play dumb.

"We desire to call into question," Xian said coolly, "your behavior at yesterday's Bluebook Day celebration."

"Ah…" he droned, "And what, may I ask, is the manner of your disapproval of yesterday's… *events*?"

Kresh wanted to burst forth in laughter, knowing how ignorant… how *idiotic* they truly were.

"With all due respect, governor," Coronil declared fiercely, "you ruthlessly executed a man in front of the citizens. You did so using the members of the Entity Project… a project that *we* haven't yet approved for disclosure."

Kresh remained silent.

"And," Barrios added, gesturing to Zedah, his voice rising in octave, "Officer Kahzak lied to us, which I would assume was under *your* order. She told us she was keeping low, waiting for your instruction, yet you announced she had intercepted a criminal."

Kresh noticed Zedah flinch when Barrios mentioned her. But he said nothing, and the Prime stared at him in silence, waiting for an explanation… for an *excuse*. It didn't come.

"I ask all of you," he said, rising from the table and placing both hands on the polished wood, "what *else* would you have me do?"

"How *dare* you?" Barrios shouted as the governor loomed over them. "We have tolerated your behavior long enough. First it was the Bluebook policy, which none of us authorized, but accepted with compromise."

"Are you questioning my judgment?" Kresh said, a wicked grin spreading across his cold face.

"Yes, we are."

"I see."

■

With those last two words, Kresh's voice chilled Zedah to the bone, its frigid tone seeping through the room with unquenchable malice. Her muscles tensed, and her mind was spinning. It had been since yesterday.

When Kresh told her what he was going to do… what he had been planning all along… where the Key truly was… it was as if her whole life had plummeted into a dark void of despair and torment. She'd already done so much wrong in her life. She'd hurt people… she couldn't forgive herself for all the things she had done… what she had done to the boy's parents…

It's wrong… it's wrong…

Her mind screamed at her, conflicted between the two separate sides of the argument. All those people in Borough III… they were all going to die. But, as *always*, Kresh's way was the way to go. Even if she didn't understand it. Even if it was wrong.

She didn't believe what her mind told her. If she refused to go along with Kresh, her life would be over. But would she be able to live with herself if she did go along with him? Would she see how much of a prospering city his plan would bring?

Or would she forever hate herself from the moment the first shell was launched?

Kresh wasn't the same man she had once known. He wasn't the caring military leader that had rescued her from the Danyorian concentration camps.

He wasn't *himself*. Not anymore.

"What are you proposing, gentlemen," Kresh asked, directing the question at Barrios.

"We are requiring your immediate resignation. This kind of behavior must be acted upon," Barrios stated with an air of triumph. The governor's expression didn't soften; rather it increased in smugness.

Increased in *cruelty*.

Kresh's smile widened, and his amusement was apparent through his face.

"You *dare* laugh at us?" Barrios spat with victorious rage. Kresh turned his back on them and glared out the window. Zedah stood as frozen as a statue, barely able to breath.

Kresh raised his right arm and snapped his fingers like a firecracker, startling both the Prime and Zedah. The six soldiers stepped forth from their positions and Kresh motioned to them. The Prime jumped from their seats, peering in horror at the soldiers stalking toward them.

The soldiers pulled their pistols from their holsters and aimed them at the council members, all of whom yelled in terror. Barrios stared directly at Kresh, who turned from the window and stared him right in the eye.

Kresh articulated, "There is a new order of things, gentlemen… a new project… and you won't be part of it."

Xian, Coronil, and Mills struggled ever harder, but Barrios maintained his gaze on the governor, his eyes locked on Kresh's cruel face. Zedah stood in horrified silence, watching the event unfold, using all her strength of will not to jump in.

"You may try to run," Kresh continued, his voice smooth. "You may try to escape… but remember… you cannot run faster than a bullet."

As quick as lightning, Barrios leaped toward the table, reached underneath, and unclipped from the wood a shimmering black pistol. He directed it right at Kresh, arming it with a sharp click.

Zedah didn't have to think twice.

Before the soldiers could make any sort of move, Zedah leaped forward and grasped Barrios' arm. The gun fired, missing Kresh by barely an inch. The bullet crashed through the window, making Zedah's eardrums throb. Barrios struggled against her with all his might, so she did the one thing she could. She drove her knee into his arm, snapping it like a twig.

His howl of pain pierced the air as the firearm fell from his hand. Zedah tumbled backward, right at the feet of Kresh, who remained stock still the entire time. She noticed him glance from her, to Barrios, and to the rest of the Prime before a cold smile snaked its way across his face. Finally, he bent down and closed his fingers around the discarded gun still lying next to Barrios, who barely stirred on the ground.

Kresh stood up straight, and Zedah heard a bullet click into place before she scrambled to her feet. The governor kept his eyes fixed on the man he hated… on the moving form finally groveling beneath him. There was a long, horrible silence in which no one, not even the rest of the Prime, attempted to move. Kresh didn't even speak before he raised the gun and pulled the trigger.

Zedah used all her willpower to hold in a scream, but the rest of the Prime did no such thing. They shouted in terror as the soldiers closed in, more gunshots ringing through the air.

Kresh watched each of them go with triumph inflating his presence. He looked like the king of the world… the king of *everything*.

Zedah's body shook uncontrollably, and she couldn't stop a timid whimper escaping her mouth. The governor stalked toward her, casting his long shadow over her small stance.

"It is time that we get on with preparations, Zedah. The fleet will be ready in a few days."

He spoke to her with uncertainty... *intimidating* uncertainty. He knew she had just saved his life, but she could tell he was still questioning her loyalty.

It took all her strength to nod before Kresh shortened his stance and gestured toward the door.

"You may go."

She accepted his dismissal immediately and hurried down the hallways.

He killed them... he killed them...

Zedah had always believed that Prime Tower, with its elegant rooms and corridors, staircases and balconies, was a place of great beauty and sanctuary. She'd always felt like she belonged, ever since Kresh had found her as a little girl after her parents died in the camps. Ever since the governor rescued her and everyone else in that hellish place. When Kresh became governor, he appointed her as officer, and trusted her with anything and everything. This building had been her home.

Now, it felt like a trap. A dark monolith constructed of hatred... cruelty... torment. A sense of terrible claustrophobia overwhelmed her as the halls seemed to press in toward her, and she turned into one of the many restrooms.

Zedah arched over the basin of one of the sinks before lifting her head and fixing her eyes on her reflection. Flecks of Barrios' blood stained the left side of her face.

I'm a monster… I'm a monster…

Tears streamed down her cheeks and splashed into the sink basin.

There's no way out… there's no way out…

Her own face stared back at her, and she was horrified with how she looked. Strands of unkempt hair hung in front of her face, and her eyes were swollen and red, jagged veins cutting through the white.

Monster… monster…

With a harrowing yell, she raised a fist and let it fly into the mirror with all the strength she had left, trying to get rid of… *herself*.

No way out! No way out!

The mirror cracked like a whip, harsh lines appearing in the glass and deforming her features even further. And now she saw it. She really did look like a monster.

The strength in her legs gave out and she crouched against the wall, hugging her knees against her body. There was no way out now. No way for her to redeem herself.

Zedah clenched her legs until her knuckles whitened. She knew there was no hope. No hope for *her*. She'd done too much wrong. Hurt too many people.

There was no way.

No way for her to climb back to the light…

CHAPTER FOURTEEN

MAY 19TH, 2492

Talon scrubbed his hair with a rag, drying off the excess moisture lingering after his shower, causing little droplets to spray in all directions. He threw it into a pile designated for their disgusting, sewer-smelling clothes.

Orson's words still rang in his head.

It's never the end… as long as you have hope… and as long as you maintain your love for others.

An almost overwhelming sense of guilt overcame him when he realized these words directly contradicted what he knew he *had* to do. But now wasn't the time. He forced the idea from his mind, but the echo of it lingered.

Castor and Amber sat in the cockpit as the ship traveled over the desolate landscape of New York. *The Independence* ascended higher as they flew, and soon they cruised above the clouds, patches of land appearing in the splitting white. As Talon gazed out of a viewing port, he could see the city and its signature shape. All five Boroughs sat in their usual places, and he saw the bare outline of Borough IV, where he'd once lived in Drudgen.

He wondered what Futz was doing right now. Not that he cared, but the idea intrigued him. The sparkling waters of the Hudson shimmered below as they sped over the city and into New Jersey.

Talon had seen New Jersey's border numerous times before, but he had never been there. As the ship descended, he noticed there wasn't much of anything. A couple small towns and roads cut through the bare-branched trees, their trunks stretching into the sky like the hands of skeletons.

They hadn't been in the air for more than thirty minutes when a towering cliff cut through the clouds directly in front of them. Castor veered the ship in its direction, occasionally glancing at the holo-device for information.

"We're close," he stated. *The Independence* drew closer toward the gargantuan wall of rock and slowed as they reached the grass-patched ground. The ship touched down lightly, less than a mile from the blinking yellow dot.

"We don't know what we're walking into," Amber said, unease in her voice. "It didn't tell us what this place is."

"It said *headquarters*," Talon restated.

"I know, but what does that mean?"

Talon and Castor shrugged in tandem, and Amber frowned. After a moment of silence, Castor replied.

"Well," he said, "We've come this far…"

Amber nodded her head ever so slightly, clearly unconvinced. Talon felt the same way; the uncertainty of this place nagged at him intensely. But there was something else… it was almost as if the place was drawing him… calling out to him.

Talon left his overcoat in the pile, knowing he wouldn't want to wear it until it was good and washed. Instead, he retrieved his sword and the holo-device.

Castor pulled the lever and the boarding ramp swung to the ground, and Talon gazed around, taking in their surroundings. The ship had landed in the grass, but large pointy rocks protruded from the dirt like horns. It was an interesting location, and the silver ship nearly blended in with the boulders, providing a sort of rough camouflage.

Talon fixed his eyes on the holo-device; it directed them straight ahead. He glanced at Castor and Amber, who awaited his confirmation, then swept around and they began the journey.

"What if this doesn't work?" Amber asked.

"What do you mean?" Talon said.

"I mean, what if the piece isn't there? What if... what if it's *gone*?"

Castor responded, "Well, then we better well hope that those shells just set *themselves* off."

Amber hung her head. "I'm sorry. I just don't want things to go wrong."

"It'll be fine," Talon reassured.

I hope.

They continued their journey in silence as they drew even closer, casting a dark shadow over the surroundings. The holo-device guided them further toward it until they stood just below, and Talon turned his head upward.

Standing before them was the gaping mouth of a giant cave, a frigid wind billowing from its depths and rustling their hair ominously. A chilling unease swept over him, and he realized that Castor and Amber must've felt the same way. He heard the rustle of their clothes as they shuddered.

"Please tell me that this isn't it," Castor said, and Talon glanced at the device.

"It is."

Castor breathed. "Talk about a deterrent."

"It can't be worse than the Lair."

He knew it could.

Castor handed Talon a flashlight and he flipped the switch to *on*, tracing the beam of white light along the walls of the cave as they stepped forward. The holo-device began its signature beep, quickening as they moved further inside.

The muggy air in the massive rock chamber made the journey feel like hours, though it was only minutes. Talon's feet sunk into the cold, wet earth as droplets of water fell from the vines hanging across the ceiling. The air smelled moist; he realized that this place must've been stewing in its own humidity long before their arrival.

The cave ended, and all that stood before them was a wall of uneven rock. The end of the cave, and yet the holo-device still beeped.

"Is this it," Castor inquired, confusion in his voice.

Talon replied, "I don't know. There's nothing here."

"Look," Amber gasped, pointing left. Vines descended from the ceiling, shielding something implanted in the rocky wall... something silver. They moved toward it, and Talon directed the flashlight toward the vines as Amber shoved the natural drapery aside. A gray, automatic door stood before them, its deformities apparent on its rusted surface.

Amber beamed. "This has to be the entrance."

"I doubt that the controls are still working," Castor reasoned. "I guess I could try to hotwire them if—"

Talon pressed the green button on the rusty control panel to the side of the entrance. The doors separated, each piece disappearing into opposite sides of the wall and revealing a dark, metal corridor.

"Well," Castor said, "Never mind."

Amber tried to laugh, but the hallway that lay before them

reeked with intimidation. Nevertheless, against Talon's own will, he began the journey forward. Dirt and grime caked the wall, and they were careful to watch where they stepped—the panels covering the floor didn't exactly look sturdy.

They arrived at a metal staircase that descended to a lower floor shrouded in darkness. The beam from the flashlight reflected off its gleaming surface

"What is this place?" Amber whispered incredulously, an earnest tone in her voice. Talon understood her curiosity; he wondered as much as she did. But again, there was that same feeling... a familiar echo.

The staircase moved further and further underground; even their lightest footsteps echoed off the metal walls. Talon kept his eyes on the holo-device, his mind anywhere but.

This was the place where the final piece of the map was hidden. After this, they would be off to find the Key itself, and once they did, they would have a chance. Talon couldn't believe they were finally here, about to find the last piece of the puzzle. But even after today, he knew they wouldn't be finished. They still had to find the Key.

"Whoa!" Castor exclaimed, his hand shooting out and clamping Talon's collar before he could collide face-first with another silver door.

"Thanks," Talon expressed. He placed his thumb on the control panel and pressed the button. The doors split open, and they were met with... black. Pitch darkness seeped through the opening—even the flashlight seemed to dim. They stepped inside, and Talon kept his hand on the wall to guide himself, until something passed under his fingers.

"I found something… feels like a lever." he said

"Let me see," Castor said, moving over to his position and wrapping his fingers around the mechanism.

He yanked downward, and a startling buzz echoed through the area as pale white light flickered all around. What Talon saw took his breath away. He finally knew where they were, finally understood what this place was.

Finally understood why it had felt so familiar.

Rows of white desks lined the room, rotting vines twisting around them like snakes. Shattered monitors rested atop the desks, and on the opposite end of the room stood a plasma screen, dwarfing the entire area with overwhelming size. Vivid lights hung from the rocky ceiling, illuminating the vast room.

But what caught Talon's eye the most, what made him understand the importance of this place, was a massive bronze symbol situated just above the gargantuan screen.

A shimmering wing encased within a gleaming hoop, glinting in the radiant light. The symbol of The Falcon's Nest. This was their headquarters. Their headquarters they had once operated from, now sitting abandoned and unused, almost as though waiting to be used again.

A sharp pain wrenched Talon's gut, and he barely noticed the holo-device cease its continuous beep. All he could feel was a sense of astonishment that this place still stood. His mind whirled with questions. Was this real? Was he really here? Was he dreaming or not?

Castor and Amber remained standing behind him, as silent as the grave, gazing around the room. This was where the Nest was stationed… this was where they worked.

This was where his mother and his father had once operated the Nest.

Talon felt Amber's warm hand rest itself on his shoulder, and it felt wonderful. To have someone there for him. To let him know it was all going to be okay.

Almost immediately, he reached up and touched her hand, accepting the comfort, accepting the compassion. But he pulled his hand away soon after. The restful feeling scared him, and he knew he couldn't let it fester.

He moved further into the space, his eyes stinging as he ran his hand along the rotting desks and stepped toward the screen.

"I wonder if it still works," Castor said. "It could give us some more information on the Nest."

Talon glanced at him with a weak smile.

"You think you can get it working?" he asked.

Castor shrugged. "Probably."

He stepped toward a v-shaped console standing before the screen, laden with switches and minute levers. Talon and Amber watched as Castor tested them out, flipping them up and down, pressing buttons and twisting knobs in organized patterns. The screen began to flicker, projecting a static image and lightening the room even further.

"Yup," Castor stated happily. "It works."

Talon expected some sort of voice to echo through the room, something of vital importance to show up on the screen.

He couldn't have been more wrong.

Security footage appeared on the screen, and the sight it revealed caused horror to course through Talon's veins.

Throngs of deranged people stampeded down the streets of

New York, destroying windows, burning buildings, and flashing obscene banners protesting against the Bluehouse Prime.

The ringing sound of the crowd's terrible shouts echoed through the headquarters, making Talon feel as though they swarmed through the very room he stood in. The footage was old, making Talon realize that this riot must've taken place before Kresh was made governor.

No sooner had he thought of Kresh than a unit of over fifty soldiers sprinted into the crowd, aiming the barrels of their guns at the rioters, who didn't stop for anything. Grain and static danced along the image as it suddenly cut to a soldier's body camera, shaking violently.

One of the soldiers shouted to a man beside him, "Orders, General?"

The man was dressed in a uniform superior to the others, his short brown hair rustling in the powerful gale. Talon could barely hear them speaking through the breaking audio and, though he'd never seen him in person, he knew who the general was.

"Hold fire," General Kresh ordered loudly.

Like lightning, the rioters barreled toward the soldiers with nightmarish fury. Fists swung, guns flashed, and weapons flew.

"*Hold! Hold!*" Kresh screamed, and the soldiers obeyed.

Talon could see in the general's face that he knew he'd made his fatal mistake. The rioters overcame them, ruthlessly attacking and showing no mercy. The soldiers were overwhelmed, and Talon's mouth parted in dread as he witnessed the destruction. Kresh stood in terror as he watched his unit die at the hands of the citizens of New York.

A loyal soldier leaped toward him, pulling him out of the way as another gunshot split the air, and the general's rescuer fell to the ground. The future governor stumbled to his feet and continued to watch as the rioters drew closer. But there was no chance. There was no hope. Kresh finally seemed to realize that.

He fled.

The connection broke, and the image on the screen went black. Talon, Castor, and Amber stood in stunned silence.

Talon already knew that what he'd just witnessed would plague his nightmares forever. But he couldn't think, his mind was a whirlwind of shock, horror, and bewilderment.

Finally… he understood. Kresh used to be a military leader, an advocate for the government. He'd refused to fire on the people, he hadn't *wanted* to, he didn't want to hurt anybody. And that was his mistake.

Talon heard Amber exhale timidly, then turned and stared into her piercing green eyes. Tears streamed down her face as she kept her eyes fixed on the blank screen. Castor, who still stood at the console, was frozen on the spot, his face pale and void of all its usual optimism.

Talon put his back to the screen and, with his arms crossed, walked at the slowest pace to the other end of the room. He wanted to curl into a ball, burrow into the dirt, shut his eyes forever. He wanted to erase the revelation from his mind.

"Come on," Castor said in a small voice to the both of them. "We've got a map to find."

It was the hardest search they had done yet, and they spent over an hour looking for the minuscule symbol. None of them said a word to each other.

Talon's arms tired as he felt around the wall, the desks, and the bottom of the plasma screen.

"It's here," Castor finally called close by. Talon and Amber stepped toward him and peered at what he'd found. Directly under the giant screen was the tiny symbol, and Talon withdrew the holo-device from his pocket.

He glanced at the others, making eye contact, knowing they were all thinking the exact same thing. This was the moment of truth. If the final piece wasn't here, if the device was wrong, all their efforts would've been for nothing.

What if it's not here?

That thought pierced his mind over and over. Everything they'd done, what if it had been hopeless from the very start?

Talon pressed the device toward the wall, heard the sharp ding, and the symbol shined bright. Two little doors separated from the wall and flipped open, revealing a cube-shaped compartment.

On a small strip of scarlet felt lay the final piece of the map.

With a heavy and relieved breath, Talon laced his fingers around the connection drive and pulled it from the compartment. Castor laughed and a wide smile stretched across Amber's face as joy overcame them all, almost making them forget the horror they'd just witnessed.

Talon climbed to his feet before immediately plunging the third drive into the final connection port. A holographic image of the Key sprang into the air, spinning on its axis before being replaced by the map of the American continent.

This time, the dot wasn't yellow. It was a vibrant red. The location increased in size, and they could tell that it indicated a state not far from New Jersey.

The Temple of Athar, Yahn.

"That's it," Amber breathed. "That's where it is."

She fell into Castor's arms, hugging him tightly as they laughed, an overwhelming sense of triumph flowing from them.

Amber broke away from Castor and quickly flung her arms around Talon. He ceased his laughter, his eyes going wide, his body stiff. She pulled away soon after, seeming to realize what she was doing.

"Sorry," she apologized.

"No, it's—it's fine," Talon reassured. He hadn't been hugged by anyone in years. He'd forgotten the feeling… the feeling of *true* care from another. Amber half smiled, and Castor stared at them both before clearing his throat.

"Okay," he said. "I guess… we're done."

Talon let his eyes sweep the room one last time, but his feelings toward it weren't the same as when they'd come in. He was content, happy even, that he'd seen this place. It brought him peace, and he wasn't sad to leave it behind.

"Yeah," he replied in a near whisper.

The three of them turned and began to ascend the dark staircase toward the cave. Castor led the way with the flashlight, leaving Talon and Amber a moment to speak.

"You okay?" she asked.

"Yeah," he said, and he meant it. "Yeah, I am."

"No one's hugged you in a long time, have they?" she inquired, though she sounded a little restrained. Talon shook his head as they exited the cave, trying to estimate the direction of the ship.

"I haven't felt like I… *belonged* anywhere since my parents died," Talon explained, and Amber seemed to be stricken.

"I didn't either," she said. "For the few years that I was on my own, I didn't have a home. I was basically a nomad. Well, I still am. The only difference is that I have Castor with me."

A light smile crossed her lips as she said these words, but there was more than just content behind it… it seemed full of pain as well.

"When you were young," Talon asked slowly, "how… how did you find Castor? What happened?

Amber turned to him with shining eyes.

"My father happened…" she said and showed no intention of going any further.

Talon immediately regretted the question. "I'm sorry, I shouldn't have—"

"It's okay," she interjected. "I'm—I'm just not ready to talk about it. I don't know if I ever will be. Even Castor doesn't know."

Silence hung over them as they drew nearer to the patch of large rocks hiding *The Independence*. Thoughts permeated Talon's mind as he thought of Amber. What had happened that had made her so closed off.

"You—you don't have to hide anything," Talon said. "I don't think it's helping keeping everything in."

I'm such a hypocrite.

But he saw a flicker in Amber's eyes, and a change in her posture. She peered at him softly, a glaze in her eyes, and stood up straighter.

"I know… you're right," she agreed, and truly sounded like she meant it. But her voice was light, almost as if she wasn't present in the moment. Her thoughts were elsewhere, and Talon could tell she was thinking. She opened her mouth to speak, but Castor suddenly cursed loudly, breaking Talon out of his own mind. Amber snapped her head toward him.

"Language, Castor!" she scolded.

"Quiet!" he exclaimed harshly and pulled them behind one of the rocks.

"What is it?" Talon asked, startled.

"Look," Castor replied. Talon and Amber poked their heads out from behind the chunk of jagged stone and peered in the direction of the ship.

Four Entities stood as stiff as boards, surrounding *The Independence* on all sides. Talon nearly gasped but figured that would be a bad idea. A black aircraft rested in the grass next to theirs, its boarding ramp lowered.

"They found us," Castor mouthed.

"What are we going to do?" Amber whispered, "We can't get to the ship."

They crouched in silence before Talon spoke.

"We'll have to create a diversion."

"How?" Amber asked.

Another silent moment, this one broken by Castor.

He said, "I'll draw them away, while you two get to the ship. Talon, you'll get to the gunner's position and shoot—"

"What?!" Talon exclaimed quietly, "Why *me*?!"

"Because it's easier than starting the ship. Amber will handle that."

Amber groaned. "Are you *kidding* me? The *one* time you're not there to control the turret, you still won't let me use it?"

Castor rolled his eyes, but immediately refocused. "Amber, you'll activate the ship. I know it sounds counterintuitive but turning on the aircraft is *hard*. A lot harder than firing the turret."

Talon protested. "But what if I hit *you*?"

"You won't. I'm faster than I look. Just make sure you aim right." But Castor's voice told Talon he was incredibly worried.

Amber cut in. "Castor, are you sure that's a good idea?"

"Yeah, it'll be fine," he responded, but he didn't sound so sure.

"I don't even know how to *control* it," Talon defended.

"Look, it has two steps. The projectile is already loaded so you just need to activate the propulsion unit—"

"English, Castor!" Amber said.

"Okay, okay… there's a gray knob on the left side of the console up there; turn that and then press it. You'll be able to control the turret and fire the bullets with the steering mechanism. There's a silver pedal under the seat—kick that to fire the missile, but save it for their ship."

Talon was lost after the first sentence. Before he could clarify anything, Castor hurled himself out from behind the rock and within vision of the Entities.

"Hey!" he yelled. The Entities whirled around and sprinted toward him faster than Talon thought possible. Castor sped away as they pursued. He'd been right. He *was* faster than he looked.

"He can be really brave when he's being an idiot," Amber sighed, rolling her eyes.

"Go," Talon whispered, and they sneaked up *The Independence's* ramp before splitting off and going to their different destinations. As Talon climbed the ladder to the gunner's position, he felt the ship rev to life, the engine making the walls vibrate with a familiar rumble.

The gunner's position was the only room he hadn't seen while living on *The Independence*, and it was the smallest room of all. A glass dome arched above him, providing maximum range of motion in the tiny space, and a leather swivel chair stood in the direct center. The turret, with its three barrels, was positioned just outside of the glass, and a square steering mechanism protruded from the console.

After a quick survey, Talon sat down in the seat, gripping the steering mechanism with his dirty hands, trying to remember Castor's directions.

Turn the knob… and push.

He noticed a miniature gray knob on the left side of the console and immediately thrust his fingers toward it. He twisted and pressed. A loud click sounded through the space, and a couple more lights lit up on the console.

Talon barely moved the steering mechanism and gave a small yelp when the turret and the seat rotated in tandem. Castor was still being pursued by the Entities, weaving himself between the boulders outside.

Fire with the steering mechanism.

Talon glanced down, squinted, and noticed two small buttons placed on the square wheel, one on each side. He aimed toward the Entities, braced himself, and pressed the buttons with his thumbs. The deafening sounds of cannon-fire split his eardrums as the ship vibrated with the force of an earthquake. He saw Castor dive behind a rock as the glowing bullets collided with the Entities, ripping them limb from limb in a shower of sparks and twisted metal.

Almost immediately, he remembered the next batch of instructions.

Fire the missile with the pedal.

He turned the gun toward the Entities vacant ship, drew a deep breath, and kicked his foot toward the pedal underneath the seat.

BANG!

A column of fiery smoke leaped from the area just below the turret, streaked through the air, and crashed into the enemy ship. A massive fireball exploded into the air as the Entities' ship split apart, the sound echoing through the cliffs.

Shock overwhelmed Talon's mind. Had he *actually* just done that? He peeled his white hands from the steering-mechanism and inhaled deeply. All the stress drained from his body, and he leaned against the back of the chair. He heard Castor's happy voice ring through the ship.

Talon descended the ladder and joined him and Amber, who smiled and laughed heartily.

"I couldn't have done that better myself!" Castor complimented, clapping him on the back.

Of course, he could've.

The shock of the moment was still setting in, but he guessed he'd finally found *something* he was good at… aim.

"What was it like?" Amber asked him eagerly, a hint of annoyance in her voice.

Talon shrugged. "More scary than fun."

She laughed, and then scowled at Castor. "I seriously want to know why you let him use it and never me."

Talon felt uncomfortable being in the middle of this situation again. There was a pause, and Castor smiled slyly.

"Because guns are for boys."

"*What?!*"

"I'm kidding, I'm kidding. But you're right," he admitted. "I guess I've been a little too restrained."

Amber scowled again. "A little?"

"Okay, okay, a *lot* restrained. But seriously, I thought you didn't like technology."

"I don't think that I'd call firing a turret *technology*."

"I definitely would."

There was another uncomfortable pause, but Amber suddenly broke into a laugh, prompting Castor to do the same. Soon, all three of them were laughing joyfully, the terror of the Entities' arrival diminishing.

"We'd better get out of here," Amber said through gleeful breaths. "They might send more."

Castor moved into the cockpit, still chuckling happily, and Amber turned to Talon.

"Well done," she said.

He shrugged with a smile and crashed into the leather seat with a big, exhausted sigh. Amber sat down next to him, Castor's laugh still echoing from the cockpit.

CHAPTER FIFTEEN

MAY 20TH, 2492

Castor set *The Independence* down near a river that looked clean enough to wash their dirty clothes in, provided they use the bar of soap from the bathroom. The sun's rays peered from behind the mountains when they finished, and they decided to stay the night by the riverbank.

The next day they soared over New York City yet again, and Talon knew that Governor Kresh was down there, preparing his fleet.

Kresh…

The thought of him sent shivers up Talon's spine. He hadn't been truly intimidated by the name before, but after seeing that footage, he didn't know what to expect.

Now, everything made sense. Kresh's wrath… his *rage* almost felt justified. After seeing what the rioters did to his unit, Talon almost didn't blame the governor for his tyranny. *Almost*.

"Are we going to talk about this?" Amber asked after a long while of silence.

"About what?" Castor said, but Talon knew what she meant, and he had a sneaking suspicion that Castor was playing dumb.

"What we saw back there… in the cave."

Castor gulped. "Oh."

"I never knew that Kresh was a military leader," Amber stated. Talon shook his head; he hadn't either.

"What those people did to his unit…" Castor began but didn't finish.

Talon gazed at their disturbed faces and knew they were thinking the same thing he was. They understood, without a doubt, that Kresh was enacting this project for revenge. Yes, he wanted further control, but revenge was his *true* goal... his true *purpose*... even if Kresh refused to see that himself.

They didn't speak of it any further. Amber climbed the ladder to the gunner's position at one point, claiming she only wanted to see if everything was in working order.

"I hope I didn't break anything up there," Talon stated, and Castor laughed.

"Nah, she does those kinds of checks regularly. I think *I'm* the one that she doesn't trust to keep things in working order."

"Oh," Talon said.

"You've got better aim than I do, that's for sure. But those missiles are hard to get," he remarked, then his voice dropped to a whisper. "I couldn't afford the two that we had, so I had to make a deal with a smuggler."

"A smuggler?" Talon repeated, impressed.

"Yup, but don't tell Amber. She still thinks that I paid for them."

"Hang on, earlier you said that there was only one missile."

Castor explained, "We used the first one on Zedah's ship... when we rescued you."

Talon shrugged and kept his eyes on the passing terrain. But Castor had given him something to think about.

Zedah...

They hadn't seen her since Blackridge. That unsettled him. Sure, the Entities showed up back near the cave, but that wasn't the same. Did that mean she had a part to play in all this? Had Orson actually defeated her, or would they have to face not only Kresh, but Zedah as well? He didn't want to think about it.

Another forty-five minutes of flight time and they were well across the border of Yahn. So far, there were no settlements in sight, but the sky shone blue and was patched with fluffy clouds. The landscape wasn't beautiful, but it wasn't disgusting either.

Expansive prairies spread across the land like a blanket, occasionally dotted with trees and bushes. There was much of the same for miles, and once Talon got a good look, he closed his eyes and rested his cheek on his hand until…

Castor breathed, "Woah…"

Talon cracked open his eyes, then allowed them to shoot open like a bullet. Standing before them was a massive wall, constructed of green-tinted metal that glinted in the sunlight. Multiple tiers were stacked atop one another, framed by the biggest pipes Talon had ever seen, a calm mist blanketing the structure. It was as high as any skyscraper in New York, stretching for miles in both directions, disappearing into the horizon. Aircraft hovered at the top in symmetrical lines, resembling tiny ants, awaiting their turn to pass over the structure. The three of them gazed up at the behemoth, keeping their eyes fixed on the numerous multi-barreled cannons positioned at the top.

"So that's why there haven't been any settlements," Castor reasoned.

"It's the Yahn Wall," Amber explained with a wide smile.

"What's it for?" Castor asked breathlessly.

"I think it was built as a shield, to keep out invaders and potential spies."

"Who would attack this place?" Talon asked, though he

remembered reading about the wall in one of his old history books.

"Other states… maybe other countries. Yahn has some of the best leadership on the continent. They wanted to build a wall to keep out others who might try to expand their borders or infiltrate from within."

"How do you know all this?" Castor asked, obviously impressed.

Amber stiffened. "My mother taught me… at home. We couldn't afford school."

Most people couldn't nowadays. Only the rich sent their children to school. Talon felt a swell of compassion for her. It made him wonder if she was feeling the same thing he always was. The pain of remembering.

Castor steered the ship upward, toward the line of ships waiting their turn. After much trial and error, he was able to secure a spot for *The Independence*.

It was only when they got up there that they realized how slow the line moved. They waited for over an hour and, when their turn finally came, Castor landed the ship gently on top of the wall to subject it to a search party.

"Where's the pilot?" one of the security guards asked in a drawling accent, raising his bushy eyebrows. Castor lifted a hand.

"*You?*" said another, clearly bewildered.

"Yup," Castor replied with a shrug. They seemed surprised and a little suspicious but didn't say any more. They wandered around the ship, inspecting anything that might violate their guidelines.

"You may proceed," said the first before exiting the ship and pressing the button to close the boarding ramp.

"Did they not notice the giant turret we have?" Amber asked, tilting her head.

"The turret isn't loaded, and we don't have any more bullets," Castor explained. *The Independence* lifted off and traveled across the immensely thick wall until the geography of Yahn revealed itself to them.

There wasn't a speck of green in sight; everything was covered by thousands of diverse buildings, and many of them spouted white steam from rustic smokestacks. They could see the strangest vehicles trudging along the various roads and streets, some of which had treads and massive wheels. Citizens and bystanders dotted the city, going about their business, like tiny bugs scurrying around on a rocky hill. A monorail snaked its way between buildings and under bridges, trains speeding along the tracks in order to get to their destination on time.

"This place is actually kinda cool," Castor said with a smile.

Amber nodded. "I don't disagree."

If Talon had to choose a place to live, this would've been it; there weren't many cities like this these days, especially in America.

"Where's the Temple?" he asked, and Castor activated the holo-device.

"It's about twenty miles northwest. We'll get there soon."

The congestion of the buildings began to thin, and soon the grass became visible again. Using the directions provided, and keeping the ship under the speed limit, they landed at the entrance to a long dirt road that led into the hills, where other aircraft stood on aged landing pads.

This was it…

Their final destination…

The location of the Key…

They gathered their things, and Talon couldn't believe they'd made it this far. They were so close... so close to finding the Key... the one thing that could stop Kresh.

"Well," Castor said, optimism in his voice. He didn't have to finish. None of them spoke, they only stared at each other. Amber pulled the lever and the boarding ramp lowered.

They made their way outside, and Talon immediately felt the warm air on his skin, the smell of healthy grass swirling through his nose. It put a little skip in his step as they traveled down the road.

Along the way they crossed other pedestrians who tipped their broad-brimmed hats and nodded happily, surprising them and making them return the nod gratefully.

"This place—" Amber began.

"Is great," Castor finished, and Talon laughed in agreement.

The road continued for a couple miles, and they occasionally glanced at the holo-device to make sure they were on the right course.

"I wonder what the Temple will be like," Castor said.

"I've read about it before," Talon remembered. He'd been thinking about it since the holo-device first disclosed the Key's location. "I think the people built it to honor the mythical god called Athar. They believe he gave them water and light and... uh... and such."

That was embarrassing, he thought.

"Well," Castor stated, "I guess that I'm the only one who hasn't read up on his history."

Talon and Amber laughed softly.

"It's not too late to start," Amber said. "I know that New York took all the books years ago, but Yahn might have—"

Castor suddenly gasped, and Talon and Amber snapped their

heads in the direction of his gaze. At the end of the road stood a monolithic temple, constructed of yellowish limestone. Four thin towers had been built at each corner of the structure, and a shimmering gold gate guarded the entrance.

It was a beautiful piece of architecture, with its numerous white columns, archways, and magnificent courtyard complete with a giant fountain. The roof of the building was a steep pyramid, a tall spire sprouting from its tip, at the top of which was a statue of a man with eagle-like wings.

Castor whistled. The feeling this building gave Talon was one of hope and accomplishment, and his eyes rimmed with gloss. They stepped through the gate and across the cobbled courtyard. The building towered over them and looked even bigger up close as they ascended the marble steps toward the door.

Those who were inside either ambled through the halls, or sat in the chapel, another beautiful sight. Wooden benches stood in rows, facing an expansive stage that bore an artistic lectern. A massive stained-glass window stood behind the stage, sunlight streaking through and casting a multicolored glow across the room. Talon, Castor, and Amber stared at the space in awe, wondering at how such a wonderful piece of architecture could still exist.

"Well," Castor began, "we've got a job to do."

Talon nodded and removed the holo-device from his pocket just before it began to beep. The three of them traveled down the Temple's massive corridors and hallways, noticing different mosaics that told the strange, eyebrow-raising story of Athar.

As the device guided them deeper into the Temple, the mosaics disappeared, replaced with rows of statues in various positions of strength, weakness, torment, and distress. Talon realized that whoever sculpted them must've had a lot of time on his hands, because they were quite good.

They turned left, right, right again, left, over and over, and Talon wondered how it was possible that this place had so many corridors. The innately carved ceiling was its own sight, and numerous skylights allowed natural sunlight to pour through in rays. The device led them over bridges, across landings, and through archways as they climbed higher and higher, and the beeping paced itself even faster.

Talon glanced upward, laying eyes on a decrepit staircase, the limestone bricks cracked and crumbling. At the top of the stairs stood a rotting, termite-eaten door with a scratched metal handle protruding from the middle. Castor and Amber didn't even notice, each of them too busy gazing at the surroundings. They stood on the highest floor in the temple, on a bridge that connected one landing with another. Amber turned her head and sucked in a breath when she laid eyes on the door.

The holo-device beeped rapidly, the sound echoing through the chamber, before suddenly stopping and enveloping them in silence.

Castor asked, "Is this it?"

"I think so," Talon declared, and slid the device back in his pocket. He turned toward the staircase and began to ascend. The door stood slightly ajar, and he forced it further open with a strong heave, the hinges whining noisily.

A musty smell immediately met Talon's nostrils, and he scrunched up his face. This place was the only underwhelming room in the entire temple. As he emerged into the space, he realized they stood in a large attic, and that no one could've been in here for years.

Besides a couple dozen wood boxes placed in the corners, the room was empty. Sunlight spilled through four windows, their sills covered in layers of yellow dust and shriveled insects. The ceiling was simple and brown, held up by supportive beams. The room was one of the most generic places Talon had ever seen, but he didn't shy away from the fact that it was rather big, and it would be very difficult to find the symbol... *if* the symbol was what they were supposed to find. The device ceased its noise, and the three of them turned to each other.

"I'm not exactly sure what we're supposed to be looking for," Talon said. "So... I guess we should try and keep an open mind."

Castor and Amber nodded, and they all began the search.

This was the final step...

Talon couldn't believe they had made it this far; his heart raced during every moment of the search. Nearly an hour passed, and with it his energy.

His arms grew weary from consistently using them to move his fingers along the walls. Later, he began to search the boxes and even the floors, and the sun cast a golden glow through the windows by the time Talon finally allowed himself to rest. He sat with his back against the wall and shut his eyes.

"Hey guys," Castor said quietly. Talon cracked open his eyelids and turned to Castor, who was crouched on his hands and knees, staring at something on the cracked floor. He crawled over to him, and noticed Amber shut one of the boxes before joining them as well.

Talon gasped and Amber's eyes went wide when they saw what Castor had found. Someone had painted something on the floor... something all too familiar.

A little blue square.

It could almost pass for an accidental splotch of paint, but Talon immediately dismissed that theory by observing its perfectly square and pointy-edged shape.

"Does this look familiar to you?" Castor asked. "I feel like I've seen it before."

Talon knew what it was. He'd been forced to see it every day while living in Drudgen. In book form... and tattooed in Alger's flank...

"It's the Bluebook," he stated. "The symbol of the Prime."

Castor's mouth parted and he inched his face closer to the square. Talon immediately withdrew the holo-device and pushed it toward the symbol.

Nothing happened.

This had to be it... this had to be the place... how were they going to activate it? The answer came much sooner and much easier than he'd expected.

Talon ran his hand along the symbol and jumped when his finger forced it just a little deeper into the ground.

His heart leaped. *A button.*

Talon placed his right index finger on the square and pressed hard. The symbol disappeared into the ground with a deep crunch as it scraped against the surrounding stone.

The room began to shake, machinery shifting beneath the floor, but to Talon, the rumble wasn't threatening. It was joyful... *triumphant*... and he began to laugh. He couldn't remember the last time he'd felt this happy.

A circular section of the floor separated from the limestone brick, lifting itself up and out of the ground. Rising from the floor was a mechanical cylinder, and it rose higher into the air before stopping at the height of Talon's stomach. The top of the cylinder split open and swung outward like a door... and a little compartment revealed itself.

They peered inside, catching their breath, flustered at the fact that the Key was finally within their grasp. The rumbling ceased, and the cylinder stopped moving.

Nothing...

There was *nothing* there...

Talon furrowed his brows, placing a hand on the mechanism, searching around it, hoping to find some sort of control or button or... *anything*.

"Where is it?" Castor asked urgently, looking at it sideways.

"I—I don't know," Talon stuttered as his hands flew faster over the cylinder. "There's nothing here."

A spike of terrible adrenaline tied a knot in his chest, and his breathing became frantic. The Key wasn't in the little compartment... it wasn't anywhere within sight.

Talon barely noticed Amber run a shaking hand over her forehead, barely noticed Castor trying to rummage through the mechanism's gears and cogs and wires, attempting to see if something was jammed or broken.

"It's not here," Talon panted breathlessly.

He heard Amber give a small, sharp breath of defeat. They had gotten this far... they couldn't give up... not now... *not now...*

Please! Just be here! Please!

Talon tore himself away from the mechanism, shoving both hands through his hair and resting them on his throbbing head. Castor straightened and stared right at Talon, who knew their last hope would be that something was broken... that something was *wrong*.

But Castor shook his head, his normally optimistic expression melting right off. The sun barely peeked at them through the window, disappearing behind the giant wall standing in the distance, darkness spreading across the sky. The blackness of the night further twisted Talon's heart, draining it of all joy... of all triumph... of all *hope*.

The revelation hammered itself into his mind. The Key wasn't here. It was gone. They had *failed*.

CHAPTER SIXTEEN

MAY 21ST, 2492

A deafening bang…
        Searing heat…
                Roars of a raging fire…

Talon shot awake with a horrible yell. His clothes clung to his skin, cold sweat acting like a magnet, his hair plastered to his face. He shivered violently as he swung his legs over the edge of the hammock, throbbing pains in his head, misery consuming him like a black cloud of darkness enveloping everything it touched.

He barely noticed *The Independence's* engine humming just beside him, and hardly paid attention to the fact that the sun wasn't even up. All the events of the day before reentered his mind, and the knot in his chest tied itself even tighter, like a python entwining itself around its helpless prey.

Talon rose from the hammock and stepped into the bathroom. He pulled off his sopping clothes and replaced them with clean ones before leaning on the sink, fixing his eyes on his reflection in the mirror. Orson had been right; he did look a lot like his father, but his mother's hair color shined bright atop his head.

It only made the pain worse.

He breathed even heavier and splashed cold water on his face. It didn't help. Talon's heart felt like it was shrinking… shriveling up. Multiple tears rolled down his face and fell into the sink.

We failed… we failed…

The Key hadn't been there… it wasn't where they needed it to be… they weren't going to save all those lives… they weren't going to stop Kresh… it was *impossible*.

It was as if he was standing in someone's cold shadow that wouldn't leave. He needed air. Talon stepped out of the bathroom, and noticed Amber sleeping peacefully in her hammock, though her face was sad. He pulled his eyes away from her, and a terrifying thought pierced his heart like a speeding arrow. He'd gone through it twice before… once with his parents… once with Alger… not again… *never*.

Castor sat in the cockpit, his hands gripping the steering wheel as he directed the ship over the Yahn Wall. Talon joined him, sitting hopelessly in the chair just opposite.

Castor spoke after a while, his voice strained and almost broken. "I don't know what we're gonna do, now."

"None of us do."

"What I mean is… if we should all find some place to… *hide* for the time being."

Talon immediately shook his head. "No."

"What else is there to do?"

They sat in silence for a short moment before Talon stiffened. He avoided Castor's gaze.

"Look," Castor said seriously, "it wasn't there… we can't stop him… even if we tr—"

"I know," Talon interjected loudly, before glancing back toward the area where Amber slept, and gently repeating, "I know."

Castor stared at him intensely. "You okay?"

"No," he snapped.

"I—I'm sorry—"

"It doesn't matter."

Castor said hastily, "Then what *does*?"

Talon glanced at him. He'd replaced his usually bright and playful face with a serious, focused one. Talon hadn't seen that from Castor before, and he assumed it didn't happen too often. But, when it did, it came out strong.

There was tense silence between them as the ship sped over the terrain, and the sun's morning rays drizzled past the Highlands. All those people in Borough III… everyone who lived there… families, workers, innocents… they weren't going to save them. Talon rubbed his forehead, attempting to crush every agonizing thought violently assaulting his brain, but to no avail.

Talon didn't know where they were going, and he had a suspicion that Castor didn't have a destination in mind, until the skyline of Manhattan appeared miles in the distance.

"Why did you bring us back here?" he asked, and Castor shrugged.

"Don't know," he responded quietly. "Just couldn't think of anywhere else."

An idea sparked in Talon's mind. There had to be some other way to detonate the shells. Orson had said they were on automatic timers that would begin their countdown when fired, but there had to be a way to start the countdown early, while the shells were still in the ships. Even without the Key.

But he couldn't bear more loss… not after everything he'd gone through… after all the pain. Borough I drew closer, and Talon finally made up his mind.

"Set the ship down at the harbor," he ordered, and Castor turned to him with a furrowed brow.

"That area's blocked off. It's where they're building the—"

"I know," Talon declared, and barely noticed Amber enter the cockpit. "Just do it."

Castor turned to Amber, who stared at him with scrunched eyebrows. She clearly hadn't heard enough of the conversation to understand what was going on.

"Okay," Castor whispered, his tone uncertain.

He veered the ship to the left as the roof of Prime Tower passed beneath them, and Talon drew breath when he got his first look at the build site.

Encased in colossal metal cages were massive silver battleships, and next to them, giant cranes stretched skyward like overgrown weeds. Talon could see the ships' elaborate designs and chiseled features. He counted twenty of them in total, all huge, but none as big as the one in the center.

The largest cage surrounded the mothership, six cranes dotted along the edges. Its silvery gray hull curved like a sharp oval and long, slim cannons lined its wooden deck, easily the most menacing sight Talon had ever beheld. He could tell the build was now complete enough for people to realize they weren't cargo ships. Was the Prime a part of this, or was it all Kresh? If it was, what had happened to the council?

He heard Amber stifle a sharp breath, and she clapped a hand over her mouth. Talon had known, ever since Orson told them, what the ships were going to do. He'd known they were going to accomplish Kresh's plan. But the knowledge still didn't prepare him for his first sight of the fleet.

His heart sank painfully, like an ocean liner crashing to the bottom of the sea. He knew he had to do something… something that could help save all those lives… something that Castor and Amber couldn't help with... what he wouldn't *let* them help with. *The Independence* touched down less than half a mile from the harbor, on the sandy bank of the Hudson River.

Now was the time... the *only* time.

Talon leaped from his seat and strode briskly to the back of the ship, intense purpose in each step. His stomach twisted, his gut churning in sadness.

"Talon?" Amber called, confusion in her voice, and Castor followed her out of the cockpit.

He wrenched on his overcoat and snatched up his sword so sharply that both Castor and Amber were shocked. Talon pulled the lever to lower the boarding ramp and bounded into the dusty air, the murky smell of the river swirling through his nose.

"Talon!" Amber cried. "Where are you *going*?"

He spun to face them, and every terrible memory manifested itself in a fit of grief and despair.

"I told you that I wouldn't be with you forever," he declared, and the both of them stopped pursuing.

"What are you doing?" Amber pleaded, beginning to break down. Castor beckoned him toward them.

"C'mon," he said. "Let's all go back in and talk about this."

"No!" Talon yelled, making them start. "I'm doing this to protect you... both of you! I can't let you come... I couldn't bear it if—"

The words wouldn't form, and Castor and Amber stood gazing at him in silence. He didn't need them. He couldn't let himself care.

Not now.

Not *ever*.

But another part of his brain wrenched for his attention. Regret?

Guilt? What was it? Whatever it was crushed his mind.

"You can't go," Castor declared fiercely.

Talon exclaimed, "You can't stop me! I'm not letting you come... you don't understand—"

"We do," Castor returned. "We do understa—"

"*I was nine years old!*"

Both Castor and Amber froze, a wave of sorrow passing over each of their faces.

"Nothing prepared me for it! I *can't* let it happen again!"

Talon spun around and began marching in the direction of the build-site when Amber shouted from behind him.

"My father was a criminal warlord…"

Talon stopped in his tracks, his head spinning. He could hear her voice breaking. But *now* wasn't the time. Not *now*.

"He was wanted by over twenty different governments… including New York," she revealed through sobs.

Not now… please… not now…

"He was on the run for years, but eventually he disappeared, and he met my mother in Hallburg while in hiding. They had me later, and I lived with them until I was seven. Nothing could've prepared me for it, either… I—I loved them both… I was happy… all I knew was happiness."

Not now… not now…

"My father never told my mother anything about his life. But when she found out who… *what* he really was, she tried to escape with me. She loved him, but—but he…"

She paused, a choking whimper escaping from her mouth. Talon still had his back toward her.

"He broke her heart… he never *really* loved her… he used her as a tool to seem normal… and—and he couldn't let her betray him."

Her voice broke like a pane of glass. Talon clenched his teeth in an attempt to stop the tears from coming.

"He caught us…" Amber continued, "and—and he…"

She didn't have to finish. Talon already knew the rest of the story. Amber had escaped her father at seven years old. Her mother, on the other hand…

He heard Amber drop to her hands and knees, heard Castor kneel beside her and try to pull her back to her feet, heard her sobs rattling his eardrums.

Their silence was only broken by the sounds of the gentle waves lapping against the shore, and Talon used all his remaining strength to turn and face them. After a short moment, he stepped forward, kneeling right in front of Amber and peering into her beautiful, grief-filled eyes. He extended his hand, gently brushing glistening a tear off her soft cheek, before one broke through his own eye and trailed down his face. Her pain cut a gash deep in his heart.

"I'm sorry," he whispered, and he'd never uttered those words more truthfully than he did now. "I'm sorry for *both* of you… you've both lost so much."

He glanced toward Castor, whose face was snow-white and devoid of all joy. Tears continued to stream down Talon's face. Amber's brokenness seeped into his own, and he gently laid his hand on the back of her neck.

Finally, he realized it. She and Castor had lost just as much as him. He knew he could relate to them, and they could relate to him.

But he couldn't think of that.

Amber peered at Talon hopefully, but he shook his head, yet

another knot overturning his stomach.

"I can't let you come," he declared. "I'm trying to protect you... I can't lose you, too."

He stood and whirled around, but Castor caught his arm.

"Are you really going to leave her like this?" he demanded, gesturing toward Amber on the ground. The pain in Castor's voice cut through Talon like a knife, and the guilt came in an agonizing wave. He was leaving them, leaving them after all they'd been through together. Leaving Amber after she'd finally revealed what happened with her father.

"Let me go, Castor."

They glared at each other for another long moment before Castor barely allowed his grip to slacken. Talon turned and sprinted toward the build-site before they could say anything else. He didn't look back... he didn't *want* to. He was doing exactly what he said he was... *protecting* them.

Talon's heart pounded against his chest as he raced toward the site, the echoing booms of the Third Borough Project growing louder and louder.

I'm protecting them... I'm protecting them...

He was going to succeed, even if he didn't make it out alive.

He turned into a decrepit alley, though kept the entrance to the build site within his view. Yellow tape blocked off the area, and a large, electronic gate stood guard.

All alone... alone...

The screaming sounds of an engine split his eardrums, and a strong gust of violent wind ripped at his hair and overcoat. He snapped his head upwards and his anger swelled. Zedah's sleek aircraft rocketed toward the build site with the fury of a tiger before slowing and descending, disappearing behind one of the ships.

When the coast was clear, Talon sped toward the electronic entrance and sneaked under the long mechanical arm he knew lifted skywards with each passing vehicle.

There wasn't a soul in sight as he crept beneath the monolithic cages overshadowing him, making him feel like an ant in a shoe box.

I can't have happiness… can't have happiness…

Zedah was here, he knew it. If he was lucky, he'd be able to avoid her. He knew that was an unwarranted hope; she'd find him… she'd find him wherever he went.

Talon rounded a corner and stifled a gasp before leaping back behind the wall. Workers dressed in gray jumpsuits and yellow hardhats swarmed the area like flies on a piece of discarded food. They stood tethered to the cranes, hundreds of feet in the air, or they moved about the deck, going over the final inspections. Talon could hear two men speaking to one another, just around the corner. Thankfully, they hadn't seen him.

"—launch in thirty minutes," said one, his voice deep and gruff.

"But they aren't finished. We need at least another week."

"I know," the other replied. "The governor said not to worry about it. The guns are operating well. He'll be here when the ships drop."

In horror, Talon stopped breathing, his throat closing.

"He must be on his way," said the second.

The two men stalked off, and Talon found it safe to round the corner. Workers still swarmed, but he easily avoided their gaze, hiding when he needed to, and crept further through the build-site.

They had said thirty minutes… *Thirty minutes.*

The words echoed in his mind, invading it, infesting it. Thirty minutes was all he had to get onto the ship, suddenly making him unsure of whether or not he could do it. He was a kid, not an army. He was young, not grown. He was fighting a government, not a bully.

Talon's thoughts jammed. Maybe Kresh… the Prime… maybe they *were* just bullies. Wasn't that what governments were? Weren't they just intimidates disguised in the glamor of wealth, power, and luxury? Tyrants who claimed the authority to decide what was right and what was wrong? He wasn't sure. He'd never experienced any *other* type of government. But he was sure of one thing; a *good* government wasn't supposed to be an oppressor.

After ten minutes and turning past another corner, he stopped dead in his tracks. There stood the mothership in all its prime glory. He felt like he'd stepped into a world of giants. The ship towered over him, shrouding him in its cold shadow and making him feel like a speck of dust. It was there… right there… all he needed was to get to it and he'd be able to shut down the operation… *maybe*.

The shells had to be loaded by now. Only twenty minutes remained until the ships would be dropped into the water, and they would set a course for their destination, less than eight miles away.

All he had to do was get inside, and that was the easy part: a rail-less metal bridge, supported by hefty beams, arched its way over the filthy river that sparkled twenty-five feet below.

The hard part would be making his way through the ship and finding the control console, if that was truly where he could detonate the shells. Talon craned his neck from side to side, making sure the coast was clear before starting the journey across the bridge. Everything stood dead quiet. All he could hear were his own gentle footsteps, ringing through the metal.

A terrible yell split the silence, echoing from above. Talon whirled around, barely bracing his sword in time for Zedah's to collide with his, the sheer force sending him tumbling to the ground.

She'd leaped from one of the banisters attached to the crane above, landing gracefully on the bridge. Zedah whipped her blade with fury, leaving Talon nothing to do but defend with all his might and willpower. His anger returned, swelling through him. He barely noticed anything, barely noticed the confused shouts of the workers, barely noticed the gleaming tears streaming down Zedah's cheeks.

The ring of metal against metal resounded through the air as they fought. Zedah struck at him, and Talon dodged, nearly slipping over the edge of the bridge. He caught himself just in time as his opponent stepped back, keeping her sword braced in front of her.

"Leave," she said. "Please… leave *now*… I don't want to do this."

Rage surged through him. Was she actually pleading with him? His anger manifested itself in the form of the question that had been plaguing his mind ever since he'd left Blackridge.

"Where's Orson?"

The words tasted like fire.

Zedah didn't answer… her face only fell, and Talon understood the worst. Tears stung his eyes, and his breaths came out in rapid gasps. All he could feel was anger… all he could feel was the tormenting inferno of misery. Talon stared at her, his face twisting itself up, his teeth grinding together, only one word coming to mind: *monster*.

Zedah pressed her lips together as he ran at her, a howling scream shooting off his lips. Again, their blades connected, and Talon could feel Zedah's arm weakening. He spun around and thrust out his foot, sending her rolling across the bridge. She didn't even try to stand, remaining crouched on her hands and knees, and Talon kicked her sword away from her with a ringing clatter.

Just one more strike… one more strike and she'll never hurt anyone ever again…

Finally, Zedah made eye-contact, and Talon nearly dropped his sword in shock. He knew the look she gave him would stay with him forever. All her misery manifested itself on her face… all her despair, all her guilt.

Don't think about it… just do it… do it now…

"Well, boy, are you going to do it or not."

Talon froze. The voice had come from behind him, and he recognized it all too well. He'd heard it before… he'd heard it in the headquarters of the Nest… he'd heard it on the video file.

Slowly, he turned to face the source.

Kresh stood behind him, dressed in the same military uniform as he'd been wearing the day of the riot. His face was twisted in an expression of raw evil, almost joyous at the display that lay before him.

"Why not do it? She deserves it."

The governor had his hands behind his back, staring right into Talon's blue eyes.

"Don't you want to… for *them*?"

What does he mean… who does he mean…

Talon's expression of bewilderment must've shown on his face, because Kresh smirked, his face twisting even further.

"I see. You don't know."

It started to come to him… the realization… the horrible truth. He knew who Kresh was talking about.

"Your parents were our main targets," Kresh explained, his voice soft. "Do you really think it was an accident?"

Talon's breathing paced itself even faster…

No! They can't have done anything! It was an accident! The explosion was an accident!

Kresh continued, "They had been upsetting my plans for far too long… so I gave the order. Isn't that right, Zedah?"

Zedah remained crouched on the ground, her face void of any kind of life, multiple tears rolling off her chin.

Stop, Talon thought, *please stop… I don't want to know… don't want to know…*

"She killed them…"

He thought he was going to black out… he wanted his pain to end… all the misery to vanish.

"*No… no…*" he whispered, his thoughts rolling off his tongue.

"Zedah was such a faithful servant of mine," Kresh said, his eyes darkening, his voice as deep as a black hole. "She never questioned me… she always did what I asked."

As the governor spoke, he reached down and wrapped his fingers around Zedah's sword, gripping it tightly in his hand. Talon was barely listening; his heart had been ripped in two, as if sliced open with a dagger. He couldn't *think*… his mind spiraled out of control. Zedah shook uncontrollably at his feet, her eyes fixed on the ground, sharp sobs escaping from her mouth.

Kresh drew in a deep breath, as though trying to contain a fit of rage. "Whether she will do my bidding now… that remains to be seen."

All of Talon's anger returned at once. He wanted to attack this man. To end him. End him *forever*.

He raised his sword and rushed at the governor, screaming as loud as his lungs would allow him. Kresh straightened. As Talon drew closer, he saw Zedah's sword flash, swing, and heard it collide with something.

At first, he felt nothing.

Then came the *dizziness*…

Then the *headache*…

Then the *agony*…

He pressed a hand to his side; something hot streamed through a slash in his overcoat. His hand was covered in a thick red liquid, his vision going dark.

All his pain—both physical and emotional—coalesced into a single cloud of darkness. Talon was sobbing, tears running down his cheeks. He heaved his head upward, barely able to pinpoint the blurry outline of the governor, who stood before Zedah. She slowly clambered to her feet and finally met his eyes.

"Finish the job," Kresh ordered, and he thrust the sword into her hand. Zedah stared at him for a long moment before shakily stepping toward Talon, whose blood continued to stain his coat.

Zedah raised her blade, and Talon shut his eyes tightly, bracing for death's embrace.

It didn't come.

He allowed his eyelids to crack open. Zedah still stood there, as still as stone.

"Finish… the job," Kresh seethed. It felt like hours that she remained in the same position, her sword raised, preparing for the fatal blow.

Then, her grip on the blade slackened, and she dropped the sword, falling to her knees and burying her face in her hands. Through the aches that stung his eyes, Talon could see how hurt she was, and the one thing he'd internally sworn he would never feel for her consumed all his emotions.

Compassion…

Compassion for how broken she truly was…

For how much trauma she had endured…

Kresh's voice rang in his ears, and it was deadly. *"Fine."*

The governor stepped toward Talon, but he barely noticed. He kept his eyes fixed on the woman who had tried to kill him numerous times… who had caused so much pain… who had killed his parents.

Talon felt Kresh's rough hand grip the back of his collar as he dragged him to the edge of the bridge. All the while, Talon stared at Zedah, who didn't return his gaze. He knew what she was doing. She was trying to cast out all her pain… all her *grief*.

Talon finally realized… he could *truly* relate.

Kresh heaved him over the edge, his body met thin air, and he tumbled downward. After what felt like an eternity, Talon crashed into the Hudson. His shoulder crunched painfully when he collided with the river. As he sank, his own blood stained the water, and the only light shining through the darkness was the sun.

But even that was dimming. A massive shape blotted it out, and a muffled splash echoed through his ears, and the shadow of a girl's hand reached toward him before he shut his eyes and let the darkness overtake.

CHAPTER SEVENTEEN

MAY 21ST, 2492

Elijah beckoned from the doorway. "Talon, come here."

Talon shut his book and leaped off his bed, shuffling barefoot over to his father. He knelt on the polished wood floor, and a wide smile spread across his young face.

"I wanted to give you something," his father stated, stepping into his son's room. Talon's mother, Hazel, appeared in the doorway and watched them, swiping her reddish hair out of her beautiful face. Talon's father sat cross-legged on the floor in front of him and gazed at his son through deep green eyes.

"You're growing up, buddy. You're getting bigger every day."

He smiled and rumpled his nine-year-old's hair. Talon laughed, jumping toward his dad and wrestling him to the ground. His mother laughed as she watched them play together, rough housing around the room, before finally knocking over a lamp. She made a face that clearly said: *thankfully, Talon doesn't have any brothers*. Talon separated from his father, and retook his seat on the floor, still giggling.

"You're growing up." Elijah restated. "I think you're ready for a little more responsibility. So, I wanted to gift you…"

He paused, stepping out of the room for a short moment. When he reappeared, Talon laid eyes on a shining object resting in his hands. A long shimmering sword.

"… *this*," he finished.

"A sword?" Talon beamed, his eyes going wide.

"Yes. It used to be mine, but I don't have a need for it anymore."

Even at nine-years-old, Talon could see that his father seemed sad, but he didn't know why.

"It's yours now. Take care of it."

Talon nodded eagerly, gently taking the weapon and placing it atop his dresser before sitting down on the edge of his bed and turning his attention back to his father. Elijah sat next to him and wrapped an arm around his son's shoulders.

"Talon," Elijah continued, "I want you to know why I'm giving it to you. When you're older, we won't be here to protect you. You'll have to fend for yourself… and it won't be easy."

Talon nodded, smiling softly. "I know… I can do it."

Elijah laughed, and Hazel smiled at her son's charming confidence.

"I know you can. The world is tough, but you're tougher. You're my strong man. In time, you will truly understand how to use the sword… in time. Nevertheless, I want you to know… it's never the end… as long as you have hope and maintain your love for others."

What did he mean by that? Talon wasn't sure—he was too enthralled with his new gift. He nodded again, and leaned against his father, embracing him tightly.

Elijah added, "But don't let me catch you swinging that around; it's still dangerous."

"Okay… I won't let you catch me," Talon said with a childish smirk. His father laughed.

Elijah ruffled up his son's hair again. "I love you, little falcon."

He stood from the bed before making his way toward the door

and exiting the room.

"Talon, listen to me," his mother said sternly. "Don't be swinging that around."

"I won't," Talon remarked. She smiled and kissed him on the forehead.

"Alright, get dressed. We're going out for a while."

"Where are we going?"

"The Guntheon Building. We have an appointment."

With a choking gasp, Talon shot upward on a solid surface, vomiting up sour river water. His vision was still blurry. Blood continued to seep from his side, and something like a white-hot knife twisted its way into his shoulder. He thought he might black out from the pain.

"You are such an *idiot*!" said a familiar voice. It was Castor, kneeling by his side as water poured from Talon's soaked clothes.

"Shut up, Castor!" Amber exclaimed. "Get a bandage—a big one."

Castor leaped up, rummaging wildly through every drawer. River water dripped from Amber's clothes as well, her golden hair plastered to her face.

Talon didn't care that he was back with them… didn't care that they were flying away from the build-site… didn't care about the pain.

All he cared about was how *wrong* he'd been.

Amber sat him down on one of the leather seats before helping him out of his overcoat and shirt, then observing the wound.

"We don't have any stitches," she declared to herself, a frantic concern in her voice.

"As if we know how to apply them," Castor said, returning with a large bandage and a bottle of antiseptic.

Amber hastily applied the solution to Talon's side, and he grimaced as a stinging sensation erupted through his waist. He glanced down at the wound but immediately wished he hadn't. It wasn't very deep, but it still bled where the skin had separated, and the area around the injury was pale white.

Amber frantically unraveled the white bandage and wrapped it snuggly around his torso until it felt like a strong, constricting hug. Talon barely even noticed the sharp pain that plagued his shoulder as he buried his face in one of his hands.

"I'm so sorry…" he choked through a breaking voice.

He knew what his father would've thought of him; he would've been ashamed… *disappointed*. He had told him to have hope, to maintain his love for others. He was the first one who had said that to him, and Talon knew that Orson had gotten it from *him*.

Talon hadn't remembered it for all these years. He hadn't remembered what his father had told him… hadn't remembered that his father wanted him to remain strong.

And how had he lived up to that?

He'd pushed people away, including Castor and Amber.

He'd shut himself off from the world.

He'd always told himself that relationships were a bad thing, that bonds only led to pain.

I was so wrong… I was so wrong…

Tears rolled off his face, and he couldn't stop them. He didn't *want* to stop them. He wanted to *feel*, to let it all out.

All these years, he'd been so wrong. He'd thought that being alone would bring him his happiness. But now, he knew why he'd been so unhappy. *Because* of the loneliness. For so long, he'd tried to achieve happiness, to obtain it *without* anyone else. But what if happiness wasn't an achievement? What if it *wasn't* obtained?

What if it was a *choice*?

After what felt like an eternity of silence, Talon felt Amber wrap her arms around him and hug him tightly, and he did something he hadn't done in over six years. He hugged her too.

He felt her tears drip onto his shoulders as she pulled away, gazing deep into his blue eyes.

"I'm sorry, too," she said through a cracked voice. "I was wrong to keep everything in… just like you said."

She turned to Castor, who knelt beside her.

Amber pressed her lips together as more tears came spilling out of her eyes and continued, "I—I was afraid that you would see me differently. And that was wrong of me… it was a judgment on you both, and it was because of what—what happened with…"

She couldn't finish. Her voice was hollow and broken, and Talon gripped her hand. Castor smiled kindly.

"You're not like your father," he said, and he wiped Amber's eyes. "You're more than he ever was."

Talon kept his eyes on him, and a sad smile spread across his face.

Castor continued, "If it weren't for the both of you, I don't know how I would've moved on. I'm who I am now because of you."

Talon stared at the two people that lay before him, love blanketing his heart like the sun blankets the day.

"I owe you both everything," he stated. "I thought I knew what I wanted… I wanted answers… but when they came, I didn't know what to do with them. And I was wrong… something *did* prepare me for it. My father did."

He turned to Amber.

"I want to live up to him. Castor's right: you're more than your father ever was, Amber. And that helped me see the truth. I'm not my dad, I haven't lived up to him. I want to but I don't know if—if I *can*."

And suddenly he was crying again. The tears fell down his face like a rainstorm, and Amber reached forward, wiping them away.

She smiled and said, "You don't owe us anything, Talon. Your father would be proud of you, I know it. If he could see you now, I know he'd be proud of who you've become."

She gripped the back of his neck and kissed his forehead. His stomach fluttered, and it reminded him warmly of his mother's affection. But different still. Almost… foreign.

All three of them simultaneously wrapped their arms firmly around one another. Talon could've stayed this way forever… now that he knew what *love* was like. Now that he knew that *love* was good.

Amber let her hand fall to his shoulder, and he flinched.

"What's wrong?" she asked.

"I think it's dislocated," Talon groaned.

Castor jumped up and said, "Why didn't you *say* something?!"

Before Talon could respond, Castor had already moved to his side, observing the joint. The worst thought entered Talon's mind.

"You're gonna pop it back into place, aren't you?" he asked.

"Maybe… maybe not."

Amber leaned forward, a serious expression hardening on her face. "You've never done this before."

"Oh—um—sure I have… it's easy."

There was a long pause, and Amber stared questioningly at Castor. Talon nodded to himself, gritting his teeth.

Take it… just take it…

Castor took a very audible breath.

"On three… one—"

SNAP!

Talon yelled. It felt as if a searing hammer had smashed itself into his shoulder.

"*Seriously?*" he grunted accusingly.

Castor shrugged and let out a timid laugh. "Oops."

The pain was already subsiding, and Talon's shoulder, though still aching and stiff, moved freely.

He looked at them both with gratefulness.

With *love*.

And he didn't try to stop it. It was the most wonderful feeling; to care for someone, and to love them.

Castor tossed him a gray long-sleeve. He pulled it on over the bandage and stood up faster than was good for him; his side twinged with pain, making his head spin.

A terrible revelation hit his mind like a meteor strike.

"They're launching the ships… they're launching them now!" he exclaimed, and both Castor and Amber's faces paled.

"What do we do?" Castor asked urgently.

"We have to stop them," Talon claimed, knowing there was nothing else they *could* do.

Amber said, "But, we don't have the Key."

"There's gotta be a way… a way *besides* the Key."

They all stood for a moment in eerie silence, knowing what Kresh and Zedah were about to do.

Zedah…

Her brokenness haunted Talon. He *couldn't* hate her anymore. He didn't *want* to hate her anymore. A swell of compassion wrapped itself around his heart, and he wanted to help her… he wanted to *save* her.

"We have to try," he stated. "We have to do something… even if we can't—"

He didn't finish.

Castor said, "We probably don't have a chance, but neither do all those people in Borough III. I'm going."

Amber stood. "Me too."

Their confident, kind faces gave Talon everything he needed. They had stood by his side for the past weeks, and he wanted to repay them in any way he could… he wanted to be with them… wanted to *stay* with them until the end.

"So," Castor said slowly, "what's the plan?"

"Get to the mothership and find the controls that'll detonate the shells," Talon said with a shrug.

"What could go wrong?" Castor asked, and Amber laughed, but it was almost a nervous laugh. Fear hung throughout the ship; Talon could feel it—they were all scared. Scared of what was to come. Scared of the potential of failure. Scared of the possibility of death. There was a moment of silence before Talon opened his mouth.

"Listen," he explained gently, "you guys have helped me so much… I hope you know that… and I've done too little to deserve it. I—I don't deserve your friendship. Not after what I've been like. But I want you to know how thankful I am for the both of you."

Amber smiled warmly as Castor raised a hand and gripped him on the shoulder.

"We're glad you're here, Talon… you'll always have a place with us." Castor said.

Amber moved up to Castor and pulled him into a hug. Talon smiled at the sight, and she broke away after a short moment, gazing into Castor's deep gray eyes.

"Thank you, Castor," she said.

"For what?" he asked.

"For helping me trust again. For everything you've done for me."

Castor smiled. "Thank *you*. You're my best friend, Amber. I hope you know that… even *if* I annoy you sometimes."

She laughed, and it was music to Talon's ears.

The three of them stood in a small circle, staring at each other in silence, soaking each other in. It took all the might Talon still possessed to tear his eyes away from Castor and Amber, silently knowing that it may well be the last time he'd be able to look at them peacefully.

Amber pulled him into another strong hug, and he wrapped his arms around her. When they broke apart, Talon moved over to Castor and did the same, and he looked surprised but gratified.

They gathered their weapons, Amber her dagger, Castor his spear, and Talon his sword.

The sword…

His father's sword that he'd gifted to him as a child… right before they died. Tears rimmed his eyes, but there wasn't an ounce of sadness in his body. He was full of joy… joy at remembering his parents so fondly… joy at the new life they had inside of him.

He stepped into the cockpit as Castor's hands flew over the controls. Talon glanced at the sword once more, knowing that his father would be glad his son was putting it to good use at long last.

CHAPTER EIGHTEEN

MAY 21ST, 2492

The Independence lurched, veered to the left, and rocketed back in the direction it came, nearly throwing Talon off his feet.

He shut his eyes, inhaling deeply. A cold shadow closed its icy fingers around his heart as the aircraft rumbled underneath his feet. The last month had been the best of his life, even though he hadn't realized it until now. Castor and Amber were the greatest thing that had ever happened to him. He'd just been too closed off to know it… too narrow-minded. Still, he was happy he was here now—with them—at the end.

Talon opened his eyes and beheld, way in the distance, the towering cranes, beams, and platforms that made up the build site. He knew Zedah was down there, but how he knew he wasn't sure, and a knot tightened in his chest. Everything she'd done, all the pain she'd caused… Talon didn't care about it anymore. All he cared about was *her*. Helping *her*.

Zedah had orchestrated his parent's deaths…

She'd killed Alger…

She'd helped destroy the Nest…

Talon couldn't hate her for it. Not anymore. He knew how she felt. Alone. Broken. As if there was no way out. As if she'd never be able to change.

A swell of compassion coursed through his blood. Compassion for what she'd been through. Compassion at the fact that she believed she couldn't redeem herself. He knew she needed help. And whether he lived or died, he was going to help her.

Talon's heart stopped. The build site had drawn much closer, and the cages that once housed such massive ships stood empty, the towering cranes as still as tombstones.

Kresh's battleship fleet streaked across the harbor in a gargantuan v-formation, slicing through the waves and leaving behind a trail of swirling seawater. The mothership sailed at the crest of the formation, as if hauling all other nineteen ships along with it, like a cruel leader forcing the weak to follow in his stride.

Something soft touched Talon's wrist and it took him a moment to realize it was Amber's palm. She laced her fingers through his and gripped his hand tightly. Despite what the three of them were about to do, Talon's heart fluttered happily. A foreign tickling ran around in his stomach. It wasn't nerves, he could tell that much. What was it then?

It was the same feeling he'd had when she kissed him on the forehead. The same feeling he'd had whenever they locked eyes. The same feeling he'd had whenever he stopped to focus on her beautiful face.

Before Talon could pinpoint the right word for it, Castor turned to speak to them.

"Get ready," he faltered. There was a pause.

"For what?" Talon asked skeptically.

Castor didn't answer and, before they knew it, he stepped on the throttle and the ship raced toward the fleet.

Amber exclaimed, "Careful! They might use their guns!"

The Independence bolted through the air like a shooting star, its engine roaring, the thrusters spitting out blue flame. As they drew closer, a realization struck Talon like a hammer to the brain.

"What are you doing?" he queried, "There's nowhere to land."

"Yeah, there is," Castor replied weakly. It took Talon a second to make sense of what he meant. The strongest rush of adrenaline clawed at his nerves, and he swallowed hard.

"That's insane."

"I know," Castor remarked, "But we can't get inside any other way. It's the only place."

He knew that Castor was right, and he sucked in a breath as they descended toward the mothership, its massive canons looking hungry for a meal. Suddenly, the guns rotated to face them.

"*Watch out!*" Amber screamed as the sounds of cannon fire rent the air. Castor swerved *The Independence* out of the way as glowing bullets zipped past, missing them by inches.

Castor shouted. "Amber, get to the turret!"

She gazed at him in shock for a brief moment, clutching the doorframe, then whirled around and disappeared up the ladder without another word.

"Have you even told her how to use it?" Talon yelled.

"Yeah, once, just have never let her try it," he replied. A deafening *BANG* split the air as the ship vibrated with the force of an earthquake, bullet strings of their own flying toward the mothership. They left holes in the shining deck, splinters of wood spraying into the air, then collided with the cannons that were still firing at them. Three of them erupted in flame, and a fourth split in two, a shower of sparks spurting from its mechanical depths.

Castor slammed a button and lowered the landing gear, steering *The Independence* toward the mothership's stern. The ship rocketed ever faster in the direction of the deck, and at the last moment, Castor yanked upward on the controls. The aircraft lurched to the side, throwing Talon against the wall, and crashed into the deck with the loudest *BOOM*.

Talon scrambled to his feet as Castor leaped from his chair, the two of them rushing into the belly of the ship. Amber descended from the gunner's position, but they didn't have time to celebrate, or check the ship for damage.

His right hand tightened around the hilt of his sword as he placed the other on the lever and pulled. The boarding ramp lowered with a familiar buzz and only now did he appreciate how fond he'd grown of the sound.

Silence…

Complete silence…

Talon bounded out into the morning air, Castor and Amber following close behind.

A haunting emptiness infested the place. The only sounds came from the rippling waves, cut in half by the bow, but not a soul was in sight. Not one person worked on the ship.

The sun glared off the reflective deck as they stepped further across it. Gun turrets had been built symmetrically along the sides, painted silver, double barrels protruding into the air. The smell of fresh paint and wood polish swarmed through their nostrils as sea spray leaped into the air.

Talon gripped his sword hilt and drew breath, his chest rising and falling heavily. Up ahead, three giant cannons stuck out toward them, aimed upward and placed directly above two glass doors. Behind the cannons stood a massive structure, sprouting out of the deck like an overgrown weed and constructed of various metals and glass. It shimmered in the sunlight as it towered over them like a skyscraper.

Castor pointed to it. "That's the bridge."

Talon nodded. He knew the bridge was the only place where the controls could be. Their pace quickened as they moved toward the doors. Amber stepped forward, wrapped her fingers around the metal handle and pulled it open, a draft of warm air emanating from the elegant hallway standing before them.

Red carpet lined floor, rimmed by wide windows on the left side, and a chandelier hung from the polished wood ceiling, casting a crystalline light on the marble wall that stood to the right. A pit formed in Talon's stomach. Kresh would've wanted the mothership to be elaborately decorated, in celebration of his plan… in celebration of what his fleet was going to accomplish.

The three of them stood as still as statues before Castor asked weakly, "Where is everyone? Where's the crew?"

"I don't know," Talon said softly, the question still haunting him as they stepped into the hallway, the soles of their boots pressing into the soft carpet.

Talon's injured side twinged with pain, and he clapped a hand over the wound, wincing quietly.

"You okay?" Amber asked.

"Yeah… yeah, I'm fine… come on."

They rounded a corner, coming to an empty doorframe, squinting at what lay before them. The red carpet continued into a large room, an oak-wood table placed in the direct center of the space. Behind the table stood a dual staircase, each of them curving upward into a second story, complete with gold railing. As they moved forward, Talon clenched his jaw; this place was more like a luxury ocean liner than a battleship.

"Hurry," he whispered, stepping through the doorframe and

into the space. Before he even had a chance to draw another breath, a sinister female voice rang from an intercom on the wall.

"Error… clearance denied."

Talon's heart dropped into the pit of his stomach. He whirled around to face Castor and Amber. Their faces went snow-white. The cold lights illuminating the battleship's interior turned a violent shade of scarlet, and a deafening alarm resounded through the room.

Castor squeaked, "Well, we've officially pissed them off."

Like lightning, they bolted through the room, right past the stairs. Talon threw himself against the shining double doors implanted in the wall and they swung open forcefully.

More red light flashed as they gaped at the massive hangar that lay before them. They stood on a metal landing protruding from the wall behind. Three stories below, the floor glistened with a shiny black gloss, on top of which rested numerous armed aircraft. Heaping amounts of white missiles lay in rows below, a diverse group of heavy machinery loading them into the cannons. Talon noticed more landings and staircases, all interconnected and leading to the very one they stood on.

As he gazed around the room, he noticed something else. The paneling on the walls was incomplete, massive pipes and gears showing through gaping holes. Wires descended from the ceiling like tangled vines, and a dull haze hung about the hangar. Talon slowly realized why the ship seemed so unfinished, remembering the conversation between the workers.

Kresh had rushed his army of builders. They hadn't completed construction, and his impatience had left much of the ship looking fragmentary. As the alarms flashed, another terrifying sight snagged at his vision.

Entities swarmed the floor below, staring daggers at them through their blazing eyes, red light reflecting off their metallic bodies. They stood like statues, their gaze as piercing as a blade, before they sprinted with inhuman speed toward the staircases.

Talon, Castor and Amber sped like bullets across the landing as twenty Entities pursued them with the fury of an inferno. With a great heave, Talon swung his sword as their pursuers drew closer, and an Entity's robotic hand flew off its wrist.

Amber yelled as an Entity grasped her by the scruff of her collar and pulled her back, preparing to drive its sharp fingers through her stomach. She twisted out of the way just in time and slashed her dagger across its throat.

Castor leaped forward as another Entity barreled down upon Amber, letting his gleaming spear unfold and driving its sharp head into the Entities forehead. Its face caved inward as it tumbled over the edge of the landing, crashing into a single missile below.

A spark ignited and the missile exploded, sending a glowing ball of fire into the air and incinerating multiple Entities. The explosion evaporated before it could reach any more of the missiles, leaving a smoking crater and the bitter smell of burning rubber.

Castor turned his attention back to the swarming Entities, threatening them with his spear. They weren't intimidated.

A voice spoke over the loudspeaker. *"Fleet will be in position in fifteen minutes."*

Talon's stomach turned over and his heartbeat jammed in his chest.

Fifteen minutes... that's not enough time!

As more and more Entities crowded the area, Talon realized the worst; they were cornered. They stood at the end of the landing… a dead end blocked by a railing. There was nowhere to go, and they were cornered by the ruthless automatons.

A startling noise made Talon snap his head toward Amber, and after a moment of stunned silence, he noticed her kneeling beside a large square hole in the wall, well covered by a thin metal mesh. An exhaust vent. She drove her dagger through the mesh and carved through it, slicing an opening into the vent.

"Hurry!" she yelled.

As the Entities drew closer, Amber dove inside, then Castor, and finally Talon. As he threw himself into the vent, he felt one of their deadly fingers graze the heel of his boot.

"Come on!" Castor called from further down the tunnel.

He crawled toward them, his sword making it difficult to move. Darkness shrouded the tunnel, except for minute green lights placed sporadically along the walls. Talon could barely see Castor and Amber's dim outlines.

A gut-wrenching noise echoed through the pipe, and he craned his neck back toward the direction of the hangar. Flashing red lights pursued them, and the scraping ring of metal against metal filled his ears.

"They're in the vent!" he shouted to Castor and Amber. He heard Castor curse, and they scrambled even faster through the pipe. The tunnel curved upward, and Talon heard Amber call to them hurriedly.

"There are wires up here! Use them to climb!"

As Castor disappeared upward, Talon wrapped his fingers around the loose cords and twisted them together like a rope. He pulled and began to ascend, silently praying that neither Castor nor

Amber would fall on top of him. The Entities roared below, and Talon's arms burned as they climbed higher and higher. It felt like ages that he was traveling upward, and he allowed his mind to drift.

He thought of his father… of his mother… of Orson. He thought of so many unnamed others who had given their lives to fight against Kresh. He knew he, Castor, and Amber were finishing what they started. They were trying to complete what others had failed to do, even if they themselves didn't succeed.

"Hurry!" Amber yelled from above. "There's another vent!"

Talon heard her drive her dagger through the vent cover and tear it open. She pulled herself through the opening, Castor going after her. Talon heaved himself out, crashed onto the hard floor, and pulled himself to his feet. They stood in a small, bland room, a control console positioned beside an automatic door.

Amber turned to Castor and said, "Can you override the controls?"

"I can try," he quickly replied. He rushed toward the console and began turning knobs and flipping switches. An ear-splitting creak resounded through the open vent as red light began to flicker through, reflecting off the walls.

"Nothing's working!" Castor exclaimed.

Talon yelled, "They're coming through!"

Castor fell onto his back and pulled himself underneath the console, tearing panels off and ripping at the wires.

"It's just a door!" Amber shouted.

"Shut up! I'm trying my best!" he snapped.

Amber drew her dagger and braced herself for the coming fight, prompting Talon to do the same.

He thought, *That's it…*

With a buzzing whir, an Entity's mechanical hand shot out of the vent and grasped the opening, heaving the mass of humanoid metal into the room.

"I've got it!" Castor yelled, and he slid out from under the console. The doors opened swiftly and the three of them stumbled through. The androids leaped forward just as Talon slammed a red button on the wall. As an Entity reached toward them, the double doors closed rapidly, trapping its arm and slicing it off in a spurt of glowing sparks. Talon doubled over, gulping in numerous breaths.

The three of them stood staring at the twitching robotic arm before catching each other's glances and spinning around, ready to continue their journey to the bridge. They stood on another massive platform, lined with a metal railing, and shining staircases positioned on each side led to the floor below.

Before Talon could step forward, before he could rejoice at the fact that they had escaped the Entities, he froze, his body going stiff as a board. His heart fell and his firm grasp on his sword slackened.

A breath caught in his throat as he gazed at the woman who stood before them, her dark hair veiling half of her face, her blade shimmering in the pale light.

Zedah glared at them through bloodshot eyes, her chest rising and falling as she inhaled and exhaled powerfully.

"Leave," she whispered. It seemed to be the only thing she could bring herself to say. Talon felt Castor and Amber stiffen as the cold sound of her voice swept over them like a frigid wind. Her face was ridden with pain and torment. Talon could see it as clear as he could his own two hands. Her knuckles shined white as she gripped the hilt of her sword. Out of his peripherals, Talon saw Castor and Amber brace their weapons, preparing for a fight.

"No," he whispered, putting a hand out to stop them.

"What?" Castor said incredulously. Talon didn't attempt to answer. After a moment of questioning whether or not this was a good idea, whether or not he was going insane, he stepped toward her.

"You don't have to do this," Talon declared when he found his voice, the words rolling out of his mouth with power. Zedah remained as still as a statue, gazing at him with eyes so broken they seemed as though they would never be fixed.

"I can't stop it now," she countered angrily.

Talon moved even further forward. "Yes," he declared. "Yes, you can… you can *help* us… you can stop *all* of this."

He was less than five feet from her now. She glared at him even more harshly, ceasing to breathe. Zedah looked so much like a standing corpse that Talon was almost sure she would never move again. He caught his breath.

She raised her sword…

Talon brought his to bear…

With cries of fury, Zedah swung, sliced, and stabbed at him, but with each strike, he deflected. Castor and Amber leaped toward them, entering the fight, attempting to drive Zedah back.

They weren't a match for her.

Zedah dodged their attempts as though they were a pesky irritant, evading their strikes, and parrying them with her own. She crouched and swung her leg out, throwing Castor off his feet. With a massive kick, Zedah sent Amber tumbling to the floor before turning her attention back to Talon.

His arms were on fire as he attempted to keep the sword within his sore grip. Zedah's blade crashed into his, throwing him against the metal railing. She lifted her weapon, preparing for the fatal blow. Before Talon could react, he heard Castor yell. His spear glinted in the light as he threw himself against Zedah, slamming her hard against the railing. They tumbled over the edge of the platform, disappearing from view.

"*No!*" Amber cried. Talon's heart fell into his stomach as he pulled himself up and peered over the railing before breathing a sigh of relief. Castor lay on the ground below, stumbling to his feet. Zedah crouched beside him, crawling toward her sword that rested just a few yards away.

Talon and Amber raced down one of the staircases leading to the floor below, sunlight streaming into the gargantuan room. They reached Castor's position just as Zedah snatched up her sword and rushed at Talon. He parried her strike so forcefully that it caused her to stumble.

Castor and Amber rushed at her with their weapons and the three of them continued to resist her. Talon hit the flat of his blade against Zedah's, twisted the handle, and her sword went spinning out of her hand. It clattered to the floor with a resounding clang.

They directed their weapons right at her chest, prepared to strike if necessary. Their adrenaline finally began to diminish as they gulped in air, and finally, Talon allowed himself to take in the surroundings.

Fifty desks lined the massive chamber, each complete with a monitor projecting fluctuating images of grid lines and numbers. The walls stood high, complete with landings, beams, doors, and even more staircases. Massive windows stood at the front of the room, letting in as much natural light as possible, and a large c-shaped console laden with hundreds of buttons, knobs, levers, and connection ports had been placed just before them. Two reactors—

one on each side of the room—vomited up white steam, their gaping shafts descending into the heart of the ship.

Everything was dead still. There was no doubt about it; they had made it to the bridge.

Talon's face went white with horror when he beheld the view provided by the windows. The bow of the mothership moved rapidly through the rolling waves, and in the distance stood Borough III, not knowing what was to become of it, not understanding how little time it had left.

The computers on the desks caught Talon's eye. Now he knew why they hadn't run into any crew, now he knew why the ship was empty. His breath stopped short as he realized that AI controlled the fleet, ordered to do one thing: get to the Third Borough.

Talon turned his attention back toward Zedah, who still stared at him with bloodshot eyes.

"Please," Talon said. "Help us… you don't have to—"

"*Zedah*," echoed a deep, blood-curdling voice. Talon's stomach turned as he snapped his head upward, his lungs catching in his chest as if they would never work again.

Governor Kresh stood at the console, staring down at them like a tiger does its prey. Talon hadn't even noticed him. His military uniform still hung about his broad shoulders, a sharp sword and dagger resting at his belt.

The governor stepped off the raised platform and strode toward them with the air of a viper. Talon knew the fleet was controlled by AI, but Kresh must've wanted to be here to fire the missiles himself… on his day of terrible triumph.

"Sir," Zedah stuttered, retrieving her sword from the ground and stumbling over to him. "Sir, I—I tried."

"You've failed," Kresh declared with untarnished rage, keeping his piercing dark eyes fixed on Talon. Tears rolled down Zedah's face, and she shook as though she were standing in a blizzard.

Kresh finally turned to Zedah and said, "Leave… *now*. I'm done with you."

"But—but sir—"

With one swift stroke, Kresh violently backhanded Zedah across the face, sending her to the floor with a crash. Talon's mouth fell open, his body stiffening as he surveyed Kresh's true cruelty… his true *wrath*. Zedah covered her face in her hands and continued to shake. The governor gripped the hilt of his sword and drew it from its sheath, its razor-sharp blade reflecting incoming sunlight. He glared at the trio who had dared to confront him… to *challenge* him.

"Zedah," Talon said calmly, and she ceased to shake. Kresh stopped, seemingly eager to see what would become of this.

Amber grasped his shoulder. "Talon, there's nothing you can do."

He ignored her, maintaining his gaze on Zedah… on the brokenness that lay before him.

"Please… is this what you want?" he asked. Zedah kept her face in her hands, still unresponsive.

Talon repeated, "Do you want this?"

She stared at him, veins appearing in the whites of her shining eyes.

"I can't stop it…" she mumbled, and Kresh's nostrils flared. Talon spoke again.

"Yes… you *can*."

She shook her head, a mixture of guilt, grief, and pain manifesting itself on her face. "Nothing I do can help me now... I've done so much wrong... I—I wish I never had. But it's too late."

Talon stared at her for a long moment before a soft, kind smile came to his face. "It's never too late to change... never too late to *turn away*."

A tear broke through and streamed down his cheek. That was the same lesson he'd had to teach himself. The same lesson he'd *refused* to teach himself. But he knew that if he could change, so could she. She stared deep into his blue eyes, and he stared right back, his gaze softening as he prepared to say one last thing.

"*I forgive you*."

He didn't *care* that she'd been the one to kill his parents...

All he cared about was helping her.

Kresh said, "Zedah."

Just her name. Only her name. But to Kresh, it *wasn't* a name... it was just another word. Zedah's gaze drifted to the governor. Her face changed, her demeanor changed.

Her *presence* changed.

It had been cowardly, it had been broken... no more.

Now, it was fierce, it was strong. Just like a raging fire.

Zedah lifted herself to her feet, stabbing her gaze into Kresh's dark eyes. The governor's chest rose and fell with each heaving breath. Talon stared at them, everything around him seeming to freeze.

Zedah raised her arm, swung her sword...

Kresh parried...

Talon's breath caught in his throat.

As Zedah fought, all her pain... all her *anguish* manifested itself into a strength fueled by redemption.

With all her might, she battled Kresh, and Talon, Castor, and Amber backed away as their swords flashed together. Kresh's face was wild with anger as Zedah ruthlessly swung her weapon, each of them fighting to kill. The governor pressed her back, away from the console and toward the desks, their blades slashing the monitors off their posts.

"*Fleet will be in position in five minutes,*" rang the voice over the loudspeaker.

"Now's our chance!" Castor exclaimed. With the console vacant, the three of them rushed forward. Talon gazed at the controls in utter confusion. It was like attempting to read a different language.

"Castor," Talon called, "can you try and figure this out?"

The rings of clashing swords echoed through the air as Castor stepped forward.

"I can try," he stated, his hands hovering over the panel. "Okay—um—how do I do this?"

He experimented with the controls, his hands flying over different buttons and knobs. Talon glanced back at Zedah and his heart plummeted. She continued to defend, but she was tiring, barely able to deliver any more substantial attacks.

Her blade slashed against a pipe, letting it spit out fluid and steam. Kresh swung at her, and when she parried, her balance faltered. Castor continued to mess with the controls.

"Hurry!" Amber said.

"I *am* hurrying!"

He slammed a button and a low beep echoed through the air. On the right side of the console, two doors flipped open, each the size of Talon's hand. A small connection port emerged from the depths of the console.

The port for the Key.

"No," Amber panted, breathing heavily. "There has to be another way!"

Castor's hands flew over the controls.

"Nothing's working!" he exclaimed. "There's nothing else here!"

He continued to experiment with the controls, but Talon knew it was no use. There was no other way…

The Key was the only thing that could save Borough III. The one thing they needed, the one thing they didn't have.

He turned back toward Zedah. Kresh fought her with the fury of a vengeful lion, stooping over her to deliver even more strikes. He threw her over one of the desks, and she barely managed to scramble to her feet before he came barreling down on her yet again.

"I have to help!" Talon said.

"Talon, no!" Amber cried, but he was running toward the fight before she could stop him.

Kresh forced Zedah toward the edge of the left reactor, white steam swirling around their bodies. He hurled his sword and it collided with hers, sparks showering through the air, using all of his strength to press her backward.

Zedah leaned backward over the opening to the reactor, sweat streaming down her forehead. She braced against him, but his larger build made it near agony. Her eyes met Talon's as he sprinted toward them.

"Stop!" she screamed, but he didn't oblige. He couldn't stop… not *now*… he had to help. Zedah grimaced as Kresh continued to push his sword against hers.

"Stop, please!" she yelled again. Talon still didn't listen. He was almost there… *almost there*. In a split second, Kresh's hand shot to his waist, and he drew his dagger.

The edge gleamed in the terrible light…

And he plunged the blade into Zedah's vulnerable core.

Talon shouted, stopping dead in his tracks, but he couldn't hear his own voice. It was as though he was tumbling through a void of nothingness, darkness pressing in and suffocating him.

Zedah's eyes widened as Kresh withdrew the dagger, stained with red, and she clamped a pale hand over her bleeding stomach. She coughed, scarlet dripping from her mouth and seeping through her fingers, staining her hand. Talon stared in horror.

Using all her remaining strength, Zedah lifted her arm and directed her index finger toward something Talon held… something in his hand… his *sword*.

He stared back at her, not knowing what she meant, pleading with her to stay strong.

All she did was nod… *once*.

With one final breath, Zedah Kahzak shut her eyes, fell backward, and tumbled down the reactor, where she disappeared into the white fog below.

It was as though an invisible knife had driven itself into Talon's heart. Tears broke through his eyes, streaming down his face and neck. His grip on his sword tightened.

"*No!*" he screamed. The governor spun around as Talon sprinted toward him, ignoring Castor and Amber's pleading yells. As quick as lightning, Kresh sidestepped his strike and pummeled Talon's injured side with his fist. His vision blurred and he screamed in horrible, bitter pain as the world began to darken. A flash of silver and the governor's blade connected with his right eyebrow, blood spurting into his eye. Kresh aimed a kick at his stomach, sending him sprawling to the floor, agony pulsing through his entire body.

Talon tried to sit up—to get his wind back—but the excruciating pain kept him down, shutting out all other thoughts. He was barely aware of Castor and Amber charging the governor, weapons in hand. Barely aware of Kresh beating Castor in the face with the handle of his sword, barely aware as he threw Amber against a desk that splintered under the force.

After a moment's horrible silence, Talon felt Kresh's iron grip clench his hair as he pulled him upward. He could feel his heated breath on his face.

His cold voice whispered, "I'm going to kill you… but not yet. This is the day that true peace is brought… and you are going to watch."

Kresh dragged him toward the console and threw him to the ground, and Talon heard him stalk toward the controls. Using all his might, ignoring the terrible concern for Castor and Amber, he heaved himself to his knees.

"I saw what happened," he groaned, and Kresh stopped in his tracks. "I saw what happened with the riot… I know why you're doing this."

The governor slowly turned toward him.

"You want revenge," Talon coughed.

If looks could kill, Kresh's gaze would've murdered him on the spot. There was a tense moment of pure, raw silence.

"You don't have to do this," Talon finally said.

Kresh immediately struck him across the face, fresh agony exploding through his head.

"You can't convert me like you did Zedah," the governor claimed. "I am doing this to make peace... to stop *chaos*... not for revenge."

The tone of his voice told otherwise.

"This *is* chaos," Talon declared. The governor raised his hand again, poised to strike, but it didn't fall. After another long, hard moment Kresh swept toward the console. Talon's arms weakened, and he allowed himself to sink to the floor. All the hope drained out of him, like the blood that had poured from Zedah's stomach.

They're all going to die... they're all going to die...

They had failed... everything had failed... Kresh was going to win. But a sudden idea sparked in Talon's mind... a sudden saying.

It's never the end... as long as you have hope... and as long as you maintain your love for others...

Their hope was gone... they were going to die, and so were all those in Borough III... *unless.*

The sword.

Zedah had pointed to his sword... the sword his father had gifted him.

What was it that his father had told him?

In time, you will truly understand how to use the sword... in time.

Using all his remaining strength, Talon rolled onto his side and peered through his blurred vision, staring toward the glint of metal that was his blade.

"*Fleet in position*," said the loudspeaker. Kresh's hands moved over the console, preparing the ships for the firing sequence, and Talon could feel the vessel rumble as its giant canons rotated to face their target.

He crawled forward, inching closer to his sword, every muscle in his body spiking with pain. At last, he extended his arm and his aching fingers closed around the handle. He turned over and pulled the weapon into his lap.

Talon caught his breath and stared, frozen in stunned shock.

He stared at a strange imprint on the bottom of the handle… something he had never noticed before.

A symbol… the symbol of The Falcon's Nest.

After a moment of bewildered silence, Talon placed his thumb on the wing and pressed hard. It sank like a button. The silver blade separated from the handle and clattered to the floor with a resounding ring. All that remained in Talon's shaking hand was the bladeless hilt.

He felt around and gasped when he found a seam. A seam running from the crest of the handle to the base. Talon forced his fingernails through it, and it opened like a little, rectangular box.

A glint of shining silver caught his eye as a small object fell from the compartment. He caught it just in time, holding it tight, feeling its rough edge dig into his fingers.

He opened his palm…

Inside it lay a silver key, looking anything but important, looking anything but impressive. Talon caught his breath, not knowing whether what he stared at was real or fake.

The Key…

He was frozen in astonishment. Now, everything made sense…

Why the Key wasn't in the Temple…

Why his father had truly left him the sword…

His father had retrieved the Key from the Temple. How or when, Talon didn't know. All that mattered was that Elijah Chambers was still with him… with him *now*. And he had been all along.

Kresh's hands continued to move over the console at breathtaking speed, his eyes in a daze—in a terrible trance. Using every fiber of his being, Talon crawled toward the governor, the Key clenched tight in his hand. He couldn't let it go, *wouldn't* let it go. It was a piece of his father… a piece of *him*.

Kresh was too busy to notice him. Too blinded by his own false triumph that he didn't notice his only threat rising up behind him. The boy whom he'd been so focused on for the last weeks. The boy whom he thought he'd defeated.

A hatch opened on the console, revealing a digital button on a shining touchscreen, and Kresh's fingers hovered over it.

The loudspeaker boomed, "*Ready to fire…*"

Talon pulled himself up toward the console… the connection port was still open. The governor paused as he prepared to fire the shells… savoring his victory… savoring his *revenge*.

Talon plunged the Key into the port… and *turned*.

Kresh pressed the button.

Silence…

There was no deafening bang. No flash of light that would've told Talon the shells had fired. *Nothing*.

Governor Kresh's brows furrowed, but he didn't turn around. He frantically began feeling around the console, frantically began pushing buttons, frantically tried everything until…

He spun around and his face went white as snow. He laid eyes on Talon, whose fingers still gripped the bow of the Key, connected to its port. And Kresh became as still as a statue. He didn't move as the realization hit him like a bullet to the skull.

His plan had failed, his revenge had failed. *All* had failed.

All except Talon.

The mothership began to rumble, vibrating as if caught in a powerful earthquake. Rolling fire burst through the mechanical doors as the reactors vomited up heaping amounts of glowing flames.

It had *worked*…

The Key had done its job…

The shells had detonated…

Waves of blistering heat surged through the room, and rageful fire sprouted everywhere Talon looked. He ignored his throbbing head, ignored the blood dripping into his eyes as he dislodged the Key from its port. He stumbled over to Castor and Amber, falling to his knees beside their unmoving bodies. He leaned against Castor, shaking him with all the strength he had left.

"Please," he yelled as he crawled over to Amber. "*Please*… come on, guys!"

Tears drained from his eyes, cutting through the ash staining his face as the inferno continued to engulf the bridge.

"Wake up!" he shouted. A wave of relief flooded through him when Castor stirred, rolling onto his back. Talon helped him to his knees as he shook himself from a dreary trance.

"Ow," he muttered before becoming fully aware.

"Come on!" Talon exclaimed, pulling at him and gesturing to Amber. Castor leaped out of the way as a flaming beam came crashing down.

"*What happened?!*" he screamed, but didn't wait for an answer, pulling Amber out of harm's way. Talon snatched up his separated blade and handle as he and Castor helped each other pull Amber up the staircase. She was barely conscious, blood trickling from her mouth.

Wait, Talon's mind yelled. He spun around and stared toward Kresh who still stood frozen, exactly as he had been a moment before. The ship collapsed around him, but he didn't seem to notice. All he could do was stand there, staring off into space, his face pale and horrified. Talon pressed his lips together, staring sorrowfully at the governor.

This is his choice… I can't make it for him…

He tore his eyes from Kresh for the last time as he and Castor hauled Amber along through the hallways. The ship lurched, shook, and rocked, and several times the commotion threw them off their feet, bringing Amber to near full consciousness.

They finally found their way to the deck and into open air.

The entire ship was engulfed in flames, and Talon caught glimpses of the rest of the fleet. Sterns protruded from the water and into the air as they sank, looking like giant gravestones, massive waves of water splashing over their burning hulls. Others were torn in half by walls of flame, their cannons engulfed in the blazing inferno. The smoke burned Talon's eyes, the scorching air singeing his eyebrows. He heard Amber cough and splutter as she leaned on him.

"Almost there," Castor choked. Sure enough, *The Independence* stood within their view. He could only hope the damage from the crash wasn't bad.

One of the three symmetrical canons above them broke from its foundation and fell, crashing through the wood, a massive hole opening in the deck. The impact nearly threw them to the ground.

Talon couldn't hear anything… the sense of hearing had drifted from him… all sounds had stopped… all sounds except the beating of his own heart.

They reached *The Independence*, and Castor used his remaining strength to slam the button, lowering the boarding ramp. They pulled Amber onto the ship, but she continued to lean on Talon.

Castor stumbled into the cockpit, the ship lifted off, and they rocketed into the sky. Through the viewing port in the side of the wall, Talon could see the entire fleet of twenty battleships as they continued to rip themselves apart, erupting in flame. The mothership stood alone.

It drifted farther and farther away as Talon stared at the bridge where they had been just minutes before. Where Kresh still was now.

Kresh, still in a trance, turned and peered out the gargantuan window. A choking breath escaped from his mouth as he watched his fleet sink beneath the waves.

He had been foiled… he had been defeated… everything had failed.

What had the boy said to Zedah?

That it was never too late to change?

For her it may not have been, she had redeemed herself.

But, for him, it *was* too late. He'd had his chance and he had refused it. There was no escape now. No way to stop what he knew his fate would be.

And he would accept it…

The boy had won fairly, playing a card the governor hadn't seen coming.

Kresh had known the Key was in the sword, but he had never

imagined the boy would discover it. He had never imagined the boy would've been *brave* enough.

He supposed that stupidity and bravery could be considered the same in some circumstances, but not this one. The child of Elijah and Hazel Chambers had outwitted him… had beaten him… had killed his revenge.

Their aircraft streaked across the sky and disappeared into the distance as he let out a short laugh.

The boy won after all.

A flash of light, searing heat, and Governor Irnal Kresh knew no more.

From the viewing port of *The Independence*, Talon saw the bridge of the mothership explode, a sphere of glowing flames rolling into the air. It teetered before leaning to the left and plunging into the waves with a splash bigger than an erupting geyser.

Amber still clung to him, breathing heavily, her face smudged with dirt and her eyes tinged with red. Talon held her close, and she gazed at him deeply before taking another big gulp of air.

"What happened?" she whispered as Castor stumbled out of the cockpit, his face blackened with ash. Talon pulled away from her. A smile came to his face as he clenched his hand harder around the Key.

"We won," he said, his voice choking, a tear rolling down his face. Amber gazed at him with a bewildered expression.

"H—*how?*" she pleaded, and Talon glanced at Castor, whose expression asked the exact same thing.

Talon's palm fell open. "With a little help from my dad."

Castor and Amber gazed at the Key in utmost astonishment, wonder flooding their faces as they stared at the little piece of metalwork that had helped save New York… helped save countless lives.

Kresh was gone…

His tyranny was gone…

It's never the end… as long as you have hope… and as long as you maintain your love for others…

His father's words repeated over and over inside his head as he gazed at the two people who had helped him through everything… who had helped him overcome the pain, the grief, the loneliness. The people whom he loved very much.

He turned to Amber, gazed deep into her eyes, and pulled her into a strong hug. She wrapped her arms around him, her hand resting on the back of his neck, and he felt her crying into his chest.

Talon separated from her, turned to Castor, and embraced him, too. They hadn't dislodged when Amber joined them, and they all spread their arms around one another with no intention of breaking apart.

Talon didn't want to let go… he *never* wanted to let go.

As tears of joy trailed down his face, Talon's mind calmly rested. He was finally, and fully, at peace. Castor and Amber were here with him, they always would be.

More tears fell from his face, and he knew he'd finally found his *true* family.

CHAPTER NINETEEN

AUGUST 29TH, 2492

THREE MONTHS LATER...

The city of Yahn, and all its rugged beauty, passed beneath *The Independence* as it cruised over the buildings at ninety miles-an-hour.

Talon fingered the collar of his new overcoat, attempting to pull a piece of loose string off the fabric. He sighed and leaned against the wall of the ship, surveying the metropolis below. A soft smile came to his face as the sun dipped behind the horizon, casting a golden glow onto everything within sight.

"Hey," Amber said as she gently moved toward him. "Are you sure this is what you want to do?"

After a moment's silence, Talon nodded. "Yeah... I'm sure."

She smiled, rested her hand on his, and the two of them watched the terrain pass by. Talon reached inside his pocket and withdrew the Key, staring at its silver surface. It glinted in the orange sunlight, and a bittersweet sensation swept over him as he realized he wouldn't have this piece of his father... this piece of *himself* for much longer. He stood and wandered into the cockpit, where Castor sat gripping the steering mechanism.

"We're getting close," he stated.

Talon nodded. He felt the ship slow as it descended toward the ground. *The Independence* touched down in the exact spot it had just three months before. Talon dropped the Key back into his pocket and glanced at his sword, its handle reattached, but deprived of any hidden contents.

He didn't need it…

Not today…

He'd already have his father with him… *and* his mother.

Talon pulled the lever, and the boarding ramp lowered. Castor and Amber stood behind him as he stepped out and into the fresh air.

"We'll be here when you get back," Castor said.

Talon snickered. "Well, I sure hope so."

Amber laughed before saying, "We can come with you if you want."

He smiled. "This is something I have to do alone."

Amber nodded before smiling back. Talon stood silently for a moment, then turned and began his journey down the road that would lead him to the Temple. The sky continued to dim as the structure came into view, its massive towers and walls illuminated by the setting sun.

He stepped through the golden gate and onto the cobbled courtyard. When he entered the building, he noticed the stained-glass window, exactly where he remembered it being. The crystalline glow cast itself around the sanctuary.

Talon turned and traveled through the Temple. He didn't need a holo-device to guide him this time—he'd unintentionally memorized the way. The statues, mosaics, and bridges passed by as he traveled through the hallways and up the staircases. He allowed his mind to wander.

He thought of Zedah. She'd sacrificed herself to help save them, and the entire Third Borough. She'd done so many terrible things, but they didn't matter anymore. What was important was that she'd redeemed herself, and that was all Talon cared about.

When he thought of Kresh, a sadness hung over him. He wished he could've helped the governor see the truth, but he'd done his best. The rest had been up to Kresh, and he'd chosen a different path.

Finally, he thought of his parents as he extracted the Key from his pocket. It almost felt like their faces were reflected in the shining metal. All this time, they had been with him, and not just in the little object he held in his hand. Their teaching, their love, *that* was what was inside him. He knew it would always be there. But would *he* be enough? Could *he* make them proud? He certainly hoped so.

The journey through the Temple of Athar felt short. He reached the limestone staircase, and saw the termite-eaten door at the top. Talon placed a hand on the scratched metal handle and pushed the door open before entering the attic space. After taking a good long look around the room, he set out to find the little blue square, crawling on his hands and knees until the symbol snagged his vision.

His fingers hovered over it for a moment.

Should I do this?

Maybe this was a bad idea after all. Maybe he should keep it.

No.

He pressed the button, and it sank into the floor.

The room trembled as the cylindrical mechanism sprouted from the stone, the doors to its empty compartment flipping open with a dull snap.

Once again, he withdrew the Key from his pocket and gazed at it affectionately. His father and mother would still be with him wherever he went, but it was time for him to let go. To move on.

Talon placed the Key in the little compartment. The mechanism, sensing the weight, closed its doors. It pulled itself downward, and

Talon smiled as it disappeared into the stone. When the rumbling stopped, Talon closed his eyes and exhaled deeply, knowing that they were always watching him… that they would never *stop* watching him.

As he made his way back through the Temple, he remembered his parents' kind faces, and how they would always smile at him with unfailing love. He traveled back down the dirt path until *The Independence* came into view, and a warm revelation settled in his mind.

Though they were gone, he knew that his parents would always be a part of him and would remain his family forever. Now, he had two new additions to that family; Castor and Amber, and he would hold them inside him as well.

Talon entered the ship, its familiar smell filling his nose, and its comforting air blanketing him with warmth.

Hey," Castor said, stepping out of the cockpit just before Amber.

Talon replied, "Hey."

"You do it?"

"Yeah."

"Well, at least no one can find it now."

Amber cut in. "I don't think anyone needs to. It didn't have any other use than what we used it for."

"Yeah," Castor continued, "but just think if someone traces it to us—"

"No one knows what we did to the fleet."

"How do you know?"

"Because they already ruled it down to some chance accident. I read it on your computer this morning, Castor. Still, no one knows what the ships were built for. I guess the workers aren't talking."

Castor groaned. "Still messing with my computer, huh?"

There was a short pause. Talon broke the silence.

"We can't go back there. Not until they rebuild."

Castor waved his hand, "They'll figure it out."

"I don't think building a government is as easy as *they'll figure it out*," Talon laughed.

"Well, I guess it's up to the people now. Kresh is gone. The council is gone."

Talon nodded, truly happy that New York was, quite possibly, facing a brighter future.

Amber said, "In that case we'll need a place to stay."

"We've survived on the ship for a long time," Castor declared, gazing around *The Independence*.

"No, I mean a *real* place. Like a city or—"

"Why not here?" Talon interrupted. Castor and Amber turned to him. He stared out the viewing port, at the skyline of Yahn, silhouetted by just a sliver of remaining sunlight.

Castor raised his eyebrows. "We can't afford this place."

Talon shook his head. "Not on our own, but we could look for work. Maybe someone will offer housing in return."

The three of them stood in silence for a moment, all quietly agreeing to this plan, not knowing—or really caring—what the future had in store. All Talon cared about was that they had each other. It was all he needed.

Amber reached up and touched the small scar running through Talon's eyebrow, all that remained of the wound Kresh had given him.

"Yeah," Talon said to her. "I kind of like it."

She laughed softly. "I do too… makes you look tough."

"Really?"

The laceration in his side was completely healed, too. They'd gotten to a doctor soon after the fleet, and she'd sealed the wound with a piece of technology Talon didn't recognize.

Amber laughed again, and then did something Talon least expected. She leaned forward and kissed him on the cheek, and his heart fluttered as she pulled away. With a soft smile, she disappeared into the cockpit, leaving him frozen and pale in the belly of the ship.

"So," Talon began, scratching at the back of his neck, "*which* one of us does she like?"

"I *told* you, she's like a sister to me," Castor stated with a smirk, his voice lowering. "She called you tough, and she didn't kiss *me* on the cheek."

"No, she said the scar makes me *look* tough."

Castor smiled slyly. "Face it. She likes you better."

"But she's known you longer!"

"Right… and if she liked me, she would have made it clear a *long* time ago. If you want any tips, let me know."

"*Tips?* You have experience?"

There was an awkward silence.

"Okay," Castor admitted. "Maybe I'm not the best person to ask for advice."

They snickered before Amber poked her head out of the cockpit. "You guys know that I can hear *every* word you're saying, right?"

"What?" Castor asked quickly. "Did we say something? I don't know what you're talking about, Amber."

Talon finished, "Yeah, me neither."

Amber rolled her eyes, a grin apparent on her face, and

vanished again. Talon and Castor glanced at each other, laughed once again, and followed her into the cockpit. They sat down, still smiling, and Talon gazed out the viewing port. He could see the massive wall in the distance, blanketed by a layer of dusty haze. Castor steered *The Independence* into the night air, and Amber was busy typing in a code on a touchscreen.

Neither of them noticed, but Talon kept his eyes fixed on them. The same love he knew his parents had felt for him, he felt for Castor and Amber. He knew that his father and mother would always be with him in his heart, and he was at peace with that.

The Temple grew smaller in the distance and, as they drifted away, Talon smiled at the truth that the memories of his father and mother were free at last.

THE END

ACKNOWLEDGEMENTS

There are many people I'd like to thank, but first and foremost, the Lord. I will forever be grateful for His word and the gift of salvation He has brought me.

Second, my parents. I am so thankful for your wisdom, love, and parental tolerance. Thank you for holding my hand and being nothing but loving to me.

My friends who journeyed with me over the pond: Rhys, Daniel, Bryan, Jess, and Maddie. Here's to more conversations about Christ, life, high-school football, college, *The Office*, and whether or not we're sus. Y'all are more than "subpar."

Thank you to my editor, Belle Manuel, and my awesome beta readers: Ethan, Danielle, Kyra, and Mary. Your feedback was so helpful, and *Talon* wouldn't be what it is without you.

Finally, my brother, Tanner, for being my best friend, joke buddy, and punching bag. I admire your creative spirit, and can't wait to read your book when it's released (yes, he's writing a book too).

ABOUT THE AUTHOR

Jayden Jelso is an aspiring author, screenwriter, and filmmaker. His love of storytelling first stemmed from a fascination with the *Star Wars* saga, *The Lord of the Rings* trilogy, and the *Harry Potter* films. He began making short films at eight-years-old, and still has a passion for it. He started writing his debut novel, *Talon*, when he was only sixteen and published it at eighteen.

Outside of writing, you may be able to spot him making a film, watching *The Office*, laughing at inside jokes, or posting about his current writing projects on his Instagram feed @authorjaydenjelso.

He currently lives in Nashville with his parents and younger brother.